HEREDITARY MAGIC

THE GATEKEEPER'S CURSE SERIES: BOOK ONE

EMMA L. ADAMS

1

I'd been having a great day right up until the omen of death appeared.

As I sat at my desk, chewing on the end of my pen over a particularly thorny essay question, the raven flew towards the house and landed on the windowsill of my room. I didn't register the bird's presence until the white stripe on its forehead caught my eye, marking him as Arden, the Lynn family's messenger.

Oh no.

Tapping on the glass with his beak, Arden shuffled impatiently in a manner that warned me that if I didn't open the window right away, he'd screech loudly enough to alert the other, all-too-human occupants of the shared house.

"What is it?" I asked, pushing the window open. "You can't be here. There are people in this house who don't know about... our family."

With every word I spoke, another thread of the life I'd carefully cultivated over the last five years unravelled. *It was nice knowing you, normality.*

"Ilsa Lynn," the raven said. "Your presence is urgently

requested at the house of Lynn at the behest of the Summer Court of Faerie."

"No, it isn't," I said. "Hazel's perfectly capable of solving her own problems."

My twin sister, Hazel Lynn, was Gatekeeper-in-training, chosen to succeed our mother as the single human peace-keeper between this realm and the Summer Court. As the non-magical sibling, I'd run as far as possible from the curse, but the breeze kicked up by the raven's arrival carried an earthy scent that promised change—and not the good kind. Magic.

The house buckled, the floor tilting underneath my feet as a tremendous crash vibrated through the foundations. I grabbed the bedside table for balance, wishing I'd kept some iron handy. Yelling a warning to the other inhabitants, I stumbled from my room and ran for the stairs.

The house split in two. Floorboards splintered, walls fractured, lines zigzagging across the plaster. I pelted down the stairs, raising my arms to protect myself. Plaster rained down in fragments, flakes falling like snow. I sucked in a breath and slammed my foot into the door, pushing it open. Nobody waited in the garden, human or otherwise, and the smell of magic was already fading. The way the house had split in the exact centre was so precise, it could only be the result of a spell, but its caster was long gone.

Faerie magic, when aimed at me, bounced right off my defensive shield. So the conniving little shits had used their spell on the house instead. For beings that prided themselves on being well-mannered, you'd think the Sidhe would have the decency to ring the doorbell before unleashing the dramatics. I muttered a few choice curses under my breath, brushing plaster dust from my eyelashes, and glanced down to find a note lying on the doorstep. Words had been scrawled in an elaborate font: "You will find the heir, Lynn, or you will all suffer a terrible death."

The note disappeared in a swirl of leaves, leaving nothing behind but the smell of earthy Summer magic. A smell I'd grown up with, and had moved several hundred miles away to escape. *You will all suffer a terrible death.* The Sidhe hadn't even signed the note. Bastards.

If I'd had magic of my own, I'd have come up with an equally non-subtle way to tell them they'd got the wrong address. Ominous death threats and the word *heir* belonged firmly in my sister's hands, not mine. My speciality was writing essays on obscure pieces of magical history for humans who'd barely come to grasp that the supernatural world existed alongside the one they thought they'd known. Twenty years had passed since the faeries exposed that hidden world for the humans to see, but they'd held my family in their grip for much longer.

I stood completely still for a moment, watching the spot where the note had vanished, then turned to face the house. "Are you guys okay?" I called to the others.

Several yelps in the affirmative followed, followed by a *caw* that sounded more like a cackle. Arden perched on the neighbour's fence, a smug expression on his face. That damned raven had arrived too late with his warning on purpose.

"Heir?" I said. "Isn't that Hazel? Is she okay?" If she'd been a normal sibling, worry would have been my first reaction, but Hazel had been scaring the living hell out of her enemies ever since she'd come into her powers. And the Summer Gatekeeper had no shortage of adversaries.

"More than you are," said the raven, fluttering his wings. "You're bleeding."

I touched my face. Red tinged my hand over its coating of

plaster dust. "This is a mistake," I said. "The Sidhe—how did they even know where I live?"

"Why is that raven watching you?" Faisal, my housemate, peered out of the ruined hallway.

"Because he knows I'm about to wring his neck," I said heatedly. "I'm *so* sorry about the house. I'll talk to the land-lord... I've no idea if faerie damage is covered in our insurance payment, but there's got to be a clause in there somewhere."

He raised an eyebrow. "Wouldn't be the first time the faeries destroyed something for fun, but I guess we can wave goodbye to our security deposits."

No kidding. I'd grown careless over the last couple of years and let my guard down. But even an iron barrier on the door wouldn't keep the Sidhe out of a place they wanted to get into. Despite the raven's dismissive comments, maybe Hazel really was in trouble. She'd never come to me for help dealing with the faeries before... probably because it'd be like asking a piskie for directions. I dealt with the faeries by staying the hell out of the way.

I picked my way through the wrecked hallway to the stairs. The raven flew ahead of me into my room, still wearing that maddeningly smug expression as though the whole thing was hilarious.

"If I stay at a hotel tonight, I'll wake up with fire imps dancing on my face, won't I?" I rescued the least damaged textbooks from the wreckage of my bookcase, shoved them into my bag and zipped it closed. My laptop joined them. No point in pretending I'd ever come back. When Faerie called, you damn well listened. Even—no, especially—if you belonged to a Gatekeeper's family. It was more than a job; it was a life commitment to keeping the peace between the Summer faeries and the inhabitants of the mortal realm. I'd signed no such contract, but the curse existed in the very name. *Lynn.*

I dragged my suitcase out from underneath the bed and tossed a pile of dust-covered clothes into it. "Great. Not like I needed anything to wear for work…" Oh, damn. I was supposed to be on the evening shift in an hour, but I wouldn't put it past the faeries to follow me to the pub where I worked and turn the weekly student pub crawl into chaos and bloodshed. Pity, because if the house was anything to go by, I'd need a stiff drink or three to face whatever the Sidhe wanted with me.

"You have terrible fashion sense anyway," Arden proclaimed, perching on the bed post.

"There's nothing wrong with my clothes," I said, glancing down at my hoody and jeans, which were also covered in plaster dust. Plain, unobtrusive human clothes couldn't hide my identity, but they signalled to the faeries that I wasn't one of their pretty mortal toys. "I'm lost on what I'm supposed to be dressing up for. If this is a hostage situation so they can probe my sister for a favour, they should probably have snatched me before I had the chance to grab this." I picked up a jar of iron filings from the bedside table and pushed it up the sleeve of my hoody before checking on my phone. No calls, either from Hazel or Mum. I dashed off a vague message to my boss about a family emergency, resigning myself to being on my co-workers' shit list for ditching them on the pub's busiest night of the week. "If Mum wanted me to come and visit, she could have just called me."

"Can't," Arden said, flapping his wings in an agitated manner. "Mother is gone."

"Gone?" I echoed. "Oh, for god's sake. Don't tell me she went into Faerie without giving a time limit again."

In Faerie, days turned into weeks, and minutes stretched into days. Whenever Mum went on one of her ambassador missions to the Summer Court, it was lucky if she returned within the same month. The Summer Gatekeeper's power could only pass to one person, so when it came to twins, it was a matter of the fates flipping a coin. My sister got heads, I got tails. That meant Hazel would be in charge of the Gatekeeper's affairs while Mum was gone, and some bright spark had decided to deliver her latest life-threatening mission to the wrong Lynn sibling.

I zipped the suitcase closed. "Arden, tell me the truth. Is Hazel in trouble?"

Getting straight answers out of Arden was like arm-wrestling a man-sized carnivorous plant, while his advice was generally about as useful as flip-flops on a mountain hike. A shapeshifter faerie tied to our family by a curse as old as our own, he seemed to thrive off winding people up.

"Everyone is in trouble," the raven proclaimed, which made no sense whatsoever. I swatted at him with the page of essay notes I'd been writing before his unceremonious arrival, and he fluttered out of the way. "Hurry up."

"I don't think so." I stood, folding my arms. There was a horrible creaking noise from under my feet. I got the message. I threw the rucksack over my shoulder, grabbed my suitcase, and ran for my life.

I didn't slow down until I'd reached the end of the road. This was a supernatural-free area of the city, which I'd chosen on purpose when I'd first applied to study at university. Now I'd finished my four-year degree course, I'd spent the last year coming up with creative ways to procrastinate on my PhD application. Hoping that if I stayed away from Faerie long enough, the curse would lift and I'd be able to leave forever. Instead, said curse had left me with two choices: stay in a hotel overnight and put more humans at the mercy of the faeries tailing me, or go to the Lynn house and get hold of someone else to handle the Sidhe's impossible request. The note hadn't carried the Summer Court's official seal, but nobody else would have reason to believe they could wrangle obedience out of me by demolishing my house.

"So is Hazel there?" I asked Arden, who flew alongside me. "Or is *she* in Faerie, too?"

"No."

"Which question were you answering?" I adjusted my rucksack. "Seriously, Arden. Just tell me what the hell's going on."

"Caw. Mother and daughter are both gone."

"Shit." When we were teenagers, Hazel had tried to run away from her Gatekeeper duties at least once a week. I thought she'd got past that habit long before I'd left home, and that she *liked* her job, or had at least resigned herself to the position. I tried calling her as I rolled my suitcase down the road, but received only the sound of a dial tone in response. *Damn you, Arden.* I wouldn't have thought he'd be messing with me if Hazel's life was in genuine danger, but with the faeries, you never really knew.

Golden light gilded the hilltops overlooking the neighbourhood as the sun began its descent, and a shadow moved in the corner of my eye. *Hey there, little faerie. Think I can't see through your glamour?* Faeries, Seelie and Unseelie alike, were given to pranking people, but they seemed to take my magical shield as a challenge. I slowed my speed, letting the four-foot-tall creature hurry along behind me, giving no signs that I'd heard its approach.

"I feel like something's watching me," I said aloud. I looked to either side, deliberately letting my gaze skim over where the creature was actually hidden. "I guess not, then."

Arden flew overhead with a disapproving screech, which I ignored.

When I reached the end of the road, the creature slipped

out behind me. I could almost feel its brewing frustration. It wanted me to scream in terror, beg for mercy, flee from its magic. I grinned. The creature craved chaos, and I was driving it out of its tiny mind. It'd snap eventually.

Sure enough—

"Lynn," murmured the faerie, fire crackling between its fingertips. The fire coalesced into a ball of whirling flames, and zipped at me with a whistling noise.

If I was as dramatic as my sister, I'd have faked screaming and running in circles, but it didn't really work when you had no power to back up the act. I made a big show of turning around in slow-motion instead. As the fireball came within a metre of me, it bounced off the shield and sailed right back at its owner. *Nice try.* The fire imp hissed and ran into the shadows, the fire dissipating harmlessly into smoke. I didn't try to chase it down. It'd become a game with the local faeries to try to land a hit on me, but they never succeeded. Our family's built-in magic-proof abilities were nothing if not thorough. It was the only magic I'd ever have, so I'd take all the entertainment I could get.

"Was that necessary?" said Arden. "It'll probably go and torch someone's house instead."

"Nah, I left a trail of iron all the way down the road." I revealed the small container of iron filings hidden in my sleeve. "I've rid the neighbourhood of fire imp infestations for a few weeks."

The raven made a disapproving tutting noise and continued to fly. I followed, wheeling my suitcase, then paused when Arden angled towards a path leading up to the peak of Arthur's Seat.

"Couldn't you have left a Path open on the ground somewhere?" I asked.

"Caw. Paths move where the Ley Line is."

"Sure they do." Not that I could actually *see* the invisible line that separated mortal and faerie realms. Most supernaturals tracked the Ley Line by its amplification of any magic in the general area. Sparks of green Summer magic shone on the hilltop where Seelie half-faeries had set up their territory on Salisbury Crag. But I was fairly sure Arden had deliberately picked this location for the Path to our house because he knew how much I loathed climbing hills.

From the high vantage point, the damage the faeries had wrought on the city was evident. Just over twenty years ago, a group of outcast Sidhe—the most powerful of all faeries—had broken through the veil between mortal and faerie realms, wreaking destruction across the globe. Civilisation as the humans had known it had crumbled as the Sidhe's magic, amplified by the Ley Line, had killed millions and dragged a huge number of Faerie's inhabitants into the mortal realm. As a result, all supernaturals had been forcibly exposed, Gatekeepers included.

With humans now rubbing shoulders with witches, necromancers, shifters and half-faeries, pulled into an uneasy truce under the regional Mage Lords, life went on. If you had no magic, you carried iron and salt, went nowhere unarmed, and kept your wits about you. The Lynn family's magic had, much as I resented it, saved my life on more than one occasion. But that didn't stop me from cursing their names as I wheeled my suitcase uphill.

"If you speak ill of the dead, they'll come back and hex you," Arden said.

I rolled my eyes. "I'm already cursed twice over. There's not much the dead can do that the living haven't already, trust me."

I reached the edge of the rise, looking out across the city. The air shimmered, the only faint sign of the Ley Line's current location. Arden flew over the cliff's edge and disappeared from sight. A moment later, I stepped after him, into empty air. The world flickered and reformed itself, and my feet touched down instantly on the path outside the Lynn house.

The manor sat on a lane which looked like it belonged anywhere out in the countryside, except if you kept walking along the road, you'd never reach your destination. You'd just be eternally thrown round in circles. Ivy covered the walls of the house in thick curtains like an illustration from a story-book, while flowers bloomed at every corner. The house might as well have worn a neon sign, proclaiming "Realm of Faerie here. Single tickets only. No returns."

The heat from the gate burned my hand, the metal baking under the blazing sun. The Sidhe rarely set foot on the Lynns' property—luckily—but Summer magic shone out of every inch of the tall manor house and wide, green gardens. I didn't blame Dad for not sticking around. This place was an eye-watering sight for someone without magic. Let alone allergies.

Surrounding the house, the forest was warm and inviting, sunshine pouring through perpetually green leaves. The flowers here never withered, even in winter, but at the other end of the fence, out of sight from this angle, the trees were shrouded in darkness, and frost coated every branch no matter the season.

And at the very end of our garden was the gate—the only known route into the Seelie Court in the mortal realm. It opened only for the Gatekeeper, so there was no way to follow and ask what in hell the Sidhe wanted with me. Admittedly, even my magic-proof shield probably wouldn't protect me from the monsters beyond the gate, eager for a new pet human to play with.

Most humans taken into Faerie didn't come back the same, if they came back at all.

I unlocked the front door. Nobody waited in the thickly

carpeted hallway. Portraits of the various Gatekeepers appeared to follow me with their eyes, as though judging me. Not unlike the real thing. From the state of the place, you'd hardly think Mum was absent. Not a speck of dust lay on the furniture in the living room, and not a single cushion lay out of place. Mum was dedicated to housekeeping spells as well as her job as Gatekeeper. As far as parenting went, though, she might have taken a few classes before my father ran away, leaving her to bring us up alone.

It wasn't his fault. Our house—or, more accurately, the gate in our garden—was designed to repel anyone who didn't belong to the Lynn bloodline, and he lasted a year before moving away. Mum didn't mind. His only purpose, in her eyes, was to provide her heir to the Lynn legacy. Meaning my sister. I was the extra. As for our estranged brother, the less said about him, the better.

As I looked around the living room, searching for any signs of Hazel's presence, a strange woman stepped out of the wall.

I jumped backwards into the sofa. "Who the hell are you?"

"Don't panic," the woman said. She was a little older than I was, mid-to-late twenties, and she'd spoken with an English accent. Her long, brown hair was tied back in a ponytail and she carried a gleaming sword strapped to her side.

She was also, apparently, a ghost.

"I'm not dead," she added, like she'd read my thoughts. "I'm travelling through the spirit realm, but my body is still alive. It was the quickest way to reach you. I'm Ivy Lane, by the way."

"I—*how* did you get here?" Sure, some necromancers could detach themselves from their physical bodies and wander around as ghosts to freak people out, but even a necromancer shouldn't have been able to find our house. Ivy's muscular build and the sword at her side indicated she was either a mercenary killer or a bounty hunter—someone I really didn't want to cross, ghost or otherwise. The blade was sheathed, but it appeared to glow faintly blue. A faerie talisman. Holy crap. "Nobody can come in here. Spirit, human, faerie, whatever. This is—"

"A liminal space," said Ivy. "It's taken me nearly a week to get around the bindings, but eventually, your pet bird helped."

I gave Arden an accusing look to cover up my shock. "You took bribery? You should be ashamed."

"I explained the situation," said Ivy. "I'm a distant descendant of the Lynn bloodline, apparently. But it's to do with your mother's mission in Faerie. The king of the Seelie Court is dying."

"And?" That was old news. From before I was born, even. As immortals, faeries didn't actually die, but the Erlking certainly seemed to be dragging out the process as long as possible.

"You might need to sit down for this part."

I've needed to sit down since you walked through the wall, to be honest. "You're a strange ghost claiming to be alive who just walked through a magical boundary set up by the *Sidhe* as though it was nothing. Do your worst."

I shouldn't have said that. When would I learn not to tempt fate?

The hint of a smile touched her mouth. "You have a point. I was supposed to speak to the Gatekeeper, but I can't cross into Faerie like this. And if you're not the heir, you can get the message to her, right?"

I nodded. "I'll be having words with my sister, believe me. So what's the issue with the Erlking? He's been dying for over a decade. At least. He'll die, and then come back like they always do."

Ivy shook her head. "No. I don't know if you know how

faerie immortality works, but it doesn't. Not anymore. It's a long story, and I don't think I can stay here long enough to tell it. But believe me when I say—the Sidhe can die. That includes the Erlking. I'm told you're peacekeepers between this realm and Faerie."

"Yeah, we are." My voice sounded distant. Our entire lives had been built around the assumption that the Sidhe lived forever. That's why the family curse was permanent. When one Gatekeeper died, the title passed onto the next, while the Sidhe endured. If the whole arrangement collapsed, I knew exactly what would happen. War. "Hazel is…" I trailed off. There were no adequate words in any human language to describe how utterly fucked we all were if what she'd said was true.

"My time's up," Ivy said. Her body had turned more transparent, like ghosts did when they came close to passing on to the next world. "Really sorry about this."

And she disappeared.

I stared after her. Hoping there'd been a mistake, and someone would come here and give me an explanation that made any sense whatsoever. The Sidhe were immortal. It was just… a fact. The idea of things being otherwise wasn't comprehensible to me. Much less that the king of the Seelie Court, who'd lived for a thousand years at least, would soon disappear forever. Now magic was out in the open, who knew what would happen if Sidhe power struggles wound up here on earth?

Dammit, Hazel. Where had she disappeared to?

"So that's what the note meant?" I said into the silence, glancing at Arden. "We—or rather, Hazel and Mum—are supposed to stop the Summer Court from tearing itself to pieces when the Erlking passes on?"

"And find the heir," Arden said casually.

I gave a slightly manic laugh. "You what? The heir will be in Faerie, if they're anywhere at all."

"Didn't you read the note?"

Find the heir. Not the heir to the Summer Court? Why would the Sidhe even consider giving a task like that to humans, even Gatekeepers?

The door clicked open behind me. Hazel stood there—my not-so-identical twin sister. We'd shared the same brown eyes before Hazel's had turned green from the Summer magic in the binding ceremony. And we had the same pale features, but my sister's forehead was marked with a swirling faerie symbol designating her position as Gatekeeper-in-training. While my hair was dark brown, hers was sun-kissed and almost blond. When she was Gatekeeper, she'd wear a circlet that looked like a crown. I wondered if she still stole the spare one from Mum when she wasn't looking, so that clients would take her seriously.

Her eyes widened. "Ilsa?"

One look at her expression told me she hadn't known I was coming. Arden had lied to me.

"Hey," I said. "You have a message from the Summer Court. Also, a ghost got into the house."

"A *ghost?*" She gaped at me. "What trouble have you got into, Ilsa?"

"Him." I jerked my head at Arden. "He implied you'd run away. And Mum was in Faerie."

"He's right about the last part," said Hazel. "I'm in charge of handling business on her behalf. So… what does he want me to do?"

I took in a breath. "You might need to sit down."

2

"So," said Hazel. "According to this Ivy apparition, the source of immortality has gone. The Sidhe can die now."

"Yep," I said, sinking into an armchair. The living room had hardly changed in five years, containing the same crooked furniture Mum refused to replace despite having the magical resources to do so, and several generations' worth of trinkets crammed onto the shelves.

"And the Erlking is dying," Hazel said, sinking into the lopsided sofa. "And *we* have to find the heir?" She didn't wait for my answer. "Well, shit."

"Pretty much."

She shook her head. "I swear, Mum didn't tell me any of this. Why did this Ivy person tell you and not me?"

"Because I was in the house. Apparently she got by the security." I gave the raven a look. Arden had perched on top of the rickety bookcase, which contained an array of dust-covered childhood board games nobody had touched since the summer our brother had run away from home. "Arden told me you disappeared and pretty much dragged me here."

"Need both Lynn daughters here!" he said reproachfully. "Very dangerous job."

"I'll give you dangerous," I said. "So there was no reason to call me. In that case, I'm off back to Edinburgh in the morning. Or rather, to find a new house, since the faeries split my last one in two, and apologise to my boss and co-workers for vanishing off the face of the earth."

"Wow." She raised an eyebrow. "I didn't know you had a house. You didn't touch your allowance at all, Mum said."

"Nope, because it belongs to Faerie. I took out a loan and got a job like a normal person, and I'm in a shared house. Or I was, before someone decided to break everything." I glared at Arden. "Happy?"

"Caw."

I flipped him off. "When did Mum go into Faerie?"

"A month ago."

"There's no way she doesn't know about this," I said. "I don't know how Ivy Lane, whoever she is, found out before we did. She said we were related, distantly. Know anything about that?"

"Nope. Maybe Mum sent her, but I doubt it." She frowned, looking more Mum-like than I'd ever seen her. I should have known Arden was talking crap when he implied she'd run away. Hazel might not have been keen on her future as Gatekeeper when we'd been kids, but she'd inherited Mum's no-nonsense attitude and commitment to getting shit done. She wasn't a teenager anymore.

"So she left nothing? Not even a note?" Wouldn't be the first time, but this whole situation struck me as someone's attempt at an elaborate prank.

"Nope. I know she's alive, at least." She tapped the mark on her forehead. "Which is more than I can say for you. You look like you just crawled out of a coffin."

"Hey!" I protested. "I had a house fall on me today, you know."

"I thought you weren't coming home at all."

I shrugged uncomfortably. Speaking to her on the phone, it'd been easy to tell her all my grand plans, but face to face, it was harder to put into words. Especially as I didn't *know* what I wanted to do with my life. Only that it in no way involved the Summer Court or the word 'Gatekeeper'.

"I was in the middle of my PhD application," I said. "But half my books are now buried in rubble."

"What're you doing a doctorate in?"

"Folklore."

She howled with laughter, the exact reaction I'd expected. "Brilliant. Bet you know more than the staff do. That's like the multilingual guy at our school who got A grades in three languages without ever showing up for class."

"Like you wouldn't do the same," I told her. "I spend all my time being a consultant on faeries for everyone I know. Might as well put it to use."

"If all faeries are allergic to iron, why did a piskie steal my phone?"

"Because iron allergies in faeries are proportionate to magical ability. Most wild fae have little to no magic, so they aren't affected by iron as much as powerful faeries are. Also, there's a common theory that faeries born in this realm are more tolerant of iron than their kin in the faerie realm. The third argument is that piskies are bloody stupid."

"There are worse things to do with your time," said Hazel. "Okay, apply your academic skills to this riddle. Why does the Seelie Court want us to find their missing heir?"

"No bloody clue." I got to my feet. "I'm fairly certain you're the one the note was directed at and they got the wrong address, but it's not like I can *call* the Sidhe and ask. It sounds like they're preoccupied at the moment."

"No shit." She looked at the raven again, her teeth running over her bottom lip. Beneath her flippant attitude, she was scared. And had reason to be. No family magic would protect any of us if the Sidhe went to war. It'd be a dick move to leave her to handle it alone, and besides, I had nowhere else to stay until I got the Sidhe off my backs. And while I'd spent so long running away, this wasn't a problem you could turn your back on.

"I'm going to check the reference books," I said to her.

"I knew you wanted to get into the library."

She wasn't wrong. The library was a sprawling room painted in calming shades of blue, with towering bookcases tucked into every corner. I used to spend hours curled in the window seat, escaping into realms where the faeries hadn't wiped out the world as everyone had known it. I'd found no shortage of bookshops in Edinburgh that reminded me of this place, but nothing quite matched the air of secrecy and hidden history that hung over these shelves as thickly as the smell of old books. The house had changed over the years as each Lynn made their own adjustments, but this room had remained the same, and was the only part of the house which felt like mine.

Hazel stared up at the closest bookcase, like she hoped the right book would fall at her feet. No such luck. Even a magical house had its limits.

"Any idea where to start?" she asked.

"Look at the labels." Grabbing the nearest book in the 'Seelie Court' section, I passed it to Hazel. "Come on, you're the one who's actually *been* to the Summer Court recently. Haven't you heard the latest gossip?"

"No. You think they'd tell a human? Mum's the one they confide in, if at all."

"And there's no point in asking the local half-faeries." Any of them might claim to be the heir in order to get a shot at going into Faerie. Not to mention foolish humans. "But I'd have thought the heir would be Sidhe."

The two of us looked around the room as though expecting an heir to leap out from behind a bookcase. Which, let's face it, was about as likely as us stumbling across the right information. What we needed was a list of descendants, but I was pretty sure we were the only family in this realm with faerie ancestry who actually had a copy of our family tree. Most faeries aren't kind enough to leave so much as a farewell note when they leave their half-human offspring here on earth. Ours left us a curse. So, you know, it could have been better.

Technically, Thomas Lynn had still been human when he'd returned from Faerie. Nobody knew the truth until he married his childhood sweetheart, had kids, and the Seelie Court turned up on his doorstep. Apparently, during his time in the faerie realm, he'd unwittingly signed all his future descendants into servitude to the Courts. His two daughters became the first ambassadors—one for Summer, one for Winter. And *their* descendants were locked into the same curse. Forever.

Nobody ever gave our ancestor the memo about not making a promise to a faerie.

Thinking about it, maybe the Winter branch of the Lynn family could help us. But I'd almost rather ask the faeries for help than visit my distant aunt. And I doubted Summer wanted their enemies to know about the Seelie King's plight, much less the missing heir. Summer and Winter had only reached a wary peace somewhat recently in human years, a peace that had almost shattered when outcasts from their own Courts had attacked the mortal realm. They still hadn't offered an apology for the whole debacle. And if Summer had no king, Winter wouldn't stay back and let them figure their shit out. They'd pounce on the opportunity to seize more power.

Suddenly my PhD application didn't seem so impossible after all.

"We could read all night and not find anything," said Hazel, pacing the row of bookshelves. "Who knocked your house down, anyway? Not the Sidhe."

"Nope." I slid another book from the shelf, checked the title, and put it back. "You know they only come here in an emergency. They'll probably show up a month late."

The Sidhe, rulers of Faerie, weren't the most reliable of people. Sidhe, pronounced *shee.* They could speak any language, possessed power beyond mortal comprehension, and the ones I'd met had been self-centred, amoral, and completely incapable of understanding humans at all. They were also murderous and paranoid, and no doubt that paranoia had tripled if Ivy was right about the state of their immortality.

There came a knock at the door.

Hazel and I both looked at one another. The Lynn house wasn't exactly accessible to anyone. Sure, Ivy had walked in, but she'd had to come here as a ghost.

"Arden?" I looked at him. "Have you given anyone else our address?"

"No." Arden ruffled his feathers, sounding insulted.

My heart sank. The only people who could even find the path to the house were other members of our family, but they needed an invitation to come in. And the Sidhe themselves, but Hazel would have sensed Summer's gate open.

"Maybe the Winter Gatekeeper found out." I walked to the door, though apprehension dogged my every step. A chill breeze blew through an open window, a startling contrast to the house's usual warmth. Grabbing the handle, I pulled the door open before I lost my nerve.

A dead man stood on the doorstep.

3

The undead leant at an awkward angle, possibly because its leg had started to decay mid-walk. Its face was greyish, its eyes sunken, and as I stared, a maggot crawled across its pallid skin. I jerked back, wishing I'd grabbed the salt shaker. But I hadn't exactly been expecting any more visitors. Least of all deceased ones.

"Nevermore!" screeched Arden.

The zombie didn't move, because he couldn't hear. Or see. They just flailed around and hit at anyone in their path. I didn't recognise the dead stranger, but dread bloomed inside me. I'd been thinking all this time about how nobody could find our house. The *living* couldn't. The dead were another story entirely.

I aimed a kick at the zombie, trying to unbalance it, but it stayed upright. A cold, clammy hand reached for my face, fingers grasping. Fighting a shudder of revulsion, I drew back and punched it in the throat. I had zero combat skills, but zombies moved slowly, and my strike sent it stumbling backwards. Then it lunged forwards again. I was ready with another kick, this time at its weaker leg. It crumpled, hands still pawing sightlessly at me. Another kick sent it flailing off the doorstep. Nothing like fighting a zombie to give you a self-esteem boost.

"Get out!" Hazel screamed, hurling a container of salt. I jumped into the hallway to avoid being hit, and the salt canister struck the zombie in the face. He went down, hard, his skin dissolving as the salt ate away at the necromantic magic keeping him standing. Reanimates, otherwise known as undead or zombies, weren't conscious beings, but they were tenacious, especially in large numbers. Luckily, this one seemed to have come alone.

"Oh, that's foul," said Hazel, making gagging noises. "I *hate* zombies. Who sent that?"

I peered across the garden, making sure there weren't any others. "Definitely not the Summer Court. Arden, did someone else follow us? Or did you give permission to everyone on the wrong side of the grave to come and visit?"

"Nevermore!" proclaimed the raven, landing on the zombie's liquefying face. "No. This one came from the grave."

"I know it came from the bloody grave, you menace," I said. "Salt will dissolve it, but this whole place will stink of the dead for a week."

"We need to get rid of it." Hazel hung back behind the door, with no apparent inclination to come and look at the zombie.

"By 'we', you mean me, don't you?" I'd always been able to handle gore better than she could—kind of funny, considering I hadn't been exposed to Faerie as young as she had—but cleaning up dead bodies hadn't exactly been on my list for today.

Hazel gave me the smile that usually translated as *can I please have the last cookie?* Or *you won't tell Mum I stole her circlet, will you?*

And I, idiot older sister that I was, caved every single time. Older by ten minutes, but still.

"Keep an eye out for trouble," I told her, and went to the shed in search of a shovel.

By the time I'd relocated what was left of the zombie to the abandoned part of the garden, I was in a thoroughly bad mood. No signs were evident of whoever had sent the damn thing, nor any other clues as to how it'd ended up in the garden. So when I returned to the doorstep to find a second unwelcome intruder, I elbowed him aside.

Or I would have, but he glided out of the way in a manner that would have made a professional dancer envious. The man was maybe in his late twenties, with light blond hair, and emphatically *not* an undead. No human could move that gracefully. I wished I hadn't ditched the shovel, though most half-faeries relied on their magic, which would have no effect on us. Still, three confrontations in a single day was entirely too many for me.

"I apologise for startling you," he said.

"Whatever you're selling, we're not interested." I moved pointedly into the hallway and faced him. "And if you're planning on making an attempt against the Gatekeeper, then look forward to spending the next hundred years as a tree."

Hazel stepped in. "Who are you?"

The stranger's gaze slid from her to me and back again. Clearly he hadn't been expecting two of us. Maybe he was one of the people looking to make a claim on the Erlking's throne. Like Hazel, his eyes were pale green, too bright for a human—a sign that his faerie parent was Sidhe. He stood at maybe six feet tall, and wore a knee-length, faerie-made coat embossed in the style of the Seelie Court. He was slightly more rugged-looking than the average half-faerie, but his pointed ears were unmistakable.

"My name is River," he said. His accent was faintly Scottish, though he spoke in the formal tones of the Court. "I have been sent here by the Seelie Court to act as bodyguard to the Gatekeeper's heir." His gaze travelled to Hazel, taking in the symbol on her forehead. "You must be Hazel Lynn. It's nice to meet you."

Bodyguard? We were faerie-proof. Literally. What in hell was Mum thinking?

I placed a hand on his arm and firmly shoved him backwards. I wasn't too worried about him retaliating. If he meant harm, the family's magic would kick in and throw him off the property. Unfortunately, he didn't budge an inch. Instead, he looked down at my hand as though he'd hardly registered that I was there.

"And you are?" he asked.

"Ilsa Lynn," I said.

"Oh." His gaze travelled from me to Hazel once again, taking in the resemblance. I knew that look all too well. He might as well have said, *right. She's the spare. The non-magical one.* I didn't even take it as an insult anymore, because I'd long since slotted those people into the category of 'we're probably never going to be BFFs'.

Coming from this guy, though, after the day I'd had? A sudden current of white-hot anger coursed through my veins, and my hands curled into fists.

"As you can plainly see," I said, through gritted teeth, "we're doing just fine here. Goodbye."

And I closed the door in his face.

The door flew open again, and though his unassuming stance hadn't changed, the air felt *charged.* Green light shimmered down his arms, with the earthy scent of Summer faerie magic. Half-faeries very rarely skipped over their family's magical talents—not that it generally made any difference to the Sidhe, since half-faeries were mortal, like us.

Go on. Hit me. Find out the hard way about our family's magical shield.

"I have been given a task, and I intend to fulfil it," he said. "The Summer Court has sent me to act as bodyguard to the Gatekeeper-in-training, and I will."

Oh crap. It wasn't his own magic that brought him here, but the binding words of a Sidhe. Faerie vows were difficult to figure out, but the one rule was that the person under the vow couldn't repeat those words to anyone who asked. Unlike a Sidhe, however, he wasn't bound to tell the truth. He was definitely under some kind of spell allowing him to come here, otherwise the house wouldn't have let him into the grounds—but that didn't mean his intentions were benign.

Dammit. Quite apart from the fact that Hazel had no need of a bodyguard, the last thing either of us needed was someone from an unknown Sidhe family tailing our every move.

Hazel stepped to my side. "I don't need a bodyguard," she said, with a polite smile. "I don't know who sent you here, but this house is not in need of any outside protection. We've got that covered."

"Then why are there traces of the dead nearby?" he enquired.

How do you know that? I'd moved the zombie, and faeries weren't sensitive to the dead. I guess I did have dirt all the way up my arm. That might have clued him in.

"You smell like you've been digging in the dirt. There's also salt all over your doorstep. There's been a recent plague of undead in the village, so I put two and two together."

"Good for you," I said. "As you can see, we dealt with the undead ourselves. We have more than enough salt, iron, and weapons in this house—which also happens to be designed as a fortress against attacks from outside forces. Including faeries of all types."

"I am no threat to you," he said, having apparently picked up on the warning undercurrent to my voice. "I'm only here to do my job."

His own voice was laced with the clear hint of a threat, or at least firm reassurance that he wasn't leaving until the Sidhe said so. *But which Sidhe?* Summer ambassadors my family might be, but I'd be a fool to believe every member of the Court was an ally.

"Listen," I said. "Whatever your orders, we have them, too. Nobody is to enter this house without permission from the Gatekeeper, and you do *not* want to piss her off."

"I don't need to enter the house to perform my task," he said. "I merely wanted to inform you of my intentions, should you see me outside at any time."

I blinked. "You're... going to stand on the doorstep? All day?"

"That was the plan, yes. Were you aware that there's a disembodied hand underneath your doorstep?"

"I am now." I kicked the undead hand out onto the path, where it flopped around pathetically. "There. You get to make yourself useful after all. I'm trusting you'll deal with the terrifying zombie hand while I clean this grave dirt off my arm?"

This time when I closed the door, he didn't open it again. Walking to the kitchen, I checked nothing inside the house had moved when he'd blown the door open. Nope. All show, evidently. He was a nuisance, but I'd dealt with worse.

"Did he say he'd been sent to guard the family, or the heir?" Hazel wanted to know.

"The Gatekeeper's heir," I said. "If he's telling the truth. Those probably weren't the words of the original vow. Why?"

She swore under her breath. "Because it means that if I leave the house, he'll follow me. How are we supposed to go looking for this missing Seelie heir with him hanging around?"

"Precisely what I was thinking." I ran the tap and set about washing the grave dirt off. Lucky Mum wasn't around to nag me for getting bits of zombie in the kitchen sink.

Or not-so-lucky. *Had* she sent River after us? Maybe he'd come to help us with the Sidhe's ridiculous quest. But he'd have come out with it right away if he had, and while Ivy hadn't actually said not to tell anyone, for all I knew, he was a wannabe faerie prince looking to sneak onto the throne. He looked the type, but most Seelie faeries came equipped with the same startling looks and bright green eyes. Noble, obnoxious, and… staring at me through the open window. I damn near jumped out of my skin. "What are you doing?"

"Checking your defences," he said. "Your house is well-protected."

"Tell me something I don't know." I dried off my hands.

"I didn't know there was a sister," he added.

"Yes. There is. She even has a name." I wouldn't normally be so rude to a guest, but most guests were actually invited, and he couldn't comprehend the violation of striding right onto our property. As much as his presence was a glaring reminder that it belonged to the Sidhe first, the Gatekeepers second.

"Ivy?"

I took a step back. "No. Ilsa. You know someone called Ivy?"

"The name rings a bell, but no. Ilsa." The way he spoke my name, in the slightly melodic tone of a half-faerie, made an irrational jolt of annoyance zip up my spine. But I was more fixated on the way he'd said *Ivy*. A genuine error, or an accidental slip? Sure, Ivy had *claimed* we were related, but for all I know, he and Ivy were both conspiring against the Gatekeeper.

"Why are you really here?" I sent a silent plea to the house's magic to give me some kind of reassurance he wasn't the enemy.

"I told you why." He gave me a dazzling smile. "If I meant you harm, you'd be lying beside that zombie."

"That's a nice comment to make to someone standing directly behind a stack of knives."

Okay, the only thing in my hands was a towel, but the knife rack was a foot away. Given how quickly half-faeries moved, though, I wasn't *too* confident I could lunge and grab one if he attacked. But he didn't have to know that. Besides, like all half-faeries, iron was deadly poison to him.

"Who's threatening who?" Hazel walked into the room behind me.

I put the towel down. "I was letting our uninvited guest know we have no shortage of iron knives in here."

"That's right," Hazel said, striding up to my side. "And that's not counting the weapons room. Were you winding up my sister?"

"No," he said. "I rather think she was threatening me."

"You appeared under the window and startled me. Besides, you showed up right after an undead attacked us. What am I supposed to think?"

"That you have enemies."

"You've clearly never met a Gatekeeper before," Hazel said. "Anyone who isn't a direct associate of the Seelie Court is a potential enemy."

"Then it's a good thing I have this." He held up a piece of paper. Or rather, parchment. The Sidhe's level of technology hadn't reached the printing press stage yet. When magic did everything for them, they probably didn't need it. Even through the window, I recognised the Summer Court's official seal on it.

"You might have stolen it," Hazel said, as the same thought passed through my head. *Great. Next we'll be talking in sync.* "What's our mother's name?"

"Flora Lynn," he said, not missing a beat. "She's often mentioned around my family's home in the Summer Court."

"So you live there?" Hazel asked. "I assume you do, if you work for them."

I looked at her in surprise. He could be the best bodyguard in all the realms and it wouldn't make a difference to the Sidhe. They hated the idea of anyone mortal setting foot in the Court. Things had apparently changed recently.

"Yes, I do," he said, his tone indicating that he'd prefer to change the subject. *Hmm. Did he get kicked out in disgrace?*

Did it matter? I should know better than to initiate a conversation with a half-Sidhe. The Seelie Court had never particularly cared for our well-being before. If they wanted anything, they just needed to ask Mum and she'd be compelled to give it to them. And if they thought Hazel and I knew more than Mum did about the Erlking's heir, they'd be sadly disappointed.

I didn't need to beckon Hazel to follow me into the living room—she knew when I wanted to talk to her alone.

"He knows Mum," I whispered. "Not that that's saying a lot..." The Summer Gatekeeper made enemies more often than she made friends.

"I don't think he's the enemy," said Hazel. "I can pretty much guarantee he didn't send the undead. Most half-faeries go into hysterics when they see a dead body. Reminds them too much of mortality."

Mortality. I didn't know where to begin with the part of Ivy's message that had kind of got buried under the *missing heir* crap. But what if he could hear us? If the Sidhe of the

Seelie Court *didn't* know they could die now, then that information might ignite a war. So many things in Faerie depended on death not being permanent.

Hazel's expression sobered like she'd guessed my thoughts. "He doesn't look like the type to go into hysterics anyway. The Sidhe only recruit the best."

"I didn't know they recruited half-faeries at all." I sat down on the sofa, fiddling with the hand-knitted throw. One of Grandma's creations. Half the stitches had come undone and I wasn't sure whether the pattern was meant to be a bird or a dog, but it was one of few things in the house which didn't have the Sidhe's handiwork all over it.

"Some do," said Hazel, leaning her elbows on the back of the sofa. "I get the impression the Sidhe pay their professional bodyguards pretty well. Didn't you see his fancy coat?"

I frowned. "River? You think he's important, then?"

"Important enough to send to guard the Gatekeeper's heir? I'd say so."

Hazel's instincts were well-honed—as Gatekeeper, they had to be. So if she trusted River... I'd reserve judgement.

"Is it possible you're projecting your past experiences onto the guy?" Hazel asked.

She knew me too well. The Lynn family's rule was: don't get involved with the faeries. Gatekeepers were supposed to be impartial. But I'd had a rebellious phase as a teenager, and back then, I was confident that Hazel and I would eventually find a way to free ourselves of Faerie forever. So I'd wound up having a fling with a local half-Sidhe. It hadn't ended well.

"No," I answered. "I think not trusting strange faeries who wander onto our property is a smart move."

Her eyes narrowed like she didn't believe me. Keeping anything secret from my twin sister was an impossibility, and she likely knew that guy had set my anti-faerie radar blaring. Admittedly, the human guys I'd tried to date hadn't been much better, but I could more or less take humans at face value. Half-faeries raised as human got some of the magic but not the amorality that came with being immortal, so we mostly left one another alone. This guy, though, came from the Courts. That meant he'd likely been raised to see humans like the Sidhe did. We were toys to them, nothing more, and the idea of leaving my sister alone with a potentially dangerous faerie in the house put yet another wrench in my plan to get the hell away and back to my own life.

Hazel shrugged. "It's fine. He can't get into the house, and we can keep an eye on him from the window."

"Not when we're asleep," I pointed out. "And he never said for how long." I looked at Arden, who perched on the sofa arm. "Can he be trusted?"

"Caw. Trust no one. Not even me."

"I *don't* trust you," I said. "You let someone through the barriers once already. I want you to swear you won't lie to us again."

"I will always obey the word of the Gatekeeper."

That was the problem. Mum wasn't here, and Arden wasn't under any binding to obey *me*. Hazel could coax obedience out of him up to a point, but as a non-Gatekeeper, the most I could do was threaten him with bodily harm.

"Then I'll ask someone reliable," I said to Hazel. "Have you seen Grandma recently?"

"Not recently, but she's still hanging around the mausoleum, as far as I know. You sure?"

"Absolutely." I'd trust my grandmother's ghost a damn sight more than I trusted the half-Sidhe intruder. "I'm not working tomorrow, but there's a limit to how long my boss will accept the 'family emergency' excuse. I need to clear this up."

"Does your boss know who we are?" She sounded sceptical.

"You think *any* non-supernatural would believe this?" I waved a hand at the house in general. "Most people stay in denial until it lands on top of them." Some of us didn't have that option. She knew that as well as I did. "I'll speak to Grandma tomorrow. If anyone has advice, she does."

4

I woke to the sensation of cold air on my neck and the horrible suspicion that I wasn't alone in my room.

Shifting onto my side, I squinted into the darkness, but saw nothing. My skin prickled. I slid out of bed, listening carefully, my feet sinking into the soft carpet. Horror movies warn you not to go investigating strange noises in the dark, but I wasn't about to stay in bed and get jumped by another zombie. The dark shapes of my furniture were all I saw, and when my feet collided with something solid, I breathed out when I remembered I'd left my suitcase at the foot of the bed. My door was closed, the curtains drawn on the window. So why did I feel like someone was watching me?

I crossed to the window and peered through a gap in the curtains, not seeing a sign of our unwanted bodyguard. Perhaps *he* was the intruder, and had been waiting until we were asleep to strike. But any intruder would target Hazel, not me, and not a sound came from the landing.

I reached for the nearest hard object—a giant hardback book that could probably knock the head off a zombie—and walked to the door.

A blast of icy air shook the room, slamming me off my feet. I landed on my back against the bed, gripping the book like a shield. A deep, terrible coldness seeped into my skin, yet the window wasn't open, nor the door. Raw, primal terror ripped through my mind, as though I stood on a sheer cliff, seconds from plummeting into an endless abyss.

Then warm magic infiltrated the room with an earthy scent. Green light flashed and dissipated just as quickly, and a shadowy figure appeared in the doorway. I lunged forwards and threw the book at the intruder with everything I had.

River caught it in one hand. He moved, the light streaming across the landing brightening the blond of his hair. I sagged with relief. He was looking at me weirdly... oh, shit. Most of my clothes had been covered in debris from the collapsing house so I'd gone to sleep in an oversized old T-shirt. Since I wasn't wearing a bra, my assets had probably been exposed when I'd thrown the book at him. I tugged my shirt into place, my cheeks flaming. But his eyes were narrowed in suspicion.

"Did you summon that?" he demanded.

Whoa. I scrambled to my feet. "What the hell are you talking about?"

A silver flash appeared in his eyes, so swiftly I was sure I'd imagined it a second later. "Don't move. It might still be in here."

"*What* is in the house?"

He frowned. "You can't see it. Of course..."

"Can't see what?"

Instead of answering, he ran out onto the landing. Either he was leading me into a trap, or he really did think there was an invisible enemy in here. Considering I'd definitely sensed *something* in my room, maybe he was right.

On the other hand—"How did you get into the house?"

"The vow I'm under compels me to protect you from harm," River explained. "The house let me inside the moment you were attacked."

"I was attacked by an invisible—*what*, exactly?"

Instead of answering, he pushed open the nearest door, which happened to lead into Mum's room.

"I wouldn't go in there. She'll know if a speck of dust is out of place."

He took a step back, shaking his head. "It's gone. Do you have the Sight, by the way?"

"Of course I have the Sight."

I'd always hated being asked. Sure, I didn't have magic, so it was logical to assume I was as short-sighted as any human. Most humans couldn't see faeries unless they wanted to be seen. Including—wait a moment. River was holding a sword in his hand, which definitely hadn't been there before. Runes glinted on the hilt. *No way. He has a talisman?*

"Just checking," he said. "If you weren't Sighted, you wouldn't have seen your attacker."

"Doesn't look like *you* can see it now either," I said. "Are you sure it wasn't just another disembodied zombie hand?"

Hazel's door flew open and she appeared, somehow looking intimidating even in her fluffy penguin pyjamas. Shimmering green magic circled her hands, and the temperature spiked as her anger ignited the Summer magic already present in the house. The mark on her forehead gleamed.

"What the hell is going on?" she asked.

"Apparently there's an invisible monster in the house," I told her. "He won't tell me what it is."

"Invisible?" she echoed. "What, like glamoured?"

"Not exactly." He stalked past her, sword in hand. "I can't sense it anymore."

"Sense what?" Hazel and I said more or less at the same time. Oh no. Not again.

"A wraith," he said, from the top of the stairs. "Think a ghost, but not a harmless lost spirit."

"What, a poltergeist?" asked Hazel, frowning. "I've been alone here for weeks. Pretty sure I'd know by now if the house was haunted."

"A poltergeist in my room?" Ghosts weren't an uncommon sight. That horrible, cold sensation I'd had, like something evil was watching me... I'd never had that feeling around spirits.

River looked from me to Hazel. "How much do you know about the Grey Vale?"

"Is now really the time for a quiz?" said Hazel. Her hands still glowed green with faerie magic. "If there *is* a ghost in the house, I want it out."

"The Grey Vale," I said. "That's the part of the faerie realm they send exiles to." And the source of the monsters which had attacked Earth. Outcasts who'd been kicked out of the Courts.

"Correct," he said, like he actually was running a quiz. "The Vale is a magic-free zone, and possibly because of that, if faeries die there, they don't come back. They linger forever. And when a particularly powerful spirit is trapped there, it turns into a wraith."

My throat went dry. *One of those was in my room? I'm never sleeping again.*

"What—" Hazel broke off. "Who told you that?"

From her shaken tone, she hadn't known. I didn't know it was *possible* for faeries to turn into ghosts. I mean, they didn't die. And in this realm, I'd assumed they faded away, drawn beyond the gates of death like humans were.

The Grey Vale. Faerie was dangerous on a good day, but the family name gave us some measure of protection from both Summer and Winter Courts. Not so much the place that belonged to neither. If it was true, someone must have sent that creature after us deliberately. And how had River managed to sense it?

"Do I have your permission to search the house?" asked River.

"Sure, why not," said Hazel. "You're already in here, and I'm not going back to bed if we're being haunted."

"Same." I switched on the landing light and walked back to my room, kicking the door inwards. After scanning every corner for evil spirits, I grabbed the hardback book and used it to prop the door open before opening my suitcase to find my clothes had cleaned themselves and folded themselves into neat piles. Living in this house had always been like having a parade of invisible servants eternally present, a luxury I'd missed more than I'd care to admit.

"Feel free to enjoy the show, dickhead," I said to the empty air as I stripped off my shirt. "You picked the wrong person to haunt."

And now I was arguing with invisible ghosts. Less than a day in this house and I'd officially lost my mind. Shaking my head, I slipped into my most comfortable hoody and jeans, giving the middle finger to the room in general in case the spiritual intruder was still lurking. My suitcase was packed and ready, and if I asked Hazel, she'd open a Path back to Edinburgh for me without a second's thought. But I couldn't get the look on River's face when he'd come into my room out of my head, the brief flash of silver light in his eyes. He'd thought *I'd* summoned the wraith? Or had he been covering up? I couldn't let Hazel handle this alone—and that was assuming I'd been targeted by accident. The Lynn house was safer than anywhere else, like it or not.

Hazel sat on the sofa in the living room, holding a mug of hot chocolate. "I made one for you."

"Thanks. Wait, do you mean *you* made it or the house

did?" I picked up the mug from the coffee table, the scent of warm chocolate somewhat soothing my frazzled nerves.

She blinked, the picture of innocence. "I'd have made one if the house hadn't provided."

"Uh-huh." The only place I'd come close to finding anything like the house's magical creations was a supernatural-run café in Edinburgh's Old Town—the one time I broke my rule not to go near anything supernatural-related if I could help it. I dragged my thoughts over to blueberry pancakes rather than angry ghosts, but even the smooth taste of warm chocolate didn't quite get rid of the creepy sensation of cold fingers trailing down my spine.

I pulled Grandma's handmade throw across my legs, taking another sip. "I think it's trying to make up for the attack. But to be honest, I'd take the collapsing house over the haunted one."

The hot chocolate scorched my tongue and I yelped. *Bloody house.*

"I don't blame you," Hazel said, grabbing a cookie from a plate which had materialised on the coffee table. "I think I'd remember if Mum had mentioned faerie ghosts can get past the house's boundaries."

"So you believe me?"

Hazel bit into the cookie. "Of course I do. You're the one who likes going into the mausoleum to talk to Grandma, and you're not scared of the dark. If you sensed a ghost, you're probably right."

"Wraith," I corrected. I'd heard the stories. Vale faeries hid in the shadows, preying on unsuspecting humans, and were drawn to carnage and misery. The Grey Vale itself was a dead end, a place drained of the magic that sustained the rest of Faerie, and the same went for its inhabitants. It made sense that without their magic, they were no longer immortal, and turned into ghosts after death.

"Do you think Arden might have left a gap in the defences?" I asked. "Because this is the second ghost to get inside in a day."

"I've no idea," said Hazel. "He shouldn't be able to—much less *want* to. We're all he has, and he's as tied to the Courts as we are."

"True." Arden's official title was the Gatekeeper's messenger, who carried messages from Faerie to whoever happened to be at the house. As a delegate of the Courts, he'd have the same revulsion towards the wraith as anyone from Faerie. "Someone here isn't trustworthy, and I'm inclined to blame our new friend."

"He did help you," she said. "Right? You said the creature came into your room…"

"I woke up absolutely freezing, and it was like an invisible force threw me into the air. He used magic on it—I assume that's what he did, but I didn't see the target. I thought he was the intruder so I threw a book at him."

"You threw a book at my bodyguard?"

"It was the only weapon I had within reach." Because I'd left the salt shaker and the iron filings I usually carried in my coat pockets, thinking the house's magic would keep out any intruders. "He didn't seem surprised at the attack. More like he was expecting it."

"Maybe it's what he was sent to protect us from," said Hazel. "I mean, it's not like magic works on ghosts. Or physical weapons."

"Then what was the deal with the sword?" I said. "That was a genuine talisman. Either he got it from his family, or he stole it. You know they don't hand out talismans to just anyone."

I'd thought only the Sidhe wielded those weapons.

"There's a simpler way for me to prove my allegiance," said River, leaning casually on the door frame. We should have known better than to gossip in the same house as a half-faerie. Their senses were generally much sharper than humans' were, and they moved almost as quietly as ghosts themselves.

He glided into the room, sword in hand. Runes gleamed up and down the hilt, and he removed the slip of parchment from his pocket again, tossing it to me. The note was written in the faerie script but I still remembered enough of it to get the gist. It was a note of recommendation signed by one Lord Torin. Must be his father.

"I know that signature," Hazel said, reading over my shoulder. She looked up at River. "Sorry for suspecting you. Nobody told me I was getting a bodyguard, and considering you appeared right after the zombie…"

"It's understandable," he said. "Your distrust will serve you well. You have some dangerous enemies."

"I don't suppose you can tell us who they are?" I asked. "You were sent here for a specific reason. You must have some idea who sent that wraith after us."

"Actually, I don't," he said. "I have a few theories, but I haven't been here long enough to determine who's behind it."

Irritation laced his tone, and sounded genuine. But my suspicions refused to be buried. It was no coincidence that someone with in-depth knowledge on the exact monster which had just attacked me would show up immediately beforehand.

"I'm betting it's the same person who sent a zombie after us," said Hazel. "I think we need a salt barrier… does it work on wraiths? It does on ghosts and zombies."

"That was precisely my plan," he said. "Wherever the wraith is now, it's no longer inside this house. I'll put up a barrier to deter it from coming back in."

And he left without another word.

I shook my head. "Salt won't do much if it already got

through the Sidhe's magical shields. Guess I have something else to ask Grandma."

It struck me that consulting a ghost when we'd just been attacked by one might not be the most logical move, but Grandma was one of the rare examples of someone whose spirit retained all her mental functions from when she was alive. Usually ghosts forgot who they were. Occasionally, if they died in a particularly violent manner, they turned into poltergeists. The faerie invasion had created an epidemic, and most families burned their dead to prevent their relatives rising again when weird spikes in spiritual activity occurred. But spirits were generally the most harmless supernatural being you could run into, and I'd been visiting Grandma for advice for years. With her help, I'd deal with both the wraith and Hazel's unwanted bodyguard in one go, and then tell the Sidhe to go screw themselves. Then I'd go back to university and actually get my shit together and put in an application. Simple.

Or not-so-simple. Staying here and settling into my designated role was the easier choice, which was precisely why I'd left to begin with. *I won't be beholden to the Sidhe. No matter how good those cookies smell.* Damn, that's how they got you. I picked up *one* cookie and went to fetch some weapons.

The house didn't actually have a weapons room despite what Hazel had told River, but Mum's workroom contained a handy collection of magical and non-magical weaponry. Knives, iron, salt, witch-made charms, even a crossbow. I'd adapted my coat sleeves so I could easily fit a container of shredded iron in one sleeve, salt in the other. Spares in my pockets. A single knife, sheathed and positioned within easy reach. For most humans, the goal was either not to get attacked in the first place, or cause enough pain to the enemy to escape and run like hell. Hence the iron, which burned out faeries' magic as effectively as salt destroyed undead.

As the dawn bathed the house in warmth, I walked into the living room to find Hazel waiting for me, wearing her official Gatekeeper's coat, green with embossed gold edges like a Court faerie's attire and glowing in the dawn light from the window. A strange pang went through me— someday soon, she'd be Gatekeeper. Five years had passed in a heartbeat, and would pass infinitely more quickly in the faerie realm. The gleaming silver mark on her forehead indicated the magic ready to spring to her fingertips at a second's notice.

River re-entered at the same time. He'd apparently found time to change outfits between patrolling, and now wore a knee-length coat similar to Hazel's. Faerie-made, by the look of things. I hadn't seen him bring a suitcase in, but faerie magic could explain away anything.

"Where are you going?" he asked.

"To the village," I said vaguely. "You don't have to come."

"I do if your sister goes with you."

"Oh, all right." Hazel threw up her hands. "Ilsa can go alone. I'll stay here. I'm the one you have to follow, right?"

It wasn't like her to sit out on the action. What was she scheming?

River's gaze slid to me. "It's dangerous."

"Compared to evil spirits?" I asked. "The most dangerous thing in town is Everett's baking. Trust me."

"The wraith is no common enemy," River said. "It knew how to breach the boundaries of the liminal space."

"I'm aware of that. I *live* here."

He still didn't move. Faeries could be bloody obstinate when they wanted to be. "If you're attacked again, I won't be able to help you."

What makes you think I asked for your help? "I appreciate your concern," I told him, "but where I'm going is a protected place."

For a moment, I thought I'd have to shove him aside to get out of the house. Considering he looked more muscular than a typical half-faerie and knew how to use the sword, I'd probably come off worse, magical protection or none.

Finally, River gave me a nod. "Come back within the hour, and inform one of us if you run into trouble. Hazel, you stay in the house." I heard him giving her further instructions as I made my way to the door, but he didn't follow to stop me.

Overbearing, much? We'd met less than a day ago and already he thought he knew the house better than Hazel or I did. Only the Sidhe had authority over the Gatekeeper's heir, and I had no doubt Hazel would set him straight on that one, whatever her plan was. As for me, the sooner I got out of this environment, the better. I might have grown up in this world, but I'd never really belong in it. I would never be Gatekeeper. And that suited me just fine. I just wished the rest of the world would accept it.

5

The Lynn family mausoleum lay on the other side of a hill, the closest geographical location to where the Summer estate would actually exist if it had a physical address. We'd attended school in the local village as we'd been growing up. Foxwood had a mostly supernatural population, and had been hidden from mortal sight before the faeries came. Now it wasn't hidden, but nobody wandered this far into the Highlands unless they wanted to end up torn to pieces by wild fae.

If Mum had been gone for a month, Hazel would have had her hands full dealing with the local supernatural community's problems. Usually the Mage Lords dealt with such tasks, but the village was small enough that it had only one small group of mages living there. Down the road from the mausoleum was the home of the necromancers, a building with blacked-out windows. They never seemed to turn the lights on, but Hazel and I had once had a running joke that they slept during the day, hanging from the ceiling like bats.

I unlocked the gate to the graveyard, a chill running

across the back of my neck. I'd never had reason to feel afraid here before. The living caused me more trouble than the dead, and iron barriers surrounded the place to keep the faeries out. The oldest grave of all was an empty one, commemorating Thomas Lynn, our great-infinity-great grandfather, who'd started this whole mess by getting himself kidnapped and taken into Faerie in the first place.

I shot a glare at the fancy embellished marble grave, then jumped violently when a hand rested on my shoulder.

"Surprise," said Hazel, appearing out of thin air.

"You." I stepped back, willing my racing heart to slow down. "Have you lost your mind? How'd you shake off your bodyguard?"

"I conjured up a glamour. He thinks I'm napping." She grinned. "Forgot I had a spare shadow-spell, too. I've been following you for ten minutes."

"Are you sure the glamour will last longer than an hour? You know what happened last time."

Faerie glamour wasn't the most reliable branch of magic. When we were thirteen, Hazel had made a fancy car materialise outside the house. She'd then driven it to town, where it had swiftly and embarrassingly vanished before she'd reached the end of the road. That's how we'd found out most of her faerie magic faded away when she travelled too far from the Ley Line. Good times.

"I'm sure," Hazel said. "He'll probably notice I'm missing at some point, but that's his problem."

Apparently she wasn't as resigned to having a bodyguard as she'd pretended to be. "Yes, it is. I won't stick around long, anyway. I'll just ask Grandma if she knows about that wraith, then go and question someone living."

"Good, because this place gives me the creeps."

Earthy scents filled the air, fresh from the rain the night before. I found this place peaceful, actually. My deceased family members didn't make snide comments on my fashion sense or implicitly refer to me as the 'spare'.

Stone gargoyles topped the family mausoleum, carved with precision. Iron had been built into the walls in a similar way to how the necromancers built their underground shelters. An odd choice considering our family dealt with faeries, who stopped bothering us when we shuffled off this mortal coil, but the extra protection did make it trickier for anyone to break in. I unlocked the brick building with another key, and slipped into the darkness.

The place might look old-fashioned, but someone had installed electric lights, which snapped on the instant I entered. Names of Lynns past covered the walls—both branches of the family. I never did find out why Grandma had decided to stick around while nobody else did, and Mum refused to elaborate on the subject. The two had had a volatile relationship at the best of times.

"Grandma," I whispered.

Silence answered. *Guess I shouldn't have expected to get lucky.*

"Grandma?" I called again, my voice echoing back at me. I dug my cold hands into my pockets, pacing to the room's centre, then back again. "Hey. I really need your help."

Silence answered. I paced again, scanning the names on the wall. Gatekeeper names. Non-Gatekeepers did get their own fancy graves but not the privilege of having their names recorded in here. The whole town had turned up for Grandma's funeral, when I was five. She'd scared the crap out of everyone by dancing on her own coffin. Unlike Mum, being Gatekeeper hadn't removed her sense of humour. But where in hell was she? She hadn't moved on, surely—Hazel would have said so. But the two rarely spoke to one another. Kind of odd that I'd been her favourite, considering my non-important status, but you didn't pick your calling if you were a Lynn.

A scream came from outside. *Hazel.*

I ran for the door, grabbing the salt shaker from my pocket. Green light flared as Hazel's magic activated. She stood with her back to the door—and a head poked up from amongst the graves.

Impossible. The place had been impenetrable for generations. Necromancers couldn't tamper with it. Nobody could.

Hazel whimpered. "I think… I think that's Great-Aunt Enid."

"Oh god." If there was one thing worse than zombies, it was *knowing* the zombies, or who they'd been in life. Not that you could tell at first glance. The flesh had rotted off her bones, leaving little more than a skeleton behind.

I cringed as bony hands scrabbled at the ground. The graves were splattered with soil, wet from the rain.

"Poor Great-Aunt Enid." I scattered the salt in front of us in a line, while Hazel conjured magic to her hands, biting her lip. "She hated dirt. I remember her yelling at me for getting mud on the furniture." I spoke more to reassure Hazel than myself. The necromancers' place was just down the road, and it wasn't unreasonable to assume a novice had accidentally summoned up a swarm of zombies. The idea of dissolving my relatives wasn't appealing, but their spirits were long-gone. I lifted the salt shaker and took aim.

Cold air slammed into me, and my back hit the door. Hazel shrieked, hands raised to defend herself. Green Summer magic exploded from her fingertips, knocking the undead back, but a second crawled from the ground to join the first. Another Great-Aunt, from the look of her tattered dress.

My stomach turned over. *They can't use magic. They're not alive.* The cold terrible energy pulsing from the undead was too close to what I'd felt in my room. Not faerie magic, but something else entirely—a power that could bypass our magic-proof shields.

"Ilsa," whispered Grandma's voice from beside me.

I jumped, spilling salt everywhere. "What in hell is going on?"

"Someone has tampered with some dark and terrible magic," Grandma's ghost whispered.

"No shit." I aimed the salt shaker with trembling hands, whiteness sprinkling the earth, but the two undead kept moving, undeterred. Horrible growling noises came from their rotting throats. "You might have shown up *before* the zombies."

"It's not working!" Hazel blasted the undead with magic once more, but it had no effect. Her Summer magic needed life to function, and there wasn't a living soul here besides me. "It's like they're—possessed."

The undead raised its hands. Another wave of icy air smacked into me, sending me flying through the partly open door. This time I landed on my back with a crash, stars winking before my eyes. I scrambled across the bare stone floor, beckoning frantically behind the iron door. "Hazel, get in here!"

A third blast of magic struck the doors, making them rattle. The lights flickered on and off, and when they came back on, Grandma's ghost appeared, faintly hovering next to the wall displaying the names of former Gatekeepers. A wooden door had appeared that hadn't been there before, its handle gleaming with silvery light.

"Hazel!" I yelled. "Get *in* here." Heaven knew if iron could protect anyone against necromantic magic, but I was out of options. Save for an invisible door guarded by a ghost.

"Ilsa." Grandma's voice was faint. "I don't have much time… it's through the door."

I lunged the last two feet towards the door, grabbing its cold handle. I'd expected to find a secret passageway, but the space inside was cramped and too narrow to climb into. Nothing was inside except for a small book lying on a raised section of stone. Pocket-sized and yellowed with age, it had a swirling mark on the cover and no other title.

"What's this for?" I flipped open the volume, but the pages were blank. I hadn't thought Grandma was losing her grip on sanity, but handing me an empty-paged book wouldn't help put my undead relatives to rest. It wasn't like we were necromancers—

An invigorating rush of icy energy pierced my veins and flooded my body. Power hummed through the book in my hands, which lit up silver-white. The pages glowed, unreadable text skimming across the blankness. Greyness infiltrated my vision, and the door flew wide, freezing cold air rushing in. The glow spread from my book to my hands, lighting the gloom. I heard Hazel screaming, but all I saw of her was a glowing outline of a person. Beyond, the undead were visible as dark spots in the gloom, pulsing with malevolent energy.

The light shot from my hands, past Hazel, right at the undead. White light ignited around their edges, and with a cracking sound, the undead fell.

I waited a moment, but they didn't rise. The greyness receded from my vision, showing only the graves, and Hazel clinging to the iron door. Slowly, I turned to face Grandma.

"What did you do?" I gasped. My body swayed on the spot and I closed my eyes, my head spinning. Though the book had stopped glowing, the white light was imprinted on my eyelids.

"Keep the book," she responded. "Tell nobody about it outside of our family." Her words rang with steel, the tone that had terrified people when she'd been alive.

"Hey—you can't leave without telling me anything."

Grandma was already fading when I opened my eyes. The outline of her face melted into the whiteness, then disappeared entirely.

In her place, Hazel gaped at me through the open iron door. "What in hell was that?"

"I… that's a very good question."

One I already knew the answer to. I had magic. I'd banished a spirit. Several of them. Only necromancers were supposed to be able to do that.

Her gaze fell on the book. "What the—?"

"Grandma gave it me." I waved vaguely at the wooden door with my free hand, and looked down at the book to be greeted by entirely blank pages again. I skimmed through, my heart sinking. "Every page is blank." Even the cover depicted nothing more than an inexplicable swirling symbol. No words.

Hazel's eyes bugged out. "She gave you *magic?*"

"I don't know what she gave me. I can't read this, and besides, you can't give someone magic, let alone if you're a ghost. It doesn't work like that."

"Our family's never been known for playing by the rules, though. Wow." She looked over her shoulder at the fallen undead, then back at me. "The undead—whatever was powering them switched off. Like their spirits were gone."

"Gone," I murmured, lowering the book and turning to face the empty room again. "Er—Grandma?"

"Is there a problem?" asked a male voice from outside the mausoleum. River. I swiftly shoved the book into my pocket. Someone had made it a convenient enough size to carry around—but why couldn't I read it?

"What are you doing here?" I asked, walking after Hazel out into the cemetery. River stood beside the gates, eyebrows raised at the undead lying in crumpled heaps. If we left them in that state and Mum found out, we'd be joining them in the dirt.

"What else? My vow compelled me to follow Hazel." His gaze slid to the graves. "Are several of your family members supposed to be lying in pieces?"

"Clearly not," I told him. "Guess the person raising zombies got here first."

"In that case, allow me to help you return them to their resting place," said River. "I also sensed necromantic magic, but when I arrived here, it'd entirely disappeared. Is there a necromancer here?"

"No," said Hazel. "This is a private graveyard for family only."

"So who banished the dead? That flash of light I just saw—"

"Family magic," I said. "Defence mechanism on the graves. Handy."

He frowned disbelievingly. "Why did you come here anyway? After being attacked by a wraith and an undead, it strikes me as a risky move." There was definite suspicion in his eyes, and I remembered the accusing look he'd given me when the wraith appeared in my room. Admitting I had some unknown form of necromancy might not be the wisest idea, especially as he was still an unknown element.

"Maybe it's none of your business?" said Hazel. "If you're volunteering to help move the bodies, though, be my guest."

"There's a simpler way." He raised his hands. Swiftly, the undead rose like puppets on strings, directed towards the rows of graves. "Which grave did she come from?"

It took me a second to understand he meant Great-Aunt Enid. I pointed to the grave, more stunned by the demonstration of actual, genuine necromancy than anything else. River wasn't just a faerie. I'd never heard of a faerie-necromancer before. I mean, anything was theoretically possible, but faeries were terrified of death, and necromancers dealt in corpses. Not exactly a match made in heaven. *Hell,* possibly.

Would he understand my magic? I opened my mouth, but a sudden tugging sensation gripped my chest. *Ow.*

Hazel got there first. "You're a necromancer? You?"

"Half," he said, directing the last of the undead back to their graves. "I didn't reanimate them, don't worry. I merely gave them some encouragement to return to where they came from."

"Wow." I shook my head. "You're wasted on bodyguard duty." That explained how he knew there'd been undead at the house.

"It's lucky those wraiths were too weak to need a circle to be banished," he said. "May I see this defence mechanism of yours?"

It might have been my imagination, but I swore his gaze briefly dropped to my pocket where I'd stashed the book.

Hazel stepped in. "It only works when we're being attacked. Kind of like our defensive magic, but without the shield. Anyway, we should go. We share this graveyard with Winter's Lynn branch, and I don't want to explain to Holly why her Great-Aunt Thistle's grave is in such a mess."

"There are more Lynns?" he asked, a note of surprise in his voice.

Thanks, Hazel. She'd successfully distracted him. All the way home, Hazel explained about the two branches of the Lynn family, and even how old Thomas Lynn had started the whole thing by getting ensnared in Faerie. That left me plenty of time to brood over the spellbook. I'd thought the only magic that ran in our bloodline was the Gatekeeper's power. The idea of having my own magic wasn't an unappealing one, but how was I supposed to figure out the book if every one of its pages was empty?

River followed us into the house again, so I slipped

upstairs and left the book in my suitcase before showering and changing out of my dirt-covered clothes. Usually I'd stop to appreciate the house's shower—which came with a dozen settings ranging from 'late to work' to 'fell in a mountain of troll dung', but the whole time I was in the shower, I was conscious of the book not being in the room with me. Like an ache in the back of my head, a constant tapping on my skull. The feeling went away when I shoved on a fresh outfit and stuck the book deep into the inside pocket of my hoody. I knew a magical item when I saw one, and the book apparently really wanted me to carry it everywhere. But if it was an important family heirloom, I sure as hell hadn't heard of it before.

I came downstairs to find River and Hazel in the living room, where the house's magic had conjured up breakfast. As I sat down next to Hazel on the sofa, she swiped a piece of toast from my plate, having finished her own. I debated snatching it back, but funnily enough, the zombies had killed my appetite. Hazel bounced back from near-death experiences in seconds, while I was still in the *I want to curl up and go to sleep, preferably without a wraith in my room* phase.

"Ilsa." Hazel waved a hand in front of my face. "You're a million miles away."

"I have no idea why." I gripped the sofa's arm with one hand like it'd restore my grip on sanity. "We just got attacked by our undead relatives. And then River *walked* them back to their graves."

"I did," he confirmed. "I assumed you would have preferred that to me reanimating them again."

Ugh. No thanks. I suppressed a shudder at the memory of those horrible throaty noises coming from my deceased Great-Aunt Enid. I'd encountered undead before—in Edinburgh, the dead seemed to rise every other week—but the city had a high number of trained necromancers, and undead weren't sentient. "Since when could zombies use magic?"

"They can't," River said. "As I was saying to your sister, wraiths are an exception to the rules that apply to regular spirits. They were able to temporarily possess the reanimated bodies of your relatives to attack you."

"Does that mean a necromancer summoned them, then?" I asked.

Hazel shrugged. "Nobody else has power over life and death."

"Except him," I said, before I could help myself.

River half-rose from his seat. "Are you accusing me of raising those creatures?"

"No, just making an observation," I said. "Those wraiths came after us with purpose. They didn't rise of their own accord. You're the only person we've met who's even heard of them."

"If I knew who summoned them, I'd have told you," he said icily, with no hint of the warm humour in his voice when he'd been talking to my sister.

"Sorry," I said, before I dug a deeper hole. Grave-deep. My phone lit up with a message from my boss telling me to explain what I meant by a family emergency.

"Who are you messaging?" Hazel asked.

"My boss." I sank back into my seat. "I doubt he'd appreciate it if I told him I'm not coming to work because our dead relatives decided to attack us."

"Human boss?" she asked. "Tell him you caught the faerie pox and it's contagious."

"I told him it's a family emergency, but that doesn't cover zombies." Or cursed spellbooks, for that matter. "It's not like he can check up on me."

Hazel stole another piece of my toast. "No, he can't. You know what happened last time a human came here."

She just had to go there.

"Last time?" said River, sounding intrigued. "Can people find this house from outside?"

"Nope." I poked Hazel warningly with my foot.

She scooted out of reach, putting the plate down. "Ilsa brought a boy home once…"

"And the house's magic decided he was a threat and turned him into a tree," I finished. "That's all there is."

Hazel cackled. "What she's not telling you is that Mum was away in Faerie at the time and neither of us could figure out how to take the spell off. He was stuck like that for hours before the house took pity on him. Don't cross the Gate-keeper, in case you're getting any ideas," she added to River, who now wore a smirk to rival her own. *Hilarious.*

I aimed a kick at her and winced when her foot connected with my kneecap. "Ow. Okay, I'm telling my boss *you* caught the faerie pox."

Hazel grabbed my phone from my hand. "Nice try. Just say you have the flu. I don't get what the problem is."

For a start, I have a cursed spellbook which seems to be connected with the dead, and I live in the most haunted city in the country.

River watched me across the coffee table. "Faerie pox? Really?"

"It's a thing." Humans could only catch the pox by kissing a faerie, not something I particularly wanted to discuss with a cute guy, faerie or not. I didn't think he and Hazel had been flirting, but he wasn't her usual type. She preferred rogues and troublemakers, not stuck-up bodyguards with unexpected necromantic talents. And there was that rule about not dating faeries. It shouldn't apply to me, but River wasn't my type either. I'd been there before, and walked away with both faerie pox *and* a broken heart.

River grinned wickedly. "I know it's a thing. I was wondering how *you* knew."

Was there a challenge in his expression? He should know better than to flirt with either of us, considering Hazel had told the exact truth about the unfortunate human guy I'd dated at school. And I'd also just accused him of working against us. Though he'd thought the same of me this morning as well…

I grabbed my phone from Hazel. "We're experts in everything to do with the faeries. And I do need to call my boss, so if you two don't mind…"

River's brows rose. "You can make phone calls from here?"

"Sometimes, if the wind's blowing in the right direction," I responded. "Don't ask me how. Same reason electricity works in the house when we aren't on solid ground—magic."

I checked Hazel hadn't sent anything incriminating to my boss and dashed off a message saying I'd had to attend a funeral. Which was sort of true, and I thought Grandma would get a kick out of it. I'd messaged my former landlord earlier offering to pay for a spell to fix the house and find alternative accommodation for my displaced housemates, but had received no response. Which probably meant I'd been blacklisted from all human-owned housing in the city for the next few decades.

Right. Let's see if I can squeeze answers out of this spellbook.

I went into the library, took out the book, and opened it. Not a single word showed on its aged pages. I flipped it upside-down, held it under the light, yet it remained stubbornly blank. "Come on, you little bastard." I flipped it over, like if I shook it hard enough, the answers would fall out.

"What in the world are you doing?" asked Hazel.

I lowered the book. "Is he gone?"

"Yeah, he's back to patrolling outside. It's not so bad

having someone else to help watch the place, to be honest." Her gaze snagged on the book's cover. "That looks like a magical rune of some type."

"I can't have magic. Not when I'm…" I trailed off, not sure how I was going to end that sentence. "…not magical."

She grinned. "Now you are. Welcome to the club."

6

In the end, I didn't get a secret handshake or initiation, just a book that wouldn't reveal its contents. Hazel and I tried three different variations of witch revealing spells on it, followed by a rare concoction that was supposed to peel away glamour in front of humans—but nothing worked. The pages remained empty. I tried writing my name in the book, but the pen didn't work. I tried another. Same result.

"Someone really doesn't want this book damaged," Hazel commented as I put the third pen onto the table in the library. "It must be magically preserved."

"Faerie magic?" I shook the spellbook, then flipped it upside-down, letting the pages fan out. "Nah, it was hidden in a building of reinforced iron. This has 'necromancy' written all over it."

"There's an idea," she said. "Maybe the necromancers' guild can help."

I snapped the book closed. "Grandma told me to promise not to tell anyone. Besides, I'm not sure I'd really count as a necromancer considering I wasn't born as one."

Only higher level necromancers could actually control the dead, zombies included. Mostly they wandered around wearing Grim Reaper cloaks and being constantly haunted by any ghost in the vicinity. It didn't look like much fun.

"What are you talking about?" River appeared in the doorway so suddenly he might as well have teleported out of thin air. *Bloody half-faeries.* I dropped my hand casually to my side to hide the book from view.

"Can you not do that?" I said. "This isn't your house, you know."

"Your sister gave me leave to enter and exit as I pleased," he said. "I wanted to ask your permission before applying a barrier to the garden as well as the house."

"If you're using iron, don't put it near the Seelie Gate," Hazel said. "The Sidhe would take it as a grave insult. Almost as much as the undead."

"Ha ha," I said. "But really—no iron. I have some, but putting it anywhere near the Sidhe's favourite corner of the garden is a great way to get yourself turned into a deer."

"Do the Sidhe come here often?" he enquired.

"Not when they're actually needed, no," I said, wishing he'd look away so I could conceal the book out of sight. The Sidhe usually only came through the gate in times of dire need. I vaguely remembered the day I'd seen the Summer Sidhe riding through our garden to war with their outcast brethren, but I'd been a toddler at the time and I had only vague recollections of the faerie invasion. I *did* know Mum had fought, and had the scars to prove it. But other than that, the gate lay mostly unused.

"The Sidhe will come when necessary," proclaimed Arden, perching on the door frame. "Human business is not their business."

I took the opportunity to slide the book into my pocket as Arden flew out of sight in a whirl of feathers.

River looked at me. "What type of faerie is he?"

"He's the Lynn family's messenger," said Hazel.

"He specialises in useless advice and delivering warnings too late," I added. "Oh, and he sometimes sits on top of doors and says "Nevermore"."

"Arden's also the only company I've had in the house for weeks," said Hazel. "Guess that's why he brought Ilsa here."

That, or he knew about the book. But I wasn't about to chase the raven down to ask, and I highly doubted the Sidhe had put the notebook of the dead into my hands.

"He brought you here?" River asked. "To help with the undead situation?"

"No," I said. "I came here to help Hazel, and I've every intention of leaving once this is over."

"Leaving?" he asked. "Don't you live here?"

"Not permanently. I have a job to go back to. What exactly did you think non-Gatekeepers did?" The words sounded more vehement than I'd intended, and I caught a glimpse of Hazel's hurt expression as she ducked her head. *Ah, crap.* This was why I'd avoided coming home until now. Hazel hadn't taken my departure well, and while we'd spoken on the phone every week, I'd held off paying a visit, knowing that setting foot in this place would bring back memories of Sidhe with pretty smiles and poisonous words who tore me down with a single look. I didn't think even Mum or Hazel understood how difficult it'd been growing up in the Gate-keeper's shadow until I'd left.

"I was told your whole family served the Seelie Court," said River. "But I didn't know there was more than one Lynn sibling."

"We have another twelve hidden in the attic," I said. "Didn't you see how many graves there were? We Lynns breed like rabbits."

Hazel choked on a laugh, muffling the noise with the back of her hand.

River turned to me, the corner of his mouth lifting. "Really? Is that one of your hobbies, Ilsa?"

Heat climbed up my neck. I'd walked right into that one, and I deserved it for assuming most half-faeries didn't get sarcasm. But at least I'd cheered Hazel up.

"Yeah, we have almost as many descendants as the Seelie King," Hazel added.

I shot her a warning look, which she ignored.

"The Erlking doesn't have human bloodlines," he said, still looking highly amused at my comment. I didn't think it was *that* funny. "Or so I'm told."

"I don't know about humans, but someone seems to want *me* to find the heir to the Seelie Court."

Dammit, Hazel. I didn't think River was a villain, but I could also count the number of people who'd got into the house without the Gatekeeper's permission on one hand, and one of those was a murderous wraith.

"What…" His brows drew together. "You've been told to find the heir to Summer? As in, the Erlking's successor?"

"Is that so hard to believe?" said Hazel. "The Gatekeeper's role is to preserve the peace inside the Court and outside it. Ensuring a peaceful power transition seems a vital part of that, right?"

Clever. She was trying to talk River into giving up what *he* knew of the Court's fragile state.

"I wasn't aware there *was* an upcoming power transition," River said. "I thought such a task would be considered too delicate for anyone other than the Sidhe themselves."

Hazel's face reddened. She wasn't used to being put down, and from his matter-of-fact tone, River didn't seem to realise he'd crossed a line.

"That's why I decided to go to the graveyard," I said

quickly. "Our own ancestors were tangled with the Sidhe, so I figured there might be clues about the heir. I guess the wraiths were sent by someone trying to stop us." It was the only connection I could think of. But did that mean someone in the Grey Vale knew about the missing Seelie heir?

"Maybe." River sounded doubtful. "I would have expected someone to tell me that when I received the orders to guard you."

He sounded genuinely insulted that they'd neglected to tell him what was going on. *Welcome to the club, River.* What with the vow binding him, he couldn't know all his superiors' motives. And he hadn't so much as alluded to the Sidhe no longer being immortal, so I assumed he didn't know about it. But if that was the case, whose binding words had led him to us? And why, for that matter, had *I* been the one to receive the order to find the heir?

"Though I can't say I know why they'd give the job to humans," he added. "It strikes me as a matter for someone within the Courts, not outsiders."

"Maybe they thought we'd do a better job than you," I said. "Aren't you supposed to be decorating the lawn?"

"I could use some assistance." He looked at me. "I feel like we got off on the wrong foot, and if we're to work together, it'd be easier if we all got along."

It'd be easier if you stopped ordering us around in our own house, for a start. If he hadn't wanted to end up neck deep in crap, he shouldn't have got tangled with our family to begin with. But the more I thought about it, the less the situation made sense. Finding out who'd tried to kill us ought to take precedence over whatever was going on in Summer.

Hazel signalled her *I need to talk to you* look again. I turned to River. "Sure. I'll get the spare salt."

River gave me a nod and glided to the door. "I'll be

outside. You never know—you might find you enjoy my company after all."

"Have fun with that," Hazel commented. "Mum left me a bunch of paperwork to deal with, so if there are no clues about the heir, I need to get a head start on that. Unless you'd like to help...?"

"I think I'll take the garden, thanks." After five years absent, my grasp of faerie languages was sketchy to say the least, and I wanted to check nothing else had sneaked in. "But seriously—why did you tell him?"

"There's something *wrong* with the request we were given," she said. "If it was a task given by the Seelie Court for our family only, I'd have got tongue-tied the moment I tried to speak it aloud. You *know* they take their vows seriously. But this quest—it wasn't one."

"You're saying someone sent us on a wild goose chase on purpose? The Erlking *is* dying. And we haven't seen any evidence to contradict what else Ivy said. If anything, this whole wraith situation proves it's true."

"Maybe our bodyguard knows."

"Precisely my thinking." I'd dealt with the dead today—I could handle an hour with River. But I definitely wouldn't be bringing up faerie pox. Or half-Sidhe lovers with intoxicating magic. *Don't even go there, Ilsa.*

I fetched the spare salt shaker from the kitchen and went out through the back door, where I found River laboriously scattering salt along the edge of the lawn that bordered the hedge. The field beyond was bare and empty, but the whole garden shone with vibrant Summer magic. I didn't blame him for removing his coat, but his faerie-made clothes clung to his tall, muscular body and left little to the imagination. I forced my gaze to the sword strapped to his waist instead. Maybe he expected a piskie to jump out of the hedge and attack him. In fairness, it wasn't unlikely in our garden.

The talisman meant the Court trusted him. Whether the Gatekeepers could do the same remained to be seen.

"You can start over there," he said, pointing at a section of hedge. "Ideally, we shouldn't leave any gaps, but the gate can remain untouched."

"No wraith with any sense would go near there," I said, shaking salt onto the grass. "I never asked—are they conscious?"

"Not in the same way regular spirits are. They're like concentrated emotion. Poltergeists and wraiths have that in common. The force of their rage allows them to do things no normal ghosts can."

Goosebumps rose on my arms, and I looked over my shoulder at the house.

"Enough about the dead," he said. "I'd like to get to know you, Ilsa."

"You've met a lot of my family. Some of the dead ones, even. Pretty sure they can give you an accurate picture."

"I can't say your Great-Aunts were keen to stick around for a conversation," he said lightly.

"Do all necromancers come equipped with graveyard humour, or is it more of a faerie thing?" Probably the former. Faeries tended to be very literal-minded, and as Hazel had rightly pointed out, most would run screaming at the sight of zombies.

A smile curled his lip. "We come equipped with a variety of talents."

Equipped… talents. Right. His smooth tone sent my thoughts plummeting right into the gutter. I shouldn't be surprised, considering all my previous interactions with half-faeries involved them either trying to seduce me or throw me in ponds. Occasionally, both at the same time.

I rolled my eyes at him. "Not subtlety, evidently."

He raised both brows innocently, but a trace of his

knowing smirk remained. "I have no idea what you're talking about."

Let him keep his innuendos. As I'd keep my thoughts several miles away from mental images of what else that smooth tongue might be able to do. It'd been a depressingly long while since I'd had any action in that department, but really.

Giving myself a mental shake, I finished the salt line. "You're sure this will work?"

"Yes," he said, moving to the next section of hedge. "Necromancers have used this technique for hundreds of years."

"That's what worries me, considering their track record for letting zombie swarms get out of hand." I turned to see him looking at me. "What?"

"I'm surprised you know about other supernaturals."

"Why? The Gatekeeper deals with them all the time. It's not like we live on another planet." I'd absorbed all the information on magic I could get my hands on, yet nothing I'd come across even came close to the spellbook in my pocket.

"You and your sister grew up here? No other family?"

"Our brother, but he left a while ago. The others are dead."

"So the comment about the twelve siblings in the attic was a joke, then?" He finished the salt line, somehow making even *that* look elegant. Faeries.

"Even twins were a surprise to everyone."

"Because there's only supposed to be one Gatekeeper?"

Why couldn't I go more than two minutes of conversation with someone and not land up on that topic? "No, because I'm the evil twin, and I actually have two heads. This is a glamour."

He appeared behind me, so suddenly that I jumped. "You seem to have missed a spot."

I swatted at him, accidentally scattering salt on his shoes. "Least I know you're not a zombie."

His teeth gleamed blindingly white as he grinned. "With this face?"

I threw more salt at his feet. "Stop laughing at me. I thought this was all serious business."

"It is. I thought you'd appreciate the distraction."

He was right. I'd forgotten all about the wraith, because now I wanted to upend the salt canister on his head. "Back to work, Mr Professional Bodyguard."

He glided back to my side. "*Can* you use glamour? Your sister said you're entirely human, and the magic only passes to one of you. It's a curious way for things to work."

Curious? No. Bloody annoying was more like it. "Nope, I just got the defence mechanism. Hit me with magic and you'll see." I'd heard variations of the same question a thousand times before and they always ended at the same conclusion. To the Sidhe, if you didn't have power, you were as good as dead, and I really didn't need to hear the same from him.

"Hit you?" he echoed. "Are you certain?"

Green light slid over his eyes, springing to his palms. Earthy power thrummed in the air, promising pain, and a lot of it. But barely a spark shot from his hands, then ricocheted ten feet into the air.

"That was pathetic." I looked into his emerald eyes and tried to ignore the way his earthy magic infiltrated my senses. "Try it. Hit me with everything you have."

Green light blasted towards me, spiralling to the right. Thorny plants sprang up where it hit the ground, twenty feet away from me. River frowned, his hands lighting up again, and took a step in my direction. The earthy scent grew stronger, overpowering the latent magic in the garden. Or maybe it was the fact that he was standing inches from my face. Green light rippled where he ran a hand down the front of the invisible shield. My skin prickled in response to the proximity of his magic. I couldn't recall anyone ever getting close enough to test the shield's exact boundaries, which made me feel weirdly exposed in a way I couldn't explain.

"I said hit me, not *stroke* me." Shit, that sounded wrong.

An amused spark appeared in his eyes. "I can do both."

Light flashed behind my head, and a buzzing noise came from the house as the deflected magic bounced off its shield. "Nice," I said. "The house will probably set a swarm of mice on you for that."

"Can it do that?"

"Mum's the one who set up the spell, so theoretically— yes. Whenever Hazel or I decided to sleep in instead of getting up early for school, she used to pre-program the house to dump ice-cold water onto our heads."

"Is that so?" Green light exploded from his fingertips, hitting the shield. Again, it shot into the air like a firework.

River stepped backwards, his gaze skimming over me. "Impressive. It's not like any defensive barrier I've seen before."

I shrugged, pretending not to be bothered by his close scrutiny of me. "I'm this close to Faerie. If I didn't have that defence, I'd be catatonic from all the magic. Nobody else can stay here for long."

"So… your father? Your sister said he moved away."

"Back to Ireland. He lasted a year. Pollen allergies didn't help."

"I can't imagine they did," he commented. "I assume you're not allergic." He raised a hand and the thorny plants he'd accidentally conjured disappeared, reforming in a line in front of the fence.

I raised an eyebrow. "You think thorns can hurt ghosts?"

"No, but I think it's an improvement." Flowers sprang to

life between the faerie thorns, a deceptive contrast to the sharp pointy stems which I knew from a former painful experience could tear through to the bone. "Your sister doesn't seem to have taken good care of the garden."

All the Summer faeries I'd met seemed to like nature more than they liked people. Though I was fairly sure most didn't also enjoy raising the dead. The flowers' petals glistened, red as blood. "Seelie magic, huh. Pretty but deadly sharp."

"You have a cutting tongue yourself." He picked up the salt shaker again. "Where do you live when you're not here?"

"Edinburgh."

"My family lives there."

"The human—necromancer one. Right?"

"Right." He nodded. "I thought you were tied to this house by magic. That's why I was surprised."

"We can't move more than ten miles from the Ley Line without side effects. But the Line goes through the whole country and moves around a lot." I shrugged, scattering more salt. "So I'm guessing you trained at the necromancer guild?"

His smile slipped a fraction. "Yes, I did, for a while. My mother's side of the family works there."

So when it'd come down to a choice between human and faerie realms, he'd picked Faerie. I guessed most people would choose piskies over zombies. "Don't you miss this realm, if you were raised here?"

Now I was asking personal questions? I really was too curious for my own good.

"Do you miss home?" he asked, his expression unreadable.

"Nice evasion," I said. "Yes. I do miss it. Missing somewhere doesn't mean you belong there. There aren't many career options available out here, in case it wasn't obvious. Actually, there's kind of only one option." Most Lynns hadn't minded being the Gatekeeper's assistant. It was supposed to be an honour to have anything to do with the Courts at all.

"So what's your ambition?" he asked.

"Maybe academia. I'm applying for a PhD."

"In what?"

"Folklore."

"Naturally. Do you get bonus points for belonging to the Sidhe?"

"I don't *belong* to them," I said. "I spend most of my time arguing with academics about the definition of a banshee, and most humans have no idea who the Lynns are." Any warmth I might have felt towards him had thoroughly disappeared. He'd spoken to me like a person, but still thought of me as a toy.

A sudden draft of cold air struck me from behind and I spun around, hearing Hazel shout from the house. Outside, the grass had begun to ripple and swirl like an ocean stirred by currents. I stared, transfixed, as the ground churned, the flowerpots under the window toppling over. Debris flew into the air and struck the window, leaving a fist-sized crack. A flurry of screeching piskies flew past like a flock of demented pigeons, and I ran for the back door. "Hazel!"

Hazel ran into the kitchen, eyes wide. "The window's broken. My magic—it's not working on it." I'd never seen her look so scared. "Is that—?"

"A wraith? I'd say so." But I couldn't *see* it.

Hazel grabbed my arm in a way she hadn't since we were five and Mum was in a temper. *Now would be a good time to come back, Mum.* I knew better than to expect a Sidhe knight to ride in on a horse and save the day, either. The Sidhe didn't help anyone except their own kind, and maybe even *they* would run from the dead.

More debris struck the house with a series of cracks. I turned back to the lawn, putting myself between Hazel and the invisible assailant, salt shaker in hand—for all the good it did against an unseen foe.

Then I spotted River, standing in the centre of the lawn as though there wasn't a monster throwing sharp objects around right in front of him. *What the hell is he doing?* Even a faerie talisman was useless against a ghost. Maybe his faerie vow was compelling him to fight it, but nothing could kill the dead.

Except...

Pale light glowed from my pocket. As my fingers brushed against the book's cover, the same odd tingling sensation from the cemetery took hold of me again. I grabbed the book and it flew open, words skimming the pages too quickly to read.

A hiss of icy air passed over my skin, and River shouted aloud as he was sent flying backwards, striking the wall beneath the kitchen window. Greyness edged in around my vision, and I saw it. Floating above where River had been, it looked like a shadow vaguely shaped like a person. No features, no limbs—just pulsing, malevolent energy. Raw fear pounded inside my head, yet my hand on the book was oddly steady.

The world fogged over, a blurred grey mist covering everything. For a second, I thought I saw Grandma's ghost at my side, mouthing words I couldn't hear. A brighter patch shone amongst the grey, a floating, vaguely humanoid shape. A being of wrath and darkness, which writhed, its mouth stretched open in a silent scream. *Oh... my god.*

Hazel's cry snapped me out of my trance.

"Hey!" I screamed, waving the book. Light shone up my arms, arced through the air and smacked into the wraith. Its shadowy form writhed with a deafening screech—then it turned around. I couldn't explain why, considering it had no visible eyes, but its attention seemed to suck all the life from the air. It'd seen me, sensed me, and wanted me dead.

My breath caught. Seeing that whirling shadow was like looking into a swirling pit of darkness. So much hate and anger rolled over me, bringing a bitter taste to my tongue. *It's trapped. It's stuck in that form.*

Another light caught my gaze from the lawn below. Several white flame-like lights—candles. That's what River had been doing on the lawn. Setting up a necromancer trap to banish the wraith. And any person who had necromantic abilities could light those candles, even from a distance.

The numbness locking my hands receded enough for me to tighten my grip on the book. A fierce power burned from my mind to my fingertips as I concentrated on the candles. Light burst from my hands again, this time directed not at the wraith but at the spirit circle on the lawn. Immediately, it came to life. The light streamed up into the air to converge around the point of the screeching, trapped spirit.

The light exploded. I fell back, shielding my eyes, head pounding, body shaking. I stared as the wraith's form dissolved, disappearing into the lights, leaving rippling grass and debris behind.

7

"Hazel?" I called shakily.

"I'm okay," she said, her voice muffled. "Is it gone?"

"I think it is."

I jumped back as the house trembled, and the bumps and tears in the wall repaired themselves before my eyes. Shattered glass vanished from the lawn. I walked forwards. River still lay against the wall, his eyes closed.

"Hey." I ran to him. "River. You okay?" He might be annoying and condescending, but I hadn't wanted him to get killed defending us.

River groaned, shifting into a sitting position. "Is it gone? I used a circle…"

Hazel and I looked at one another. "Yeah, it's gone," I said.

"I haven't faced one that tough before." He climbed to his feet. "Bastard really didn't want to let go of the mortal plane."

"Are you okay? Come in. I think the house is done repairing itself now."

"Repairing itself?" He blinked, then shrugged. "I need to check the garden."

"Not if you have a concussion, you don't," Hazel said.

"I don't," he said, climbing to his feet. "I have healing magic, in any case. It's fairly essential in this line of business."

"Because your vow forces you to stand in the way if your client gets attacked?" asked Hazel.

River looked at her. "Occasionally, but it depends on the circumstances. I've never had a client threatened by the dead before. I thought I hadn't finished speaking the banishing spell when it hit me." His gaze was questioning—penetrating, even.

Did I want to tell him what I'd done? It seemed only fair to. But when I opened my mouth to speak, what came out instead was, "I'll finish the salt lines. Just in case there's another one."

I put my hand in my pocket to show him the book, and my hand… stuck. I tried to pull it out, and a wrenching tug gripped my chest, my fingers locking around the book seemingly of their own accord. I let the book go, and my hand came free. Had I imagined seeing Grandma? I'd say no, but there wasn't any sign of her left.

"I didn't sense anything else," he said. "It must have been waiting nearby until we came back to the house. I shouldn't have left you alone." He addressed Hazel. "I can only offer my apologies."

"I'm not hurt. You're the one who got flung into a wall." Hazel looked at me again, and seemed to be communicating something with her eyes. "I didn't even see what was attacking."

But I did. At first I hadn't, but when the book opened… the grey light I'd seen was the spirit sight. I knew it as surely as I knew my own name. But the necromancers saw the world that way all the time, not just when they used magic.

River walked to the candles set up where the spirit had

vanished. They looked like regular candles but made of some sort of plastic rather than wax, and edged in iron.

"So is that how it usually is when you banish spirits?" I asked, watching him pace the circle as though checking the spirit was gone. "You set up that—spirit circle?"

"Yes," he said, back in serious business mode again. "It's effectively to keep a spirit caged in one place so I can use a banishing spell on it. No matter how strong they are, they're no longer bound to the world of the living. That means the veil constantly tugs on them, pulling them towards the gates."

"The gates to the afterlife?" asked Hazel.

"Nobody actually knows what lies Beyond, but yes," he said.

I hadn't seen any gates, but the whole thing had happened so fast. My heart still raced, and the image of that creature exploding into light replayed behind my eyes. I knew necromancers. They'd been everywhere in Edinburgh. Like many old cities steeped in history, it had no shortage of spiritual activity. They even made tourist attractions out of it, in the world before the faeries had invaded and everyone gained more experience with ghosts than they'd ever wanted. The Ley Line in particular was close to the veil…

The veil. The *Vale*. Whoever had named the place must know both worlds. The Grey Vale was a physical plane, though, a separate part of Faerie itself. The necromancers' veil was the part of the spirit world visible to people with the spirit sight. Nobody aside from advanced necromancers knew what lay on the other side of the gates of death, the place known as Beyond…

There was a flash of silver light above the circle, then all the flames went out.

"Nice," Hazel said. "If I threw something into the circle—"

"Please don't," River said. "I used to train novices. There's only so many times you can tell them not to put things in the summoning circles before you start losing the will to live."

"So you're a certified necromancer?" I asked. Working for the guild was one thing, but only the best were tasked with the tricky and dangerous business of introducing new necromancers to the spirit world.

"I am, yes." He crouched down beside the candles and began to move them into a sack that he must have conjured up from somewhere.

"Aren't Guardians the top level?" asked Hazel.

"Technically. Guardians are the only necromancers who can pass between the gates and the veil, but nobody can do that without permanently leaving their living body behind."

"Is that your life goal?" I asked. "Guarding the gates of the dead?"

"Not quite." He picked up the last candle. "You have to be dead to take that position. It's not a life goal so much as a death one."

"Very funny. So you prefer being a human shield?"

He rose to his feet. "Generally my assignments involve guarding objects, not people. The Sidhe are fiercely protective of their possessions."

"Oh, fun," said Hazel. From what I'd heard, the Sidhe were as fond of stealing from one another as they were of attempted murder. "So this is probably light entertainment for you, if you've been anywhere near the borderlands."

"How'd you guess?" River said. "The borderlands were my first assignment. Ilsa, should I leave the candles outside the house?"

I'd turned away at the initiation of faerie talk. "Why ask my permission?" I said. "I don't own the place."

Hazel gave me a vaguely puzzled look, but I ignored it. It wasn't worth feeling insulted that River was capable of having a conversation with my sister without implying she was the Sidhe's property.

"Do you think another wraith will show up, then?" she asked him.

"Possibly," said River. "You're not to leave the house again today."

"Excuse me?" I said. "It attacked us right here. Logically, we're no safer staying in than we are going out." Wraith or none, answers weren't here—about the heir or otherwise. And I needed to speak to Grandma's ghost again, if just to tell her that it'd be helpful if I could talk to River about my newfound magic.

One look at River's face told me he wasn't budging without a fight, and I'd had quite enough conflict for today already. Besides, I was certain Grandma had appeared next to the house. Maybe she was still here.

"Can you sense any more ghosts?" I asked River.

"No, I can't. I'd tell you if I did."

Hmm. Maybe she'd hidden herself from him. Considering he'd decided to start ordering us around again, I didn't blame her.

"Is that your spirit sight?" asked Hazel, with a not-so-subtle glance at me. Maybe she figured I wanted to tell him. But he didn't take the hint.

"My spirit sight allows me to sense if anyone living or dead is in the general vicinity, yes."

"Then why didn't you pick up on the wraith?" she asked. I'd been about to ask the same question, as unwise as I knew it was.

Sure enough, River's eyes narrowed. "Because for some reason, I can't detect those monstrosities until they're right on top of us. It's like it bypassed the veil altogether."

"So the salt didn't do much," I observed.

"It stopped the wraith from getting into the house," he

said. "Which is likely why it decided to unleash a frontal assault on your defences. If you two had been inside the house, you'd have been fine."

Hazel folded her arms. "Right, so I'm supposed to hide. Its magic shouldn't have been able to touch me."

"That wasn't faerie magic, it was death energy," he said. "Otherwise known as necromantic power or kinetic energy. Like a highly powered poltergeist."

No kidding. Poltergeists broke stuff. The wraith had put a dent in a magical house with more defences than almost anywhere. And it was the third one we'd encountered in a day. One thing was abundantly clear: the person who'd summoned it wanted one or all of us dead. River thought he'd banished it. But he hadn't. *I'd* done it. Somehow…

Hazel beckoned me into the living room when I returned to the house to deposit the empty salt canister.

"You did it," she said in a low voice. "Didn't you? It wasn't him."

"You've got it. Also, I can't tell him."

"Nor me." Her gaze dropped to my pocket. "Seriously. I tried to ask you in front of River, and it's like the words—stuck. Must be a spell on the book."

"That's what I thought," I said. "I need to talk to Grandma. Maybe she knows why we have necromancy in the family."

When it came to supernatural hierarchies, mage and faerie magic tended to come out on top, while witch and necromancer magic came second to any other magic in the family. So most hybrids lived in one world or the other, not both the way River seemed to. Then again, it was fitting that our family, which didn't entirely belong in Faerie *or* the mortal realm, had links with necromancers. Still, we were tied to the Summer Court, and I'd thought our family's magic rested in life, not death.

"Life and death are intertwined," Arden interjected, when

I said this out loud. "You cannot separate one from the other."

"Of course you'd talk in riddles," said Hazel. "That won't help us now. Why did she give the magic to *you?*"

"That's nice," I said, a little stung.

Hazel winced. "I didn't mean it to come out like that. But it's weird."

"Yeah, it is," I muttered. Maybe the person who'd created the book had decided the Gatekeeper had enough power of their own, and it was only fair that someone else had a shot at developing magical abilities. Sure would have been nice if this had happened when I was a teenager, so I wouldn't have had to go through puberty while watching the Sidhe's magic transform my sister into a powerful magic user, while I remained an ordinary human. Admittedly, any type of magic came with a sting in the tail. Like murderous wraiths, for instance. "Perhaps the book's set on a timer to awaken once per generation and target a non-Gatekeeper. It's not like Morgan is a contender."

Hazel grimaced like she always did when I mentioned our estranged brother. He'd reacted to not being Gatekeeper by running away and turning to a life of crime, and Mum pretended he didn't exist most of the time. "No, I suppose not." She sighed. "I'm going to shower."

"Have you told Dad, by the way?" I asked as she left the room.

"No, of course not," said Hazel, over her shoulder. "He doesn't need to know every time Mum goes jaunting off to Faerie. And it's not like he can do anything about the wraiths. We'll be fine."

Let's hope so. Dad didn't get in touch often, but telling him killers were after us would cause unnecessary panic considering he didn't have any magic of his own. He wasn't so much inattentive as eternally absent. Possibly, I took after him, because I'd only spoken to Mum a handful of times in the last few years. We'd argued before I left, and while I hadn't disappeared off the face of the earth like Morgan had, I spent entirely too much time justifying my decision to leave. It'd taken me a while to conclude that maybe she envied that I *had* the choice, unlike her and Hazel.

I caught sight of my blurred reflection in the newly repaired window. An odd silver light gleamed over my forehead, and I frowned, walking closer. *What in the world is that?*

I ran to the hall mirror to properly look, and gasped. A thin cut snaked down my cheek where I'd been hit by debris in my collapsing house, but more significantly, a pattern of swirling silver lines appeared on my forehead like an elaborate tattoo. I walked right up to the mirror and rubbed it with my sleeve. Then I touched a hand to my face, followed the line with my fingertips. The skin felt slightly raised.

When did that happen?

I walked to the sink in the kitchen and ran a cloth under the tap. Then I pressed it to my face. My reflection on the inside of the now-fogged window still wore the mark. It hadn't faded at all. Soap had no effect. It only irritated the skin, and left the mark intact.

My heart started beating fast. *No. It can't be permanent.* For the last five years, I'd been relatively free of the questions that plagued me in Foxwood, because nobody at the university had ever met my sister. I didn't have a lot of friends, but that was by choice. Not because I had "I'm cursed" written in blazing ink on my forehead. For the first time since the attack, tears stung my eyes, and a bitter taste coated my tongue. I imagined Hazel, twelve years old, waking up to the same sight—not difficult, because I'd witnessed it. She'd screamed in wild delight, running up and down the halls, not knowing or caring yet that the mark was one of the signs the Sidhe usually put on things that belonged to them.

The one thought that had carried me through the last eleven years was knowing I was my own person, not someone else's. And now a similar mark gleamed across my forehead in a swirling pattern of lines.

Wait. I know that symbol. I pulled the book from my pocket. The swirling lines on the cover hadn't moved, nor did they glow like before—but the symbol was definitely the same. I didn't know it. Whatever faerie tongue it was, it carried no translation that I knew of.

One thing was clear—whatever the mark was, it meant trouble.

8

"What's wrong with your face?" asked Hazel, when she came downstairs to find me in the living room. I lowered the sci-fi paperback I'd been attempting to read—spaceships and explosions, no faeries and curses, thanks—and she gasped as my hood slipped down. "What *is* that? Holy shit."

I put the book on the coffee table. "I guess it's like a faerie mark. It won't come off." I pulled some of my hair forward into my eyes. I'd needed a haircut for weeks, but hadn't had much in the way of spare cash. "I need one of Everett's witch charms to cover it up."

Agnes and her husband Everett were the only people who might have skill enough to hide a spell signature. I'd never seen anything close to it—except the Gatekeeper's mark.

Arden fluttered down to land on the arm of the sofa. "You won't remove that mark with a spell."

"What?" I looked at him. "You don't know what the mark means—do you?"

"The mark is the Gatekeeper's."

"I'm not the Gatekeeper. I don't even know what this

magic is. I can't actually *read* the book it came from." I pulled it out of my pocket. Apparently I could speak freely about it in front of Arden, but he was family.

Hazel sucked in a breath and pointed at the book's leathery cover. "Look."

"I know it's the same symbol," I said. "But it's not the faerie language."

"No," she said. "I've been trying to figure out where I saw something like that before, and I *have* seen similar runes recently. On River's sword."

"Seriously?" I stared at her. "But he's not—"

"It's not death magic," she said. "Not like, the corrupted outcast magic, anyway."

"Definitely not," I said with a shudder. The Grey Vale beasts that ended up stranded in this realm… if they had any magic at all, it was a darker version of Summer's or Winter's. While Summer drew on life magic to thrive, the darker version fed on life force. There were skin-eating faeries and beasts that sucked the blood from your veins while your heart still beat. Winter magic thrived as the seasons turned to decay, but its darker version fed on despair and hate, and creatures like hellhounds grew more powerful the more death there was in the area.

I didn't gain strength from the magic. All I'd done was banish the spirit, in the same way a necromancer would. It wasn't Summer or Winter magic, in any shape or form that I knew of. So why did I have a faerie mark?

"I can't go out like this," I said. "Does Mum have any disguise charms? She must have rearranged her desk, because I couldn't find any."

"Sure," Hazel said. I got up and walked behind her into Mum's workroom. Of all the rooms in the house, it was the messiest, filled with an array of weapons and tools and miscellaneous magical ingredients. While the faerie-made weapons were conspicuously absent, Mum had left no shortage of witch spells behind, since they didn't work in Faerie.

"Here." Hazel held up a teardrop-shaped necklace. "One of Everett's illusion spells. It's been here a few weeks, but it should work."

I put the necklace on and walked to the hall mirror. Immediately, the mark faded into the background, leaving smooth skin behind. When I ran my finger over my forehead, I could still feel the slightly raised pattern, but it was no longer visible.

"Thanks," I said to Hazel. "It's a good job Mum had it. I just wish she'd told me about all this."

"Yeah," said Hazel, biting her lip. The unexpected nervous gesture made her look younger. "She'd better have a *really* good reason for ditching us. As for Grandma, *she'd* better have a good reason for not telling us—anything."

"She didn't have long to speak, I don't think," I said, touching my forehead. "But there aren't any other ghosts to ask. I need an actual source, from the Court or… I don't know. Do the Sidhe have anyone designated to deal with the Grey Vale?" I didn't think so, somehow. They'd been as taken by surprise as we had when the outcasts had invaded this realm and waged war against the supernaturals here.

"Mum might know," Hazel said. "The Sidhe generally avoid discussing the outcasts if they can help it."

The door opened and River walked in. I lowered my hand and turned my back on the mirror, hoping he hadn't seen.

"There's a problem," said River. "I've been in contact with the local necromancers, and apparently they picked up some unusual necromantic activity coming from this direction."

"They detected the wraith?" That might lead to unwelcome questions. I'd never spoken to the local necromancers, but everyone knew about their ongoing feud with the village's other supernaturals. We tended to stay out of one another's way at the best of times.

"You spoke to them behind my back?" said Hazel. "If the local supernaturals are involved, they're supposed to go through me."

River must think the wraith's threat was more important than our family's secrecy. That or the way the wraith had vanished had raised his suspicions after all.

"I'm just passing on the message." He put his phone in his pocket. An old model, covered in a heavy plastic case probably to stop the metal touching his bare skin. I hadn't realised he had the necromancers' contact details, let alone that they actually used them. There wasn't much chance of a phone signal from the afterlife.

"Thanks," Hazel said to him. "I really appreciate you telling all the local supernaturals that the Gatekeeper's heir failed to stop a ghost putting a dent in her house."

"I didn't tell them that," River said. "It's inevitable that someone would have picked up on the aftereffects. I'm told there have been a few other incidents of undead attacks in the area lately."

"I told you that," Hazel said. "Who was the local necromancer head again? Graves, right?"

"Greaves," River said. "I'm told he's not fond of the nickname."

"I'll speak to him in person and set him straight, then," I said. Maybe I'd even find someone at the necromancer guild who knew about the book. As much as I'd wanted to avoid attention, it seemed sensible to ask an expert about whether it was possible for a non-necromancer to have necromantic magic.

The necromancers' guild was so far on the outskirts of town, it was almost part of the fields, down the road from the Lynn family mausoleum. Around the guild, the fields were abandoned as their owners had fled during the faerie invasion, untouched by the life magic covering the Summer estate. A medium-sized building with blacked-out windows housed the necromancers of this region. Rather than making for the building, however, River pushed open the gate into the graveyard alongside it. The earth was fresh, like it had been recently disturbed.

River walked down the row of gravestones. "This is what the call was about," he said, indicating the surface of the nearest grave. A symbol appeared above the grave, a swirling silver pattern. Then it vanished.

I couldn't breathe.

The same symbol marked my face.

Hazel stepped forwards. "Looks like a spell. Are the necromancers even here?"

Never mind that. What in hell was the symbol that had appeared on my face doing in the necromancers' graveyard?

"This is a spell signature," said River. "According to the necromancers, they traced its source to the Ley Line. And this mark looks just like yours, Hazel."

"No, it doesn't." She lifted her hair to show him. "What exactly are they accusing us of?"

A stooped figure appeared from behind the grave. For an instant, I thought he was a ghost—but he didn't have that odd shimmer about him that the dead did.

"Mr Greaves," said River.

'Graves' seemed a more appropriate name. He looked so old and frail it was a wonder he could stand, or hunch, anyway, looking at the trampled earth around the headstone beside him.

"What did you do?" he demanded. "If this mark is yours, one of you cast a necromantic spell and raised my predecessor from the dead."

Oh shit. That's what he thought we'd done?

"We aren't necromancers," said Hazel. "And that mark isn't mine. I'm the Summer Gatekeeper's heir."

"And your sister—"

"Can't use magic," I said.

"Maybe don't accuse us of crimes we never committed. You don't want to make an enemy of the Gatekeepers, Graves," Hazel said.

Graves narrowed his eyes at her. "It's Greaves, not Graves. And don't think I won't teach you your place if you continue to insult us." His voice was deep and gravelly with a spine-chilling quality that made me want to slowly back away.

"Perhaps we might talk to the spirit, if he's still here?" River cut in.

"Exactly," I said, determined not to let the old man intimidate me. "Pretty sure the spirit can set the record straight."

Abruptly, the world went grey, and the graveyard disappeared, blanketed under thick fog. Three figures stood out—River, Greaves… and a blank white space.

I backed away by instinct, feet bumping against a headstone. Fear prickled every inch of my skin. The white light grew above the grave until it was human-height. Features became distinct, like a camera coming into focus, and I realised it *was* a person. An old man, who might have been Greaves's twin. His father?

The ghost watched me. "So this is the Gatekeeper," he said.

9

"We need to ask you a question," I said, before Hazel could anger Greaves any more. Or the spirit, come to that. But the old man didn't have the same scary vibe as his living son did. His semi-transparent shade hardly came up to my shoulder.

"I didn't come back from the dead for young upstarts like you to make fun of me," muttered the ghost, and about-turned, like he intended to walk through a door. Except there wasn't one. Just his grave. An unexpected flash of pity went through me. I knew how spirits had trouble adjusting to reality. Even necromancers, apparently. "I came to speak to the Gatekeeper."

"That's my mum, and she's not here," said Hazel.

"Not *that* Gatekeeper." His gaze fixed on me, and I froze.

So did the others. The living Mr Greaves locked into position, his mouth half-open, while River's body stiffened, too. Hazel was completely still, one hand slightly outstretched. *What the hell?*

"Don't look at me like that," said the spirit. "It's tempo-rary. Looks like you can't speak of your title to anyone living.

Whoever made the spell forgot to include the dead in that arrangement."

"I…" I gaped at him. "You know about the book?"

My second question: had he used necromancy to freeze Graves and the others? Unlike raising the dead, I could think of a few scenarios where that sort of power would come in handy.

"I know. I'm not the only one," he said. "You're in danger."

Seriously? His timing for warnings was about as useful as that bloody raven's. "If you know the book, can you tell me why I can't read the damn thing?"

"Patience," he said. "I never expected to be raised from death, much less subject to a questioning by one of the living. It's been over a decade since I had a conversation, least of all about that book."

"You talked to Grandma? You must be able to sense her, if she's a ghost. Wait—first question is, do you know who raised the undead who attacked us?" I couldn't reel in my questions. I craved answers like oxygen, and to be honest, the cold clinging fog was starting to make my hands go numb. Was I *in* Death, or was this what the world looked like with my spirit sight switched on?

"One question at a time. Yes, I've spoken to your grandmother. Yes, I can sense her if she's nearby, but not at the present moment. No, I don't, because I've been gone for over a decade. Next question."

"Er…" Questions bubbled to the surface and I sifted them over in my mind. "Who put that mark—spell signature—on your grave, when it wasn't me who raised you?"

"Absolutely no idea. As I said—I only just woke up."

"But you know the Lynn family."

"I do. And I know that the power you've picked up is potent and dangerous, too much so for you to access all at once."

"The book's completely blank," I told him. "How am I supposed to learn how to use its power if I can't read it?"

I shifted as his gaze roamed over my face—and I knew, when his eyes went wide, that he'd seen the mark. In the spirit realm, somehow, I couldn't hide it.

"So the mark doesn't lie," he mused. "You have an unfortunate gift, Gatekeeper."

"I'm not Gatekeeper."

"The gates of Death are open to you, Ilsa Lynn."

Ice trailed down my back. "Look, I have something important to do for the Seelie Court, and whoever's sending the dead after me and my sister is getting in my way."

The old man's eyes narrowed at those words. "Yes, your family is known for its devotion to our… neighbours."

Of course necromancers didn't like the Sidhe, or any faerie species. They believed faeries didn't have souls, while faeries feared death like nothing else.

"My family," I said. "Not me. I'm *not* a necromancer either. I'm here to help my sister and for no other reason. Got it?"

He looked aggrieved. "Being one of us really isn't that bad. Modern language has caused people to forget the original definitions of magic, but 'necromancy' doesn't literally mean 'death magic'. It means conversing with the dead, not raising them."

"What, like we're doing right now?" I rubbed my hands together in an attempt to warm them up. "Or am *I* a ghost?"

He raised his eyes to the sky. "I retired from teaching a decade ago. If you want to learn basic necromancy, the guild might have a guidebook lying around somewhere."

I sincerely doubted the living Mr Greaves would let me wander away with the necromancers' property. "Isn't *this* a guidebook?" I tapped my pocket where the book was hidden.

"Not for amateurs."

Now the dead guy was sassing me. Wonderful.

"If I'm an amateur, then it's because nobody at any point in my life decided to warn me that I have necromancer ancestry." I folded my arms across my chest. "That's why I got picked, right? No human can have the spirit sight otherwise."

"I'm glad to hear your mother didn't neglect your education," he said, in a bored voice. "I am not, however, the person to ask about that book. You're a necromancer by all definitions, but that book of yours belongs to another type of magic entirely."

"Faerie?" I self-consciously touched the mark on my forehead. "How about the Grey Vale? Have you seen *that* place?"

"Of course I've seen it," he said. "All of us who've passed through Death's gates in recent years have seen the part of Faerie where nothing and nobody ever dies." He gave a frankly creepy laugh. "I've met a few spirits who talk of the horrors on the other side. There's a reason it's unwise to use necromancy on the Ley Line. And yes, that includes your magic, too, Ilsa."

He snapped his fingers. Everyone unfroze.

"You must know we aren't necromancers," Hazel said to him. "So why blame us for bringing you back? Are you sure a ghost didn't just sneeze somewhere and wake you up?"

"Your impertinence does you no favours." The spirit rotated on the spot. "I didn't *see* who raised me, but their magic apparently carried your signature, if that mark is to be believed."

My signature. It should be impossible. But the living Mr Greaves's forbidding presence made me reluctant to question him further. More to the point, Hazel apparently hadn't heard any of the words we'd exchanged. Nobody looked shocked to have been frozen. *Did they not notice at all?* That spirit had some seriously powerful magic.

Advanced necromancy, or something you could only do when dead.

"That's complete bullshit," Hazel said. "Not only did we do nothing wrong, we were attacked on our own property. We're peacekeepers, Graves, and whoever tried to kill us is threatening my job as well as my family's lives."

"I can't move from this spot," said the ghost. "You'll have to ask my successor if you'd like someone to look into your issues with the dead."

The living Mr Greaves narrowed his eyes. "I'm more inclined to assume the two of you are making up elaborate lies."

"We aren't liars," Hazel said heatedly. "Someone raised the dead in our mausoleum, too. Can't you look into that?"

"My people are already investigating the situation at the request of one Holly Lynn. I'd suggest you leave before you implicate yourselves further."

Well, damn. I'd forgotten Holly and the Winter Lynns might have words to say about the state of their dead relatives' graves.

"Neither of us was responsible for raising any ghosts," I said. "But we can find out who did."

I didn't add, *or we'll all be in a grave of our own by the end of the week.*

10

I'd planned to revisit the necromancers the following morning and demand answers, but Arden derailed my plans. I woke to a racket which sounded like a swarm of vultures fighting over a corpse. Pushing the curtains back from my bedroom window, I saw River pointing his sword at Arden, who flew overhead with a scroll clamped in his beak, squawking loudly. *Oh, boy.*

"Hey!" I shouted through the window. "Arden, cut it out!"

I just about had the presence of mind to grab a dressing gown before dashing downstairs into the hallway. Hazel got there first, opening the door and running outside.

"Don't stab the messenger," she told River.

River glared up at Arden, his blade extended in such a way that suggested it'd take little effort to cut the raven out of the air. Arden dropped the scroll on River's head and flew off.

"What the hell was that about?" I asked, smothering a laugh at River's expression.

"He sneaked up on me," River said, lowering his sword and retrieving the scroll. "I apologise for disturbing you."

"Menace," said Hazel, shaking her head after the bird. "What's that note?"

I took it from him. "It's addressed to you, Hazel."

"Crap," said Hazel, as I passed the scroll to her. "Winter's ball… it's the solstice. I forgot all about it."

I groaned. There were two events every year of immense importance to all faeries living in the mortal realm—the summer and winter solstices. Due to some bizarre tradition, each event came with a grand event held on the territory of one of the Lynns, and the summer celebration was held on Winter's territory, while our family hosted the winter one. Probably because Summer's power was at its peak right now and they thought it was unfair. Their timing couldn't be worse if they'd tried.

"What happens on the solstice?" River asked, sheathing his blade. His fair hair was dishevelled and if the shadows under his eyes were any indication, he'd spent the night sitting out on the porch again.

"We go to the Winter Gatekeeper's house and pretend not to hate each other for one evening," I said. "Or rather, Mum and Hazel are supposed to go and deal with Holly and her delightful mother."

Holly and I had actually been friends once, until Mum and her fellow Gatekeeper had had a dramatic falling-out. I still wasn't quite sure what they'd argued about, only that the result was a week of droughts and heat waves followed by blizzards and frost. Their feud came to an end when a contingent of Sidhe had appeared and yelled at everyone for using their magic for trivial purposes, then put another curse on us for good measure to stop us from murdering one another. We hadn't really spoken since. Despite what the old ghost had said, I hadn't seen anyone near the cemetery the day before, so I'd assumed Holly had reported the state of the place to the necromancers and then left.

"We can't get out of it," said Hazel, heading back into the house. "Maybe Holly has some pointers about dealing with zombies."

"You don't think Holly might know about what's going on?" I suggested, waiting for River to enter then closing the door firmly behind him.

"Maybe," said Hazel. "Perhaps Aunt Candice and Mum had another falling-out and she summoned the wraith in vengeance."

"If you suspect these people, I need to speak with them," River said, as we walked into the living room.

"You can't attack our relatives," I said. "I don't see why they'd do this, anyway. All of us are bound in a truce that prevents any Lynn from inflicting damage on another. That's the second part of our curse."

"But summoning wraiths doesn't count," said Hazel. "Not that they can do necromancy anyway. Holly's an only child and all the magic she has is the Winter Gatekeeper's. She and Aunt Candice are peacekeepers like us. Same goals, different Court."

"I'd like to speak with this other family of yours if possible." Despite his polite tone, River seemed tetchier than usual. He also seemed to have borrowed the sci-fi paperback I'd been reading yesterday since it'd disappeared from the coffee table, but that was the least of my grievances. I'd hoped—ridiculously—that today would be the day we'd sort out this whole mess and I'd be able to go back to my old life. But leaving Hazel to face Winter alone wouldn't be fair, especially with the slightly sticky issue of the Summer Gatekeeper's ongoing absence.

"Feel free to talk to them at the ball," I told River. "But we can't have them find out about Summer's missing heir."

"I still think someone gave you the wrong information,"

River said. "We should focus on bringing down whoever is out to do you harm."

"The last thing they did was raise a harmless old man from the dead," I said.

"That wasn't the person who summoned the wraith," River said, an assessing look on his face. "Apparently, it was the person who banished it."

Oh hell. Now would be a great time to lift the spell stopping me from speaking, Grandma. I'd tried to ask River some indirect questions about necromancy at dinner last night, but there was no indirect way to say *by the way, a random sort-of-necromancy handbook that might or might not be evil picked me as the vessel for its magic.* Whenever I got remotely close to mentioning it, my jaw would lock like I had a mouthful of thick toffee. I swore the bloody book was laughing at me by the time I retired early to bed in frustration.

"There's someone we *could* ask," I said. "Agnes."

Hazel frowned, then her gaze briefly went to the place on my forehead where the mark remained invisible. The spell wouldn't last forever, and despite what the old man's ghost had said, I had no intention of walking around as a beacon to anyone with the Sight—spirit or otherwise.

"Who?" asked River.

"The most knowledgeable person in the village." I rubbed the back of my head, realising I'd left the spellbook in my room. That'd explain the faint tapping sensation on the back of my skull. "We'll leave in an hour. That okay, Hazel?"

"Sure," she said, though she shot me a concerned look. Wait… if I couldn't mention the book to anyone outside of our family, how in the world was I supposed to explain the mark to Agnes and Everett?

I'll find a way. I retreated to my room, finding the book where I'd left it in the pocket of my hoody. At once, the ache in the back of my skull faded. "Attention seeker," I told it. "I know you've been hidden in the mausoleum for years, but that's no reason to—"

I broke off with a gasp as the book glowed faintly, and something flickered on the page. My gaze caught the word *amateur* before the letters disappeared just as quickly.

"You *can* talk to me?" I flicked through the book again, but no words appeared this time. Anger pulsed to my fingertips. "You're just fucking with me on purpose, aren't you?"

Its silence was answer enough. I let out a low growl of frustration and tossed the book onto the bed. Then I showered quickly and shoved on a fresh outfit, stopping only to grab a breakfast bar on the way out of the house. Arden's message had hammered home how easy it'd be to get ensnared in the Sidhe's trap and end up stuck here forever, trapped in a never-ending cycle of quests, balls, more quests, ad infinitum. No thanks.

The moment we stepped outside the house's boundaries, rain began to fall. The grey sky sharply contrasted the sunny warmth of the Lynn estate, and Hazel grumbled under her breath as we walked. Living on Summer territory made genuine Scottish weather come as a shock, but I was used to it by now. We passed by the necromancers' place and continued down the lane towards the main village.

"Who exactly did you want to visit?" asked River. He didn't wear his Court clothes but a knee-length grey coat that looked human-made. "I've spoken to the necromancers, but I can't say I know anyone else in the village."

"Agnes is a witch," I said. "Part witch, part mage, possibly. She won't tell us. I need to buy some spells from her."

"I thought your magic was enough that you didn't need hedge witch spells."

"Some of us, maybe." There was an ongoing rivalry between the local witches and necromancers that the Gatekeeper had often had to step in to resolve, so River had probably heard some of the rumours. Witch charms were portable and most people with magic could use them, not just witches, so it was common for humans to be wary of them, but not someone like River. His sword wasn't on full display, but I knew he must have it handy.

"Have you considered there might be another supernatural from the village behind the attacks on your life?" he said.

"Not Agnes," I said firmly. "I thought you said it was almost certain a necromancer who did it."

"That doesn't mean they don't have accomplices. I don't think it's wise to draw any more attention," River said.

"You think the necromancers haven't spread word about the old man coming back from the veil by now?" I said. "Besides, *everyone* knows who the Gatekeepers are. If it really bothers you, I'll talk to Agnes, while you and Hazel go and… I don't know, look for runaway zombies. Agnes isn't a huge fan of necromancers *or* faeries, so it might be easier that way."

For a moment, I expected to have to argue. Then he nodded. "Fine, but don't mention the wraith."

Sure I won't. Getting rid of the mark was my priority, for now.

Agnes and Everett's shop was nondescript on the outside —off-putting, if anything, with cracked glass in the windows and what looked like claw-shaped gouges on the door. Agnes always said a dragon was responsible. I never did figure out if she was joking or not.

River gave it a distrustful look. "There's a lot of iron in that place. I can sense it."

"Look, they don't like faeries," I told him. "I'll be out in half an hour."

I pushed the door inward and stepped inside the dark little shop. Despite feeling cupboard-sized, it was full of more shadowy corners than a small square-shaped room had the right to have. Shelves housed various artefacts—books carved with runes, glimmering jewels, and a million varieties of portable charms.

A clap of thunder sounded and I jumped. Agnes appeared behind the desk, her white hair braided and a friendly smile on her lips. Both she and Everett were ancient—maybe even older than the head of the necromancers. Certainly old enough to have known Grandma when she was Gatekeeper. And they had enough magic between the two of them to set the whole town on fire if so inclined.

Agnes's hands folded on the counter. Chalk lines dusted her leathery skin, remnants of recent spells. I'd never been able to pin down the exact nature of her gift, but Agnes's magical skills seemed to know no bounds.

"Ilsa," said the old woman. "What can I do for you today?"

"Haven't you heard?" I'd assumed some of it would have reached her by now.

"Heard what?"

I drew in a breath and gave an abbreviated rundown of the situation. I didn't try to bring up the book, but I did tell her about the undead and the necromancers, and the increasing suspicion that someone with necromantic powers wanted to bump us off.

"Necromancers," Agnes said. "That explains why I didn't know. Old Greaves and I had a disagreement some months ago."

Agnes didn't really do 'surprised'. I'd long suspected the Sidhe themselves could walk in here and Agnes would offer them tea and her husband's potently magical cupcakes.

"Might Greaves be behind this?"

"Not a chance. This is advanced work—dark magic, reanimating the dead within the Lynn graveyard."

A chill crept across my shoulder blades. "Yeah, well. Mum's gone, and instead of telling us where she is, the Seelie

Court sent us a bodyguard who also doesn't know what's going on. I don't suppose you know when she's coming back?"

"No. She never said." She frowned. "It seems to me that you've been singled out by someone with a grudge against your family."

"I figured," I said. "There's another reason I need your help. I have this mark on my face, and I'd like to cover it up."

"I thought that was it." She tilted her head sideways, her gaze on my forehead. "That's remarkable. Take the charm off."

My hand automatically jumped to the necklace around my throat. "You—know what it is?"

"I don't, but I can guess what it means. Those who attacked you weren't regular spirits."

"Faeries." Huh. So I could say *that* aloud. I looped the necklace over my head. "I didn't know you could use necromancy on faeries."

She squinted at the mark in that penetrating way that made me feel like she could reach into my head and pluck out my thoughts if she desired. "They're living beings, same as us. As for those foul wraith creatures, however, they're an abomination."

"You know about wraiths, then?" A small measure of relief rose within me, despite River's warning not to mention the attack. "One of them got into our estate."

"And you banished it."

My breath caught. "You must have spoken to…"

"Can I see the book?"

I gaped at her for a moment, then reached into my pocket. To my immense surprise, the book came free in my hand and didn't get stuck like when I'd tried to show it to River.

"Interesting." She looked at the cover, then my forehead.

"That mark won't come off, Ilsa. When did it appear?"

My heart dropped. "After I used magic to bind the wraith —with the book." I flipped it open. "It goes blank unless there's a wraith or undead breathing down my neck or it feels like messing with me. So—do you know what the symbol means?" I ran a fingertip across the cover, tracing the swirling lines.

"I don't, but I can hazard a guess that the symbol is not from this world."

"You mean—Faerie."

She gave a nod. "Yes. There's a certain type of text that can only be read by someone with faerie blood—Sidhe blood."

"River." But he hadn't recognised the mark when it'd appeared as a spell signature. "He's a half-faerie, and I have no idea who sent him to guard us, or why. Maybe to stop the wraiths, because he's part necromancer as well. But that thing was far stronger than any of us. I only banished it because of the book."

"Is that so?" She raised an eyebrow. "This bodyguard—is it possible he might be a spy for the other side?"

"He's definitely from the Summer Court," I said. "I thought he was the enemy at first, but he's bound by a vow to protect my sister. I'm wondering if Mum sent him, because she knows something's going on involving the dead."

"This started with the undead attacks in the village," she said. "But you weren't at the house. You said the Summer Court brought you?"

"A faerie knocked my house down," I said. "They dragged me home on a mission that might be a ruse, might not."

"Which is…?"

I weighed the options. By now, I was fifty percent sure there was no heir at all, and that someone had wanted to fabricate a scheme to bring me back to the Lynn house. "To find a missing heir to Summer's Court. I don't suppose you've ever met anyone called Ivy Lane? She knew something, too." It seemed more and more suspicious that the whole thing had begun with Ivy's ghost showing up. But I still couldn't work out how it all connected, since faeries and death generally went together like elf wine and fireworks.

"I know the name," she said. "There are rumours of a human with faerie magic…"

"Who can turn into a ghost?" This just got more and more bizarre.

"Anyone can leave their body with the right magic, but with no guarantee of returning. It was a great risk she took, travelling along the Ley Line."

"To warn me," I said. "It sounded like the situation in Faerie might be pretty dire, but it's the solstice ball tomorrow. I can't let the Winter Lynns find out any of this."

A clap of thunder made me jump backwards, and Everett appeared at Agnes's side. His grey beard was clipped short and he had a friendly smile. He and Agnes shared several talents—such as the ability to see through most magical illusions—but while nobody knew the extent of Agnes's abilities, Everett's were more straightforward. He apparently came from a long line of illusion mages revered for their talents, which when combined with witch magic made for a lethal combination.

"How much of that did you hear?" I asked.

"All of it," he said. "Interesting… I haven't seen that mark in a long time."

"I need to cover it up," I said. "At least until I've worked out what it means. Arden said it couldn't be removed with a spell."

Agnes said, "He's correct. If that's the case, nothing here will remove it. But we *can* hide it. I'll check in the back."

She disappeared behind the counter.

"So you have the book." Everett looked down at it. "You have a very interesting family."

"You're telling me."

"I won't speak of this to a soul," he added. "Agnes and I know the dangers of the Courts of Faerie well enough not to provoke those who care not for mortals… yet this book of yours is something else entirely."

"I wish I could read it. Do you have a spell for that?"

He shook his head. "No. Not if it doesn't want to be read. It's the type of magical object which adapts itself to the skill level of the user, I imagine."

"And my skill level is zero." I rolled my eyes. Amateur indeed. "Grandma wouldn't tell me anything. Why did nobody tell me she was a necromancer?"

"She wasn't," said Agnes, walking back into view.

"You knew her, didn't you?"

The old woman inclined her head. "For a time. As Gate-keeper, she often came to me for advice on handling disputes between supernaturals within the town. She never mentioned the book, but it's an ancient one, perhaps as ancient as the Lynn curse."

Hmm. I'd never known anyone else in *our* family to have any magical talent aside from being Gatekeeper. But I'd also I'd never had the chance to consider a future where I had magic of my own. Here, surrounded by it, I couldn't deny that some part of me was drawn to it against my better judgement. Maybe the same part of me, long buried, who'd *wanted* to come back to the Lynn house.

"What about… the other branch of the family?" I glanced over my shoulder. "I haven't spoken to Holly in years. Have you seen her recently?"

"I haven't spoken to Miss Lynn in some time, nor her mother, but talking to her might be a good idea. Their magic has natural ties to death."

"Wait..." I said slowly. "When the wraith appeared, it went cold. *Really* cold. I figured that was because it came from Death. It's always freezing around necromantic magic. But... wraiths are concentrated magic, I'm told. Might it have been from Winter—the faerie, when it was alive?"

"Perhaps," she said.

Maybe the Unseelie were involved. It'd be in their interests to stop us from getting to the heir—if there was one. But would the Winter Lynns risk a thousand or more years of peace when the Sidhe could permanently die? I didn't know enough about the situation in the Courts to make a judgement call on that one. I *did* know that the Winter Gatekeepers were sworn to keep the peace as much as we were, and betraying that oath meant death.

Agnes handed me a necklace with a teardrop-shaped stone. "This is an updated version of the spell you already wear. Everett's best work. It should last a few weeks... I'm afraid witch charms aren't made to be permanent. But if you need anything else, you need only ask."

"Thank you." Slipping the spell into my pocket, I said, "Can you get me some basic disguise spells, as well?" Hiding the mark might not be enough. If I wanted to do any more poking around, maybe I was better off putting on a mask.

She went to unlock a cabinet. "Yes, I can. How many do you need?"

"Two," I said. "One for Hazel and me... maybe one spare. I don't suppose you know anything else about the nature of this mark?"

"I'm afraid not," said Agnes, lifting the spells from the cabinet and re-locking it. "I imagine the book will tell you, when it feels you're ready."

"It isn't alive," I said. "Seriously?" You couldn't put a soul inside an object. I knew *that* much, at least.

"Everything about that book confounds me, to be honest,"

said Agnes. "Keep it hidden."

"I will. Thank you." I paid for the spells, put the book back in my pocket and the spell around my neck, and left through the door. As I did, a curtain of rain lashed down on me, and a feathery shape nearly crashed into my face.

"Bloody hell, Arden." I stepped backwards as the raven righted himself and flew off. He didn't usually come to the village, but maybe he'd come to check up on us. Zipping my pockets tight, I huddled in my coat and went in search of the others.

I found them in a coffee shop, hiding from the rain. River got to his feet the moment I reached them. "Got what you needed?" he asked.

"Yeah. Wish I'd bought a weather-proof spell. Are you two done here?"

"We are," Hazel said, moving towards me. Maybe she didn't want anyone seeing them together. Oh well. She'd kept him out of my hair while I questioned Agnes, which was the plan. Unfortunately, I had no more answers than before, and I'd never heard of a spell Agnes didn't know about. Next time Grandma appeared, I'd corner her for a proper conversation. Or maybe I'd use the shadow spell to sneak into the necromancers' guild. They strode in and out of Death at will, so there must be a way to track a specific spirit...

River stopped abruptly, frowning. "There's someone nearby."

We'd reached the village's outskirts, where houses gave way to fields and farms. A faint earthy scent reached my nostrils. Summer magic... but not quite.

Three figures appeared from nowhere in front of us. Faeries, long-limbed, sharp-toothed. River tensed up, his hand slipping to his sword.

"Gatekeeper," said the faerie, extending tentacle-like limbs. The others did likewise, circling us. Trapping us.

11

Hazel raised her hands and blasted a wave of green Summer magic into the enemy, while River whipped out his sword, rushing them. I raised my arms to shield my face from their jabbing hands, and when the first fae turned on me, I grabbed its arm, my hand covered in iron filings from my sleeve. It let out a thin, reedy scream. Long, spindly and tree-like, they didn't quite look like traditional Summer wild fae. Their eyes were huge and staring, their mouths curved and cruel, their hands long and taloned. Whatever they were, I'd never seen them before, but some weaknesses were universal to all faeries.

I grasped a handful of iron flakes in my palm, flinging them at the enemy. The fae creature dodged aside, hissing as the iron's close proximity burned its skin. I needed to get closer to better aim, which would put me at their mercy. One fae shook off Hazel's attack, long arms reaching for her. She danced out of reach, her hands glowing with green light.

Similar light surrounded River's blade as he appeared as little more than a blur on my right hand side, moving in a lethal dance that should have taken out all three fae at once.

But somehow, they dodged, as surely as they avoided Hazel's flaring magic. Green light struck the earth, thorns springing up as her Summer magic spun a trap, but the plants died the instant they grew, withering to dust.

I threw more iron fragments, my other hand grabbing the short knife in my pocket and tugging it free. If they could dodge even River's sword, these creatures were leagues above my skill level, but the iron would still hurt if I could get a good stab in. Green light lit up Hazel's hands, shining from the mark on her forehead, yet every attack had little effect on any of the enemies.

"Who are you?" Hazel demanded. "You're not from Summer—you're spinning a glamour."

Shit. She was right. And it'd have to be one hell of a glamour to fool the three of us. I narrowed my eyes, gathering more iron, trying to see—*there.* The spindly faeries warped before my eyes, bodies twisting into contorted, shadow-like shapes as their glamour peeled away.

Vale faeries. Outcasts.

A spindly hand appeared behind me, wrenching my arm back. One of the fae had slipped unseen behind my back, and its other hand grabbed my neck, bark-like fingers gripping tightly. I gasped, my breath sputtering, but I couldn't get at the right angle to stab it with my weapon hand incapacitated.

I thrust my elbow back, missed, then trod on the fae's foot. It was like stamping on a tree root, but my boots were thick enough to cause pain. Its hand momentarily relaxed on my neck and I released iron fragments into my hand, grabbing the wrist of its tentacle-like arm. The creature hissed in pain, its grip loosening enough for me to wrench my knife hand free. As the iron tore away at its defences. I stabbed it in the arm. Sap-like blood spilled from the wound and I pivoted out of the way, its talon snagging my foot. I'd never fought and bested a shape-changer before. Usually they attacked alone and ran when things got nasty.

"Who sent you?" I kicked out, tugging my foot free. "Tell me who you're working for."

Hazel's harsh scream made my head snap up. She struggled in the grip of the beast she'd been fighting, whose hands had locked her in place. Summer magic didn't do much good against creatures who fed on its power, like these did. *I think I know what they are.* Wherever death stealers went, they left corpses in their wake. But I'd *never* seen more than one of them fight as a team before.

River cut down, his blade freeing Hazel from the trap, and she sprang backwards with magic at her palms. Our shielding abilities didn't extend to deflecting grasping tentacles. River's sword flashed over and over, severing tentacles in a wave, but there were just too many.

And it still hasn't peeled off all its glamour.

Tentacles lashed, teeth snapped, and the creatures kept growing, thwacking my hands aside as I cut desperately, trying to get through to where they held Hazel captive. She screamed, magic flaring from her hands, but it disappeared as quickly as she summoned it. Cold horror took hold of me. I'd seen how quickly those monsters could drain the life out of someone.

Not Hazel. Never.

Iron shards flew from my hand, piercing the closest fae's leathery skin. I needed to get up close to its gaping mouth in order to kill it, and the three of them had effectively woven a net around us. A tentacle hit me in the face and knocked me backwards, my feet skidding in the mud. In its true form, the death stealer was a purplish black colour like a bruise, its head sunken into a huge suction-like mouth. All three had reached their final form, their tentacles entwining.

Mum's face flashed before my eyes and I took aim,

hurling the knife at the beast's mouth. At the same time, it spat a flood of slime at me.

Thick green slime splattered my feet, but the knife sank between its teeth. The flailing beast let go of Hazel, who dropped to the slime-covered grass. River leapt in with one vicious stroke, decapitating the death stealer. Its tentacles went limp, its mouth sagging, and it slumped onto the grass.

The remaining two death stealers made horrible growling noises, tentacles reaching and swamping their fallen brethren. *Ugh. They're devouring it.* Poison-coloured light spread across their tentacles, closing the gap in the web. One enemy had fallen, but now its companions were even stronger than before.

River staggered backwards, sword cutting wildly with none of the finesse he'd previously used. The creatures were draining our energy—and I'd lost my best weapon somewhere in the monster's mouth.

I lunged forwards, and my knees buckled. My slime-covered boots had stuck together. The slime the creature had spat at me moved as though alive, binding my legs, creeping higher. *This is how they devour their prey.* "Hazel, run!"

Hazel's hands splayed. Magic swirled around her, gaining momentum like a whirling green tornado. The air crackled with power, the light growing brighter until all I saw was a green haze.

Then she let go. Green energy engulfed the patch of ground where we stood, sending both living and dying creatures flying. I fell to my side as sharp thorny vines burst to life from the damp soil, forming a shield above my head. I lifted my head and saw River was protected in the same way.

Hazel's hands were spread wide... and dead pieces of tentacle surrounded her. Broken, shattered into fragments like a boulder dropped from a great height. *Whoa.*

"Take that, you bastards." Hazel swayed and fell to her

knees. "Ilsa," she said, half-crawling towards me. "I'll undo it—"

The plants lifted, retracting into the earth and removing the barrier over my head. I twitched my leg and found it slime-free. Sighing in relief, I kicked the slime away, and got to my feet. "Thanks, Hazel." I hadn't seen her use her power to its full extent in a long time, especially away from the Ley Line, and I'd forgotten it was quite that volatile.

"Thanks for freeing me from that monster." She shuddered. "That was too close."

River pushed the plants aside, his eyes wide and blood streaking his face. "I've never seen magic like that."

"You're welcome." Hazel groaned, lifting her head from the earth. "That hurt more than I thought it would."

River wiped slime from his sword onto the damp grass. "I thought you used magic all the time."

"At home. We're too far from the Ley Line here." I shot a concerned look at my sister. "Our magic needs the Line to function effectively."

Hazel tried to stand and fell flat on her face again, groaning.

"Whoa," I said. "Take it easy."

"I wasn't about to let them kill you," she croaked. "Ow. My head."

"You just saved our lives," I said. "I should have guessed they were Vale creatures, not Summer. Are you okay to walk back?"

"I can carry her," River offered. "We should get back as quickly as possible. There might be more of them."

I knew she was exhausted when she didn't object to him picking her up and slinging her over his shoulder. I kicked the last of the slime from my shoes and trudged after them, burying my shaking hands in my pockets. *That was too close.* Nobody except a highly adept magic user would stand a chance against that many death stealers, and probably not even then.

The Vale outcasts didn't usually work together. Every creature there was out for their own survival only. They shouldn't have reason to go after us Gatekeepers, much less as a team. Someone in the Vale had made deals with the dead *and* living to target our family. And if it was the same person who'd set the death stealers on us, they must know we'd managed to finish off the wraith.

Maybe they even knew about the book.

12

The instant we crossed the Ley Line's boundary on the hilltop, Hazel came to alertness, instructing River to put her down. He did so, and a moment later, the familiar shape of the Lynn estate sprang into existence. I tried to quell the rush of relief—we'd been attacked here, too, after all. But I couldn't help it. The house and its magic brought a sense of comfort and familiarity, wrapped in the smell of baking and flowers. I didn't even have the energy to be annoyed with its blatant emotional manipulation. Hazel made for the living room and collapsed onto the sofa, while I sank into the nearest armchair. After checking the doors and windows, River did the same. He looked almost as exhausted as Hazel did. Several moments passed before Hazel lifted her head.

"They were waiting for us," she said. "Why not attack us in the village? Because there'd be witnesses?"

"Maybe." I swallowed. "The death stealers... they don't normally wait before attacking. I never thought they were intelligent enough to set up an ambush either."

"That's because they were following orders," said Hazel.

I know. Monsters like those didn't use magic to attack, which let them circumvent our defences. My body ached from the beating I'd taken, though the house's magic had taken pity on me and wiped every speck of dirt from my clothes. And Hazel's. It'd even done so for River, too. Next he'd be a permanent fixture in our house. That was all we needed.

Wait, *our* house? That'd be the house's magic working on me again, trying to tempt me into staying. I'd been intending to call landlords in Edinburgh who catered to supernaturals today, but now…

I'm *a supernatural.* I used the word so often I'd never thought of applying it to me… but it fit. With renewed energy, I pulled out my phone, saw another message from my boss, and exhaled in a sigh. Work and studying… it all seemed so distant. Someone had tried to kill us, and now I couldn't imagine walking back into that old life again as though nothing had changed at all.

"Oh, thank the Sidhe," Hazel said, as several plates appeared on the table. "I was beginning to think the house was going to let us starve."

"It wouldn't kill you to make your own lunch." I grabbed a plate of sandwiches and took a bite of one of them, suddenly ravenous.

"I'd really like to know how you survived the past five years, considering you didn't used to be able to turn on the microwave without setting the kitchen on fire."

"I did that *once.*" I bit off another chunk of tuna mayonnaise sandwich. "I'm domesticated as hell, thanks."

"Pfft." Hazel leaned over and poked River in the shoulder, where he appeared to have dozed off. "Poor thing's been awake for two days."

"I'm awake now." He blinked a couple of times and picked

up another plate. "Is anyone ever going to explain where this came from?"

"Magic." Hazel waved her hands dramatically. "Haven't a clue. You'd think I'd be able to use this sort of conjuring trick away from the house, but it only works here. Guess the faeries get a monopoly on all the free cookies."

"Chocolate chip cookies don't exist in Faerie," I pointed out. "Neither does coffee. Must be why they're always sleeping." I took another bite.

Hazel snickered. "When they're not partying or declaring war on one another."

Or seducing humans.

"Your magic really is something else," River remarked, biting into the sandwich.

"Perks of putting your neck on the line for the Sidhe." Hazel shifted in her seat, the atmosphere abruptly sobering. This was hardly the first time our lives had been in danger, but it was definitely the first time Mum hadn't been around to help. The Sidhe might not have our backs, but she always had.

Nobody spoke for a while. When River broke the silence, he said, "Hazel, I must apologise for failing in my duty to protect you. I didn't see the attack coming, but that's no reason to have let them surround us like that."

"No worries. They were sneaky bastards." She rested her head against the cushions and closed her eyes. "Don't worry. I'm not planning to move from this sofa for about a year."

River watched her for a moment, then turned to me. "I never asked—are you hurt?"

"I'm fine." I glanced at Hazel, who'd apparently fallen asleep. "I wish we'd found out who sent them."

"Believe me, so do I," he said darkly. "Vale beasts don't normally cooperate with one another. Whoever sent them is breaking the rules of both realms."

No kidding. There appeared to be no rule our enemies wouldn't break—including the laws of life and death itself.

"Have *you* ever been to the Vale?" I asked him.

A moment passed before he said, "Yes. It wasn't a pleasant experience. That realm is poison to any faerie. It drains the very essence out of us. Nobody in their right mind would deliberately choose to go there."

"The Sidhe know about this, don't they?" I asked quietly. "They just don't give a shit unless it directly affects them. So you had to come here and handle the wraiths because nobody in the Court would lift a finger to do it. That's why you were chosen. Right?"

"It's why I volunteered," he said. "Few faeries have even set foot in the Vale, and none are accomplished in necromancy."

Because the Sidhe can't die. Except they can, now.

"Is that what you were telling Hazel about when she pretty much ran away from you in the village?"

"No, she thought we were being watched," he said. "Something about the Gatekeeper not being allowed to date faeries…"

"Oh, that. Yeah."

He waited as though expecting me to say something more.

"Well, we all belong to the Sidhe, so they don't want to share their property." *Dammit, Ilsa.* Why did I even go there?

He raised an eyebrow. "I didn't mean to imply your sister and yourself have no free will of your own. The two aren't mutually exclusive. I was merely quoting what I was told… that the entire Lynn bloodline is the property of the Sidhe."

My fingernails dug into the sofa arm. "We don't tend to appreciate being reminded."

"Noted. I apologise. I was misinformed on the subject. Your sister mentioned your brother managed to leave…"

"Somehow." I shrugged. "Haven't seen him since I was fifteen. The only people who *technically* belong to the Sidhe are the Gatekeepers, and believe me, if you meet Mum, you wouldn't know it. Unless you've already met her."

"She visited my father's estate a few times to speak with other messengers," he said. "I can guess where your sister gets her attitude."

"Mum's the rule-follower. Grandma's rebelliousness skipped a generation. But she's good at the job. They all are, in the end. Pretty sure the contract demands it."

He looked thoughtful. "A contract. That's why it includes only one of you."

"Yep. Lucky us. Do you have any siblings?"

He shook his head. "I have half-siblings on the faerie side of my family, but we never grew up together."

"So you grew up here, and then got an invitation to Faerie?" There was no other way for a half-faerie to get into the Courts. Being offered a talisman was like winning the lottery.

He shrugged. "The option was open. I was luckier than most."

Not my business, I guessed. "I was just surprised. They're polar opposites. The spirit world and Faerie."

"They have more in common than you'd think."

You're telling me. Apparently I still couldn't mention the book or my newfound powers. Agnes and Everett had known, but River... as much as I knew he was still working for the Court, it wasn't fair to keep him in the dark.

Since when did you care? He's your sister's bodyguard. But somewhere between the necromancers' place and home, he'd lost his superior air and just looked sleepy. Or maybe it was those ridiculously long eyelashes of his.

"I'll speak with Mr Greaves again," he added. "Maybe you'll come to an understanding. I believe it's misguided of us to ignore the necromancers' advice. We'll talk to them at the earliest opportunity once I've ensured the danger has passed."

Ah, there it is. "Might as well. We can't stay holed up in here forever. It's the solstice ball tomorrow, for a start. If Hazel goes, you'll have to join her. I assume you have experience of faerie balls, right?"

"I don't want to alarm you, but Court faerie revels have a tendency to end with someone dead," River said.

"That's why we don't go to them," I told him. "This is run by the Winter Gatekeeper. You'll be carrying your talisman, anyway. Where'd it disappear to?"

"I keep it close." The sword appeared, leaning against the sofa beside a suitcase. So that explained where his spare clothes had come from.

"Neat trick," I said. "Did you borrow my book? The one I left in here."

"It's yours? I can put it back."

"No, it's fine. Just don't fold the page corners down. That's sacrilege."

He grinned. "I won't. The Court doesn't come with good reading material, unless you like thousand-year-old murderous ballads which sometimes curse you if you speak them aloud."

My brows rose. "Yeah, no thanks." One book with an apparent life of its own was quite enough for me.

"The library's yours?" he asked. "Your name's written on every bookshelf."

"I was a possessive child. Most of the books have my name in them, too, so I could tell if Hazel swiped one." I glanced at her. "Are you actually planning to sleep at some point? I'm guessing you have your faerie magic running on autopilot to compensate, right?" He'd been bleeding, too, but the wounds had healed. Healing magic could be used as a substitute for rest up to a point, but it wasn't unlimited. And those creatures had come too close to wiping all us out.

He ran a hand through his hair. "Yes, I do. I assumed the two of you would go more than a couple of hours without one of you running into trouble, but so far, I've been wrong." He looked at Hazel's sleeping form. "She's not going anywhere, is she?"

"Nope." *But I am.*

His breathing evened out and he was asleep a moment later. I waited for a second then leaned forward, waving my hand in front of his face. No reaction. Faeries were capable of dropping off to sleep in a second, I knew that, but there was something oddly endearing about the way he sat there, entirely unconscious to my presence. I wouldn't push my luck. He was a faerie-trained bodyguard and doubtless had more tricks up his sleeve.

Hazel's eye cracked open, and I jumped. "That was poetic." She rolled her eyes. "Faeries."

"How long were you awake for?"

"Long enough to work out you were flirting with him."

"No, I wasn't. I wanted to make him think we were all getting on fine so I can go and talk to Grandma without him hovering around."

She wriggled upright on the sofa. "What, now?"

"It won't get dark for a long while yet. If Grandma won't appear here… I have to speak to her again. I might not get another chance." If we showed up at the ball without Mum, all our enemies, living or dead, would know that the Gate-keeper was missing in Faerie, if they didn't already. They'd have an open shot at both of us.

I went to the workroom and replaced the iron filings I'd lost in the battle, adding two knives and a canister of salt. As an afterthought, I grabbed a shadow spell. Of all witch spells, they were probably the most useful—disguise spells that caused the person to blend into shadow, as Hazel had done when she'd followed me to the mausoleum. They weren't too effective on open roads or fields, places without shadowy corners to hide in, but it was a gloomy enough day that it might give me an edge.

Like all Agnes's spells, the shadow spell came in the form of a piece of jewellery—in this case, a bracelet. I snapped it on, and when I left the house, I rotated the bracelet once, and my body melted into shadow. At least, it was supposed to. With the sun beaming down onto our territory, anyone would be able to see I was there.

Past the gate was a different story. Rain lashed down, soaking me to the skin in seconds. I tugged my coat tight, shivering. At least the mausoleum would offer some shelter. Several uncomfortable minutes of skidding along muddy paths later, I halted beside the cemetery gates.

Holly Lynn leaned on the gate, conversing with two black-cloaked necromancers. All three spoke in hushed voices, their words lost in the patter of rain. I ducked out of sight, glad I'd worn the shadow spell. How was I supposed to sneak in and talk to Grandma with those three standing in the way? Maybe they were talking about the mess the wraiths had made of their relatives' graves, but the cloaks and hushed voices set my nerves blaring.

Wishing I'd bought an eavesdropping spell, too, I inched closer. Holly had her back to me, but the family resemblance would be uncanny if Holly hadn't cut her hair short and dyed it jet-black. Her eyes were tinted with blue Winter magic as Hazel's were tinged with green, and the mark on her forehead was almost identical. Unlike us, she was an only child. Her mother, Aunt Candice, was a nasty piece of work. While the Gatekeepers' designated roles were to help the other supernaturals as well as the Courts, the Winter Gatekeeper had a habit of turning anyone who tried to ask her for favours into ice statues, so they usually came to Mum instead.

Holly walked away from the two necromancers, heading back up the hill the way I'd just come. I kept still, waiting for them to leave.

"I can see you, Lynn," said one of them softly. "The rain doesn't hide your footprints."

Ah, crap. The two necromancers turned to face me as though I wasn't invisible at all. They weren't people I knew, either. Both were men. One had a long scar on his face, one had a mullet haircut, but they were plain-looking enough that I wouldn't have picked them out of a crowd.

They moved at the same time. I shifted on my feet, weighing the odds of taking one of them down. Possibly. They were both bigger than I was, but I was also invisible.

I lunged, tackling one of them in the chest. He lost his balance in surprise, crashing into the fence—but didn't give ground. Alarm blared through my mind as the second grabbed the back of my coat.

"Lynn," he said. "Got a grave marked out for you right here."

"Hey!" I squirmed, fighting his grip, but his partner grabbed my legs. With one heave, they threw me *over* the fence—right into an open grave.

13

I yelled, my hands clutching nothing but dirt. My feet hit packed earth, bringing me to a halt in a deep trench. I reached for the edge but my fingers grazed the wall, and soil came away in my hands. There were no hand holds. I tried jumping, but other than making a complete tit of myself, all I managed to do was bring more rain-soaked soil into the hole.

"Grandma?" I whispered. "Come on. You gave me your power and ran away. I need answers. I also need a way out of this grave."

There came the sound of scrabbling fingers against the earth wall.

"Back off," I warned, my voice rising. *Oh god.* Revulsion clawed up my throat, horror coursing in my blood as undead fingers poked through the soil. I threw salt at it, and the hand withdrew, its fingers dissolving. The hands continued to scrabble, more earth collapsing. My heart raced faster. If I made any sudden movements, I'd be buried alive.

An undead hand broke through the earth, dead fingers reaching where my face had been moments before. I backed into the opposite wall, and a hoarse cry escaped when hands grabbed at me from that direction as well. Crushing panic rose within my chest, and my hands fumbled the salt canister, tipping salt into my palm. I hit out at the zombie, my hand coated in salt, and knocked its wrist aside.

Which of my relatives was that? No—don't think about it. I grabbed the undead's hand in salt-covered fingers and squeezed, bone disintegrating under my touch.

Don't think about it, don't think about it... Swallowing bile, I dug my free hand into my pocket for the book, running my fingertips over the cover. A shiver ran up my spine, not from the zombies but the tingling sensation of the book's magic. It sparked along my hand, calming my racing mind enough to think clearly. More power flowed into my palm as the tingling intensified. *I'm controlling it?*

Silvery light skimmed over my palm, and the zombie's hands withdrew into the earth as though burned. I held my breath, but the magic continued to flow over my fingertips, glowing bright as a star. Then, greyness overlaid my vision. I'd tapped into the spirit sight. The real world was muted in shadows as the grey filter descended, but my hands glowed faintly. If I was able to see my reflection, I'd be a glowing ball of light like the others had been when I'd spoken to the ghost of old Mr Greaves.

As though prompted by my thoughts, the image of his floating face came to mind, and I sensed his glowing spirit in the graveyard across the road. I blinked, the greyness fading. Heart racing, I opened the book—but its pages remained as blank as ever.

"Come on," I hissed, but no response came. At the very least, I hadn't sensed any more zombies—but since when could I sense *people?* The spirit sight usually took years to effectively train, and most necromancers couldn't do much more than see ghosts. I'd been able to see spirits before the book had landed in my hands, but not tap into the spirit realm itself. Light skimmed over the book, tingling at my fingertips. Necromantic energy… the power to banish spirits beyond the gates of Death. Even faerie ones.

I closed my eyes, trying to grasp that sensation again when I'd picked up on the presence of the necromancer's ghost nearby. When I opened my eyes again, the world was grey, hazed over. My hands glowed. And so did the person standing nearby… no, walking towards me. I slipped the book into my pocket, blinking the greyness away.

"What are you doing in there?"

Of all the people to discover me standing in an open grave, River would normally be bottom of the list. But I'd *sensed* him, through some other awareness than sight, before I actually saw him. I'd known it was him without even seeing his face.

"Reflecting on life," I said, hoping he hadn't seen the glowing light. "I'm stuck. Mind giving me a hand?"

He lithely jumped over the fence and looked down at me. "How did you climb in there? I can't say I've met many people for whom standing in graves is a desired pastime."

"Aside from the dead."

"Most of them don't do much standing."

"I meant *un*dead. Pedant." But I took the hand he offered me, letting him pull me halfway out. He deliberately pulled too hard on my hand, forcing me to stumble against him or else trip over the edge again.

"Careful now," he said, his lips inches from my ear.

My feet wobbled, but I held onto my dignity. "Jesus, what do you do, bench-press coffins?"

"Deadlifting."

I groaned. "You were saving that one, weren't you? You even scared the undead away."

"I have to confess, I mistook you for a reanimate for a second there."

I stepped away from the grave. "How flattering. Did you know your people were the ones who threw me in there?"

That shut him up. "What?"

"What I said. The two henchmen dudes."

River's brows rose. "Henchmen?"

"Big guy with the mullet, smaller guy with the scar on his face. I caught them hanging about here talking to my distant cousin. I was waiting for them to leave when they jumped me out of nowhere, saying there was a grave with my name on it. Evidently." I gestured to the grave, which thankfully, did *not* have my name on it. Or Hazel's. "You know them?"

River's mouth flattened with sudden anger. "No, I certainly don't know them." And he marched in the direction of the necromancers' place.

"Hey—wait!" I hurried after him. "Do you really think they'll have stuck around? That place is locked up. Where in hell is Hazel, anyway?"

"Waiting for you in the rain. Go and join her. I'll deal with this."

"Er, no. They tried to bury me alive."

"Precisely." He marched up to the necromancers' doors and knocked, loudly, several times. Nobody answered.

"Can't you sense if people are inside? Isn't that how your gift works?"

He took a step back from the door. "Yes. There's nobody inside." He spun to face me, anger saturating his expression. He actually looked pretty frightening, with green faerie magic flaring from the blade in his hands—whoa, he'd drawn that thing fast. "How did you know that?"

"I worked it out." I also knew that with my spirit sight on, I had the ability to sense people in the same way. And I hadn't sensed Grandma at all. "C'mon. I'm soaked and freezing, and Hazel *hates* standing outside in the rain. Let's head back."

He lingered a moment, casting a furious look in the direction of the guild, then turned away. Hazel waited in the shadow of a tree, eyes widening when she spotted me.

"What happened to you?"

"Two necromancers threw me in an open grave. They were talking to Holly, outside the graveyard, and they saw through my shadow spell."

"*Holly?* Are you okay?"

"Just a little bruised." Not to mention pissed off.

"We should leave," River insisted. "Talk on the way back."

Hazel didn't argue. She moved closer to me as we walked uphill. "Maybe Holly's involved after all."

"She didn't see me," I said. "The necromancers attacked me after she left. But she sure *looks* guilty. I'll corner her at the ball."

"If our bodyguard lets us go after today."

"Why did he drag you after me?" I asked in an undertone. "Doesn't exactly fit with his promise not to let you get attacked again."

"You wouldn't believe how much iron he made me put on. I feel like a Christmas tree. He was really worried *you'd* been attacked. And he was right."

"What?" I frowned. "Surely he guessed I'd go off alone. One of us has to look for answers. Besides, falling into a grave is far from the worst thing that's happened today alone."

"Well, I suppose you two ended up cuddling there in the cemetery. I saw."

"We weren't cuddling."

She grinned. "Sure. He's concerned about you. It's kind of cute."

"There's nothing cute about being buried alive." I dug my hands in my pockets. "He also said I looked like a zombie."

"You're deflecting. That means you like him."

"That's not deflecting, it's fact. Also, I don't like faeries, especially Court ones. Our ancestors would turn over in their graves."

"Is that what Grandma did?"

"She didn't show up this time," I said. "Instead, two necromancers tried to kill me. And I'm going to call them and give old Graves a piece of my mind as soon as I get back."

"There's no need," said River. "I'll call them myself."

Damn. Had he heard? Maybe it was for the best that he didn't get any ideas, but by now I was far past the point of comparing him to the Sidhe. They'd have probably filled the grave in if they'd found me buried alive with zombies. *Nice job there, Ilsa.*

River pulled out his phone before we reached the house, and by the time Hazel had unlocked the door, I wondered how I'd ever thought he'd been raised in Faerie. The curses he levelled at the necromancers on the other end of the line would have put a troll to shame.

I figured I'd get him alone to apologise properly once he'd hung up the phone, but I'd forgotten how bloody difficult it was to get hold of a half-faerie who clearly had no intention of being cornered. Every time I saw him in a room, he'd disappeared by the time I caught up. I glimpsed him through the window, but nothing more than the earthy traces of magic remained when I got outside. And he still hadn't returned my paperback. Figuring I could corner him on the porch while he was on overnight bodyguard duty, I gave into exhaustion and headed to my room for an early night.

Maybe it was the glowing book on my bedside table, casting silvery shadows everywhere, and perhaps it was the wraith's lingering presence, but I woke in the early hours as widely awake as though the house's magic had dumped a bucket of ice water on my head. I grabbed the book, running my fingertips over the surface. If I could tap into the spirit sight there in the cemetery, there was no reason I couldn't do it here.

Grey light filtered across my room, spreading throughout the house, and two pulsing silver lights within showed me Hazel, sound asleep, and River… floating above the ground. Whoa. I let go, my heart lurching. Had he seen me? More to the point, he'd looked like an actual ghost. A necromancer power, maybe?

Curiosity got the better of me. I shoved on my hoody with the book deep in the pocket, and headed downstairs. Halfway down, I tapped on the spirit sight again. Maybe soon it'd be as easy for me as it was for River. Hazel was still asleep. River… wait a moment.

I half-ran into the living room, peering out the window. River sat on the porch, leaning against the wall, eyes closed. I frowned, tapped on the spirit sight again, then swiftly turned it off. I'd forgotten his necromantic powers extended to being able to sense whoever was in the vicinity at any given time. *So that's how it works.* He was conscious in the spirit realm while being in a dead sleep in the waking world. That was one seriously useful power. Too bad I'd probably blown all chances of him giving me pointers, even without taking the book's reluctance to show itself into consideration.

Arden fluttered down to land on the arm of the sofa. "You're alive," he remarked.

I stepped out of view of the window. "No thanks to you. Where have you been for the last day?"

"Me? I was making sure nobody took advantage of your absence when you decided to go gallivanting off to the village." The raven fluffed his feathers.

"You mean, nearly dying. Several times." Annoyance

flared. "Did you know about all this when you dragged me here? You said this was about finding the heir to Summer, but that's not true, is it? There's no reason for necromancers to be involved in the Seelie Court's business."

"Times change in the Courts and outside them."

"Tell me the truth," I snapped. "You were swooping around the village yesterday while we were being attacked."

"Caw." He flapped his wings, and I lunged at him. The raven disappeared in a flurry of feathers, causing me to over-balance, and fall into… River.

"Ah—shit. Sorry." I let go of him, heat rising to my neck. Pity this newfound magic hadn't given me the grace and elegance of a faerie. "I didn't see you there."

"That's because you're standing in the dark. Are you still planning to attend this event tonight?"

I took a step backwards. "Yes, I am. Best case scenario is we get answers, then everyone leaves us alone."

"Including me." His tone was neutral, not hostile, but he clearly expected a response.

"Not that I don't appreciate the effort you're putting in, but I prefer it when people aren't trying to kill my sister and me."

"Understandable." He paused. "I don't want to alarm you, but I found out why the necromancers disappeared yester-day. One of them was murdered."

I stared at him. "What? Seriously?"

"I'm still getting the details. I thought you should know it's not a good idea to bother them today. I'm waiting for an update."

His phone buzzed and he tapped the screen, swearing under his breath. "The same mark we found on the old necromancer's grave yesterday was spray-painted at the murder site."

It took every ounce of willpower not to raise a hand to

touch the mark hidden on my forehead. Cold horror flooded my body. *Someone's framing me.* And I couldn't tell him. The words were there, on my tongue, but they wouldn't come out.

"For fuck's sake," I said instead, half at the book, half at Grandma's non-existent ghost.

"What's going on?" Hazel called from upstairs.

"We're in the shit," I shouted back. "Now someone's murdered one of the necromancers and stuck a mark that looks like ours on the murder site."

Hazel swore at full-volume and ran downstairs. "Those bastards. Please at least tell me the person who died was one of the pricks who threw you into a grave."

"Unfortunately not," River said. "But I can't get through to Mr Graves—I mean, Greaves—as he's otherwise occupied."

Hazel and I looked at one another. "They need to know you were attacked," Hazel said, running a hand through her dishevelled hair.

"Not if we get arrested."

"We have an alibi," she said. "When did it happen?"

"While we were in the village," River said. "No, we don't have an alibi. And the fact that Ilsa sneaked out immediately afterwards doesn't help at all."

"You can't blame me for that," I said, forgetting all about apologies. "They can't seriously think one of us murdered someone."

"It looks like an undead committed the murder, but apparently they sensed the presence of a rogue necromancer. Someone operating on the Ley Line."

"But we're not—" I broke off, dread crawling up my throat.

"Exactly," he said. "I'm an outsider in their eyes, and I fall under suspicion due to my connection with you. Add in the mark that looks like your family's, and it doesn't look good for you."

"Holly and those other necromancers did it," I said, my hands curling into fists. "We should have chased down the necromancers and reported them."

River slid the phone into his pocket. "The murder took place on the other side of town."

"But—" Dammit. "If it was someone on the Ley Line, Holly's family are the only other people in this area. And the mark *isn't* ours."

Not our family's, anyway. But maybe it was. Whoever was faking the mark knew about my magic—and Holly definitely hadn't seen me use it. Maybe she'd found out about it in some other way, but it begged the question of why she'd want to bring us down. The Courts *needed* the Gatekeepers to survive. And I'd done nothing at all to provoke anyone before I'd been dragged back to the Lynn house.

"No," said Hazel, shaking her head. "Holly and I are on the same power level, and I wouldn't know how to fake a magic signature. I can paint a mark or a glamour or even a witch-style illusion, but I can't make it come to life like that. It looked like... I don't know. The only other similar kind of magic is witch magic, and Agnes and Everett have a monopoly on all spells of that type."

Unsurprisingly, River's attention sharpened. "I told you asking for their help was a bad idea."

"They didn't do it," I said. "Why would someone with more power than anyone else in the village decide to piss off their allies? For that matter, why bother framing us at all if it's the same people sending faerie assassins after us? If we're dead, it doesn't matter if it looks like we murdered anyone or not."

"Good point," said Hazel. "Whoever's doing this seems

determined to discredit us in every way possible. Do they want us dead, in jail, or—what?"

The doorbell rang, loud and clear, reverberating through the house.

River approached the door. I was behind him in an instant. "Don't you *dare* let them in."

"I'm going to look at who it is." He stopped as Hazel elbowed past him to peek through the spy hole.

Hazel whirled around. "It's Holly."

"Holly?" Oh no. I hadn't reckoned on her coming here in person, but of course—she had free run of the territory. The truce forbade any of us from harming one another, but if she'd brought undead or another wraith with her—

The door flew open, and I prepared to stand my ground. Holly crouched on the doorstep, hands shielding her head, while Arden flew at her in a blur of feathers.

"Call him off!" she yelled, as the raven pecked at her with more viciousness than I'd ever seen him show towards another person. She appeared to be alone. No undead. No necromancers, wraiths, or fae assassins. Even her magic was turned off, and she screamed when Arden's beak tore open the skin of her hand. "Stop it!"

Arden gave her one last peck and flew to land on Hazel's shoulder. From her expression, the action was as bewildering to her as it was to me.

"What the hell is your bird's problem?" Holly asked, wiping her bloody hand on the leg of her jeans.

"We've had a lot of trespassers lately," I said. "As you should know, since I saw you at the mausoleum yesterday right before those two necromancers tried to murder me."

"What are you talking about?" she said.

"What my sister said," Hazel cut in. "You're the one summoning undead as well as trying to kill us, right? If you have a problem with me, say it to my face, but do *not* involve my family."

Whoa. I gaped at her, momentarily speechless.

Holly ran a hand over the scratch marks Arden had left on her cheek. "I'm not working against you. We're both Gatekeepers. Why would I do that?"

I narrowed my eyes at her. "You can cut the bullshit and tell us the truth. It'll make things easier for all of us."

"Seriously," said Hazel. "The murder accusation was overkill. And *death stealers?* Really?"

"I just came to remind you of the solstice ball this evening." She stepped backwards, wiping more blood from her face. Her hands were bleeding, too, and a thin sheen of sweat stood out on her forehead. She was the picture of innocent confusion, but I wouldn't be fooled, not after I'd seen her with those necromancers. "You can't accuse me of absurd nonsense. We have a truce."

"You blew that truce out of the window when you set undead on us," I said.

"I think you'll find *you're* the ones being accused of raising the dead down in the village. You have a necromancer living with you." She eyed River behind us. I didn't turn around to see his expression.

"We've been attacked multiple times by the dead in the last week," Hazel told her. "River's here to help us defend ourselves."

"As if you need help," Holly said to Hazel. "If you make trouble at the ball, my mother will turn you into redcap bait. The whole town's saying you're summoning the dead, and killed a necromancer, and the necromancers' reports back it up."

"Does it have to do with why *you* were talking to them?" I asked. "Your two henchman friends tried to bury me alive yesterday."

"Feel free to take your accusations right to my mother," said Holly.

Oh, crap. Not only did I hate Aunt Candice, Mum wasn't here, and Hazel's power wasn't as strong as the Gatekeeper's. If our distant aunt was in any way involved… we were in a world of trouble.

"Are you seriously threatening to tell on us to your mother?" said Hazel. "Guess it's true that your own magic isn't worth shit."

Holly stepped forwards, and stopped, cursing under her breath. Green light shone from Hazel's palms, while blue light shone from Holly's. At this rate, Mum's and Aunt Candice's argument would get a second round. Sure, I wanted to get answers from Holly, but since neither of them could harm the other, all fighting with magic would do was wreck the garden.

River glided between them. "If that was a threat against the Gatekeeper, I'm going to have to intervene." Green light snapped to his fingertips. "I should warn you that faerie magic isn't all I can do, and unlike you, I'm not under any agreement not to harm anyone."

The earthy scent of his magic brushed my skin, along with a cold sensation like fingertips trailing on the back of my neck. Coldness fogged the air, a chill similar to when the wraith had appeared, and a faint white glow surrounded River.

"Stop that!" Holly snapped, stumbling backwards over her own feet. I'd never seen her intimidated by another magic user in the slightest, but she looked up at River as though he'd conjured up her worst nightmare from her head. Her face paled and her eyes were wide, terrified.

"See you at the ball," she said, and stalked away, vanishing the instant she passed through the gates.

"Thanks," said Hazel. "She's probably going to go and wail at everyone that we threatened her now."

"She threatened us first," I pointed out. "What did you do to her?"

"Showed her the veil," River answered. "I considered raising that undead you buried in the garden, but I didn't think it wise to make her more suspicious about my intentions."

"Little late for that," Hazel said. "I can't believe you did that. That's a top tier necromancer skill."

"I suppose it is." He closed the door behind him.

"Is someone going to explain what 'showed her the veil' means?" I asked, re-entering the living room. "Like—what, made it look like she had the spirit sight?" Ghosts sometimes had the ability to make themselves seen by people who were usually oblivious to the presence of the dead, but I hadn't known human necromancers might be able to do the same.

"Essentially," River said. "Most people don't like it when you show them what awaits after death."

"That's *really* creepy," Hazel commented. "And effective." She grinned. "She's never going to forget that, is she?"

"Probably not," said River. "It's not something I generally use as a first tactic, but given her immunity to magic and the threat she presented…"

"I had it handled," Hazel said.

"No, you didn't," I said. "We can't fight her with magic. She's got people on her team, framing us for murder. If we don't clear our names, it won't matter what she's planning when we get arrested."

"You won't get arrested," said River. "Not if I have anything to do with it." I had no doubt he'd try. Maybe the vow binding him would force him to step up and take the hit if we were locked in jail, even. If he was a top tier necromancer, what in the world had motivated him to give it all up for this? He must have good reason to get himself locked into a faerie vow. Maybe his family in Faerie…

Okay, Ilsa, that's enough speculating. You already said you don't like him. Even if I'd lied to shut Hazel up, so what? He was only here on the orders of a vow, and once this was over, he'd go back to Faerie never to be seen again. They always did.

"Look," I said. "The necromancers can raise the guy who died and ask who killed him, right? Then we'll know who left the mark there. It'll prove we weren't responsible."

Hazel nodded slowly. "Okay. You're right."

I turned to River. "Can *you* raise him?"

"Not without them detecting it, and I don't think it'll help matters if *I* use necromancy on the Ley Line."

"Shit." I considered our options, remembering what else I'd bought from Agnes and Everett. "They should at least listen before arresting the Gatekeeper's heir."

"Not you, though," Hazel said, worry furrowing her brow. "It's not worth the risk."

"Don't worry," I said. "I've got it sorted."

They both stared at me for a moment. I frowned. "What?"

Hazel shook her head. "Nothing. What's the plan?"

14

"Disguise spells," said Hazel. "You have got to be kidding me."

"I got them from Agnes," I said, looping the necklace over my neck. "Can't say I know who I'll turn into, though."

Hazel shrugged and put on her own necklace. "I might as well just use glamour," she said. "That's more powerful."

"It won't work on faeries. You know that." I clicked on my spell.

"And these will? Are you certain?" Hazel gaped at me as the disguise rippled over my skin. "You... okay, that *is* strong. Good thinking."

"Told you Agnes was a genius," I said. My voice came out croaky. Whoa. That was different. I looked down to see wrinkled hands and old-fashioned clothes. Then I looked at Hazel, who now resembled a man with a grey beard and similar attire.

"Holy shit," she said. "We're Agnes and Everett."

I grinned. "It's perfect."

"I'm an old man," Hazel said faintly. "You know what, I'd rather use glamour."

"Even my spirit sight can't pick up on you," River commented, pacing around me as though he could see right through the disguise. "It's quite... uncanny. I'd worry the house's magic won't detect who you really are."

"Nah, nothing can fool the house," said Hazel. "Or Arden. But it's enough for the necromancers. I didn't know your spirit sight could see beyond glamour."

"Most necromancers can't," he said. "I can sense how many people are within reach at any moment, and I have a general impression as to whoever's in the vicinity. If I focus on one person, I can usually tell if they're using a glamour or disguise. And I can tell if they're living or dead."

"Wow." Hazel shook her head. "You're full of surprises."

"No more than the two of you." River looked between us. "You're aware any other higher necromancer will be able to see through those disguise spells of yours?"

"Yes, I am," I said. "It's just a surface charm so we don't get ambushed again. Everyone with a jot of sense knows not to cross Agnes and Everett."

And with that, I left the house, doing my best impression of Agnes's fierce stride and wishing I had her ability to jump out of the shadows to back it up. Better than walking in the mud. It wasn't raining this time, but yesterday's weather had left slippery paths and muddy trenches all the way down the road to town. Thankfully, nobody confronted us on the way to the necromancers' place, but before I could knock on the door, the spirit of old Mr Greaves materialised.

"You shouldn't be here."

"The necromancers think we murdered someone," I said. "You must know we weren't anywhere near wherever the necromancer died."

"My successor thinks otherwise," he said. "It appears you

were sighted near the town hall, two streets down from the murder site. All three of you."

"But… we weren't there." I looked at Hazel and River, then back at the ghost. "Is someone using—?"

"A disguise, or a glamour," Hazel said. "Humans are easily fooled—but the necromancers shouldn't be."

"Not if someone else got hold of those spells," River said from behind me.

I shook my head, disbelieving. "Agnes wouldn't. No way. Can't the necromancers raise the murder victim and question him? That'll prove we didn't do it."

But not if the enemy had transformed to look like us…

"Normally, yes," the spirit said. "However, as of yet, the necromancers have been unable to recall his spirit. It seems he's already passed beyond the gate."

My heart sank. "Seriously? How's that possible?"

I already knew the answer. *Because a necromancer committed the murder. And they can control spirits.*

"Because they're covering their tracks." Hazel crossed her arms. Or rather, the old man she was disguised as did. I'd have laughed at how Hazel-like the mannerism was if the situation wasn't so dire.

"Can you see anything?" I asked. "You can see Beyond, can't you? Doesn't that let you see into places we can't get at?"

"Technically," said the spirit. "Now I'm back from the gate, I'm bound here. It's an insult, really. They expect me to be a consultant on spiritual matters. I'd had enough of that when I was alive."

"But you can move around, can't you?" I asked. "Can't you go looking for the killer yourself, or at least the person who brought you back?"

He frowned. "I wouldn't know where to start. The Ley Line is incredibly volatile. No spirit can go near there without being swept beyond the gates—if they're lucky. I've only been able to stay because I'm tethered here."

Damn. "But—I'm almost certain the other Lynn family is behind this," I said. "They live on the Ley Line, same as us, and we saw Holly Lynn talking to some necromancers yesterday. When they spotted me, they tried to bury me alive. I don't suppose you've seen those two necromancers recently? Guy with the mullet and another with a scar. Couldn't you sense they were attacking me?"

"That's not how it works. I can only get a general impression of who's in the area, and the defences on your family's mausoleum don't help."

"So you can't sense Grandma?" I said, throwing caution to the winds.

"No," he said, "I can't. And you need to leave. You seem to have an alarming habit of implicating yourself in the very crimes you're being accused of."

And he disappeared into fog, fading away. Nothing remained behind but the gate and the building with the blacked-out windows. I debated turning on my own spirit sight, but not with people potentially watching on both sides of the grave.

"That's because someone set things up that way," Hazel said, but he didn't come back.

"And we're going after them at the ball tonight." Regardless of the danger. There seemed little point in antagonising the necromancers, and we needed a plan of action in case the Winter Lynns played their hand. Somewhat difficult, since I didn't know *what* game they were playing. "River, can you sense anyone else close by? Living or dead?"

He shook his head. So the other necromancers weren't around, and presumably Grandma's ghost wasn't either.

She didn't go beyond the gates and leave me alone, did she?

If all else failed, I'd fall back on my well-honed research

skills. Once we got back to the Lynn house, I made for the library, grabbed all the available books on necromancy and the Lynns' history, and began methodically searching out the relevant sections and dismissing each book as it yielded no information. At the very least, I got to brush up on my knowledge of necromancy and all things magical, but as the pile of discarded books grew, so did my suspicion that this was a version of history not recorded by Gatekeepers past—and that if I wasn't careful, I'd be joining those forgotten Lynns six feet under.

I moved the heap of books aside to find River had returned my sci-fi paperback without my noticing. He'd left a note: *I borrowed the sequel. I hope you don't mind.* He had absurdly pretty handwriting. I looked out the window, where Hazel and River faced off against one another with practise swords. Despite River's obvious advantage, speed-wise, Hazel had been trained to go head to head with faeries ever since she'd been chosen as Gatekeeper. I winced at the crunching noise when the wooden sword connected with River's ribs. I hoped he knew what he'd got himself into.

Hazel's gaze snagged on me, and she winked. I stuck my tongue out at her and picked up the notebook I'd been using to record my findings, occasionally looking up whenever there was a particularly loud cracking noise. If I kept my eyes on the page, I could pretend I was fifteen again, listening to Hazel and Mum practise magic and swordplay while hiding in here under a stack of paperbacks. I shook my head at myself for painting nostalgia-tinted rainbows over a seriously messed-up childhood, and got on with my research.

I didn't notice the sounds of sparring had stopped until River tapped on the half-open window. Mud smeared his face and his nose was dripping blood. "Your sister fights dirty."

"So do the bad guys. Need our first aid kit?"

"The bleeding's stopped." He ran a hand through his hair, which was plastered to his forehead with sweat. "We're leaving for the ball in two hours, by the way."

"I know. Thanks for returning my book, by the way."

"No problem. I take it books are your weapons of choice?"

You have no idea how right you are. "Knowledge is. Unfortunately, we're lacking in that department, too. At this point, I really don't think the Sidhe are behind this. Not directly, anyway. This has Mum's eternal grudge against Aunt Candice written all over it."

He frowned. "Grudge?"

"They had a major argument when we were kids," I said. "No clue what it was about, but that's when the truce kicked in. The person trying to kill us is doing it in such a way as to get around the truce. I'd blame Holly, but Hazel and I haven't even spoken to her *or* Aunt Candice in years. Maybe Mum ticked her off before going into Faerie and we happen to be in the way of her revenge."

"Maybe." He looked doubtful. "It seems foolish to gamble with life and death stakes over a petty grudge."

Life... and death. The book. Holly couldn't possibly know about it, right? It'd been hidden from sight until Grandma had shown it to me, and Holly was the same age as me. Unless her mother had known…

"Who even knows how these people's minds work," I said to River. "I'll keep an eye on the clock. Best way to get answers is to wring them from Holly herself."

Two hours later, all I had for my trouble was a scribbled account of our misadventures so far, recorded in a spiral-bound notebook for some future Lynn to find. If the book chose someone else, at least they'd be forewarned this time.

When I went looking for the others, I found that Hazel

had set up a circle that covered a section of the lawn. River stood watching her, arms folded across his chest.

"You're using a witch spell?" I asked her. "Why not spin a glamour?"

She looked up from her handiwork. "Because witch spells last longer. I'll need all my magic if we get into trouble."

"Just how many people are coming to this event?" River wanted to know. "It's harder for me to use my spirit sight to pick out threats in crowded places."

"Haven't a clue," I said. "People show up from all over. Half-faeries in particular, but other fae living in this realm, too. There'll be at least a couple of hundred guests. And yeah, I think it's a bad idea us going at all, but it's better than staying here and doing nothing." I hated being backed into a corner, and walking onto Holly's territory put us entirely at her mercy. But it also put us in the best place to get direct answers, or at least contact with the perpetrators. With the book, Hazel's magic and River's talisman, we were hardly defenceless.

"It's held right beside the gate into the Winter Court," said Hazel. "The Vale beasts won't dare go near the place. That's why it makes no sense for her to work with them to begin with."

"Then it's not worth the risk," River said. "Certainly not for you. If I could go there alone, I'd take care of the threat."

"I'm *not* helpless," Hazel said, anger flashing across her face. "My magic is at its peak right here, and that includes their territory. Plus there's the truce stopping her family from harming me. If anything, *you're* more in danger than I am, so get off your high horse."

"I don't suppose you know how much trouble you'll be in if the Sidhe perceive that any of us have actually committed these crimes?" River said. "Forget jail—we'll all be executed. So please at least try to take this seriously."

Instead of answering, Hazel activated the spell circle. A swirl of leaves surrounded her, stirred by a sudden breeze that lifted the hair from my head. A moment later, she walked out clad in a leaf-coloured dress that shimmered when she moved, as did the circlet on her head. She glowed all over, golden light blending with green Summer magic.

A jolt of unexpected jealousy shot through me, more unexpected because I'd long since buried any wish to take her place. No… it was the sheer majesty of her magical facade. Like looking at one of the Sidhe, the dangerously terrible power that made you want to bow down and worship them. I didn't feel that, and I couldn't, because our family's magic made us immune. But it didn't stop the knot in my chest from tightening when River looked at her. I found myself averting my eyes, not wanting to see his expression.

"Come on, Ilsa," she said.

"No thanks."

"Do you actually have any suitable clothing?"

No. I didn't. It wasn't like faerie balls had been a part of my life in the last five years. I'd long since accepted I'd never be one of the sleek and graceful Sidhe, but my hair was hand-cut and uneven, and unlike Hazel, I didn't make a concerted effort to stay in shape. I was softer and curvier than she was, and didn't particularly want to wear something that revealing, especially surrounded by impossibly beautiful faeries.

Hazel grabbed my arm. "Chill. You'll look fine."

She knew me too well. I gave up resisting and let her drag me into the circle of leaves. Immediately, warmth spread through me, down my limbs to my fingertips. When I next looked down, my ratty jeans and hoody had been replaced by a deep-green dress that was positively modest compared to Hazel's. But from the way River stared, you'd think the Sidhe themselves had rode through the gates.

"What?" I said. "Is there a problem?" Shit—my mark hadn't exposed itself, had it? The witch spell was still around my neck, for all the world like a regular necklace.

He shook his head. "Nothing." He turned away, but my skin flushed from the heat of his brief stare. Not the calculating one of a faerie looking to entrance their prey, but pure unadulterated need. Had anyone ever looked at me like that before? I didn't think so. But now was hardly the time to get any dangerous ideas. Dangerous in a different sense to walking into Winter territory, that is.

"Is there a time limit on this spell?" I asked Hazel.

"Worry not," said Hazel, with a cackle that sounded more like an evil witch than the Gatekeeper's heir. "It'll turn back into your clothes at midnight. Don't worry, you won't turn into a pumpkin."

"Have you already been drinking?" I rolled my eyes at her.

"Only one drink. If I show up half-intoxicated, I have an excuse to turn down their offers of potentially poisoned beverages. You clean up nicely. Your turn, River."

"No thank you," River said. "I can glamour myself if need be, but I don't intend to draw attention."

Hazel apparently missed the warning note in his voice, because she laughed again. "You're lucky it's a faerie event. Watch out the humans don't throw themselves at you, pretty boy."

"Hazel," I said. "We need an alibi for why the Gatekeeper isn't with us. If it was on our territory, we could get away with pretending she was in bed with flu or something, but somehow I don't think they'll go for that."

"Precisely why I think this is a bad idea," River said, with an oddly protective note to his tone. Directed at me or Hazel, I couldn't say.

Arden swooped in and landed on Hazel's shoulder, a self-important look on his face.

"You decided to show yourself?" I asked him.

"Of course," said the raven haughtily. "It wouldn't do to leave you alone. But for Summer's sake, can you try *not* to draw attention to yourselves?"

"Like they won't pay attention to us anyway," I said. "Especially after our argument with Holly. It wouldn't surprise me if she'd planned some form of revenge."

Like an angry wraith, for instance. But what we were missing was a motive. I didn't blame River for being suspicious. And thanks to the book's spell, I couldn't tell him that the person who'd accidentally raised old Mr Greaves and caused heaven knew how many side effects… was me.

"Arden," said Hazel. "Your time has come."

"I beg your pardon?" said the raven.

"You're a shapeshifter," said Hazel, still grinning. "A master of impersonation, and bound to serve our family."

"I also can't leave your territory," said Arden, fluffing his feathers.

"Yes, you can," I said. "You came to find me."

"What?" yelped the raven, fluttering off Hazel's shoulder. "You can't force me to impersonate the Gatekeeper."

"Need I remind you there's a threat to our security?" put in Hazel, sounding disconcertingly like Mum.

"Isn't that a good reason for me *not* to come?" he asked.

"No," said Hazel. "The house is protected. Ilsa doesn't have magic and we're walking into enemy territory. We need to show them we aren't vulnerable."

I stared in open astonishment. Hazel was not only worried about me, she was strong-arming *Arden* of all people into helping.

"Oh, all *right*," snapped Arden. "But you owe me for this."

And he transformed into a woman, tall and proud in elegant shades of green, a silver crown atop her head. Honey blond curls cascaded down her back, and she had one of

those ageless faces that might have been twenty or forty—
more fae than human, almost. But a face I knew as well as my
own. The Summer Gatekeeper.

"This had better not take long," she said, with such Arden-
like mannerisms that the spell broke and I looked away. *No.
Mum's not here. It's up to us to handle this alone.*

"C'mon. Let's storm Winter's castle," said Hazel.

15

Though I'd put on a thin jacket over my dress, I shivered as we walked down the path from our home, the opposite way to the village, and turned right. The path shimmered and changed, and ahead of us lay the Winter estate. It might have been our house's double, except instead of bright green foliage coating the outside, the whitewashed walls were bare, almost aggressively lifeless. Frost-coated hedges swept over the fences, branches sharp and covered in poisonous-looking berries.

Arden walked at our side. Once I'd got over the initial shock, I had to admit the spell was a good one—a *really* good one. Arden's walk was our mother's. So was his voice. It actually creeped me out a little. Arden had used a similar spell when messengers came to the house and Mum didn't want to speak to them, but would it fool the Gatekeeper of Winter? The two weren't friendly, but it would only take one wrong word to rouse her suspicions.

A wave of snowflakes fluttered past as we walked through the front gate. The sounds of chatter reached us, along with an eerie tune that suggested Aunt Candice had hired a faerie band again. At least Hazel and I were mostly immune to the side effects of faerie music.

"Good thinking," I said to Hazel, jerking my head in Arden's direction. "He can divert their attention while we snoop around."

"Not to mention my magic works perfectly fine—and Holly knows it," said Hazel. "Pity I can't teach her a lesson, unless I drop a tree branch on her. Or throw her into the fountain. Unless you'd like to do the honours, River."

He shook his head. "I'm still an associate of the Summer Court. They wouldn't be pleased with me for violating Faerie's peace agreements as well as yours."

"Then we'd better hope they're on their best behaviour." My nerves spiked. Since all the local half-faeries, half-Sidhe included, were likely here, we'd be the least of the attendees' focus—but the solid weight of the book in my shoulder bag didn't quite quell my sense of foreboding.

What we needed was proof that Holly and her mother were responsible for the necromancer's death, the wraith, and the swarm of recent undead. Holly had definitely been speaking to those necromancers who'd attacked me, but there was no way the living Mr Greaves would believe us without proof. And River looked just as guilty thanks to his own necromantic powers. Even the Court might not take his word for it. There'd been no witnesses to the attempts on our lives. Unless we found and apprehended those necromancers and forced them to confess to what they'd done.

"You might at least pretend to be in the party mood," Hazel said, prodding River in the side. He wore a slight glamour that darkened his hair and slightly altered his features in order not to be recognised if we ran into Holly. It wouldn't fool her if she saw him close up, but would at least get him into the party without drawing attention.

He shot Hazel a frown. "It's all of our necks on the line.

And if I spot any enemies, I'm getting both of you out of there."

Hazel strode forward and rang the doorbell. The smooth pine-wood door swung in immediately, and a wrinkled old redcap beckoned us inside. The Winters kept faeries as slaves rather than putting a spell on the house like Mum did, in an apparent attempt to play up to every available stereotype of the Winter Court. Not that Summer couldn't be ruthless and cruel as well, but they at least tried for a pleasant façade.

We passed through the hallway, which again, was remarkably similar to home—even the faces in the portraits. The resemblance was uncanny, considering how many generations had passed since the two branches of the Lynn family had split. I'd always thought I got my darker hair from Dad's side of the family, but there was a woman in one of those pictures who could have been my sibling.

I shivered, drawing my arms around myself and wishing I'd brought a thicker coat. Icy air swirled in through an open window like air con turned up to max. Eerie white lights dotted the hallway, showing only the path ahead and leaving the rest in shadow.

Hazel made a disparaging noise. "Could they be any more obvious? They might as well have a sign on their roof saying "We're the culprits.""

"Quiet," I hissed.

"This way," said Arden in Mum's voice, beckoning ahead.

"Damn, I thought it was really her, then," said Hazel in an undertone. "What the hell's up with this hallway? Feels like we've walked a mile." She walked along, tottering a bit in her heels. Still pissed, apparently. *Not good.*

"It'll be a spell," I said. "You know they like their theatrics."

I just hoped *we* weren't the star attraction. Arden might look like Mum, but he didn't have any of the Gatekeeper's power. All he could do was shift forms or turn into a bird and peck people's eyes out. The lights grew brighter, until a door finally waited at the end, leading into the garden.

The rippling lawns of the Winter estate were almost entirely coated in snow. Frost glittered on leaves of draping plants, which would reveal sharp thorns or creeping branches if we got too close. The forest at the back of the garden was shrouded entirely in darkness, masking Winter's gate from view. A frozen fountain played in the centre of the lawn, near which a group of eerily beautiful fae with pointed ears and sapphire eyes lounged. The sight of human men leaping into the ice-cold water made my own teeth chatter.

"Nixies," muttered Hazel. "Make sure River stays away from them. Their magic causes any heterosexual human male in the general area to strip and dive into the water. I mean, I assume he likes women. Half-faeries aren't usually picky, and he likes *you*—hey, maybe both of you should go for a swim. You do need to chill out."

"Hazel, shut *up*. What exactly were you drinking?"

"Elf wine. Because it might have escaped your attention that we're fucked halfway to the faerie realm."

"One of us is." I gave her a warning look. "Please at least *try* some self-control. Why are there even humans here at all?"

"Because someone likes entertainment." She indicated a group of half-faeries laughing at the humans shivering in the fountain. "Nasty little shits. Lucky River's not like… where is he, anyway?"

"Keeping his distance, avoiding attention, and doing everything we're supposed to do. Did I mention avoiding attention?"

The crowd seemed to have doubled in the last few minutes, from armoured half-Sidhe to pointy-eared redcaps, imps and tiny piskies. A group of dryads had literally taken root in one corner, their bark-like skin making them look like part of the scenery. Redcaps wandered through the crowd, handing out drinks. I knew better than to trust anything the faeries offered us for refreshment. Too many cautionary stories began with mortals unwittingly wandering into Faerie, accepting food or drink, and ending up pledging their soul for all eternity. Not that they needed us to do that. They had us already, and they knew it. It looked like half the faeries in the Highlands were here. Most of the guests were faeries, but some humans wandered around, expressions dazed. And…

I stopped dead, seeing a group of people in cloaks a short distance away.

Hazel saw, too. "Didn't know the necromancers came to faerie parties."

It's the bastards who attacked me. They couldn't be discussing their evil schemes out in the open… right?

Hazel stiffened. "Ilsa—was it them?"

"Yep. Holly's sidekicks," I muttered. "All right. I'm going to—"

A dark-haired female figure stepped out in front of us. "Thought I heard my name," said Holly. She was stunning, of course, her blue dress the colour of a waterfall in full flow. Her pale skin glittered and snowflakes studded her midnight-black hair. While I felt like a kid playing dress-up, Holly owned the not-quite-human, not-quite-Sidhe look.

"We wondered where you were," said Hazel. "Seeing as it's your party. Didn't know you'd invited your necromancer friends."

"We aren't friends," she said. "The necromancers have some interesting things to say about *you*. Where's your bodyguard?"

"We don't have a bodyguard," I said. "We're capable of fighting our own battles. And that includes false accusations and attempts to frame us for crimes we never committed."

She shrugged. "You *look* guilty. Just passing on an observation."

"You bitch," hissed Hazel. "You made a deal with the dark Sidhe to break the peace agreement, didn't you? Why?"

Holly blinked innocently. "The outcasts aren't permitted to enter here. Judge for yourself. Every attendee has magic."

"That's not what we meant and you know it," Hazel said heatedly. "You sent assassins after us from the Vale."

Her eyes widened. "Excuse me?"

"And those two tried to bury me alive." I indicated the necromancers… but they'd gone. The pricks had slipped out of sight while Holly had diverted our attention.

"Where's Aunt Candice, anyway?" Hazel asked.

"I could say the same for your mother," she said witheringly. "Well?"

"Didn't you see her come in? She's over there." I pointed towards where Arden had begun to circle the crowd on the yard, in full-on serious Gatekeeper mode, knowing how much trouble we could get into if anyone guessed the truth. "So don't try anything. And remember we know what you did."

Those necromancers… River and Mr Greaves hadn't been able to find them because they'd been hiding right here. The Ley Line hid them from his necromantic powers.

Magic sparked into Holly's eyes, which glowed blue. "Don't push me—either of you."

An icy breeze blew from her—a threat she couldn't follow through, because she couldn't harm either of us. That's why she had people acting on her behalf, but it was impossible to wring the truth from her without leverage. And we had none. *I'll catch those necromancers instead, then.*

"See you around," she said, and with another rush of Winter magic, she was gone.

Hazel made to run after her, but I caught her arm, shaking my head. "Hazel—"

"I'm not getting out of this without finding out what she's doing."

"Great idea, but you've been drinking, and besides, we can't harm her even if she's guilty."

She shot me a furious look. "If she destroys the peace agreement, it's one step away from a war. I'm *not* letting that happen on my watch. No way in hell."

The crowd moved, surging around us, and it became difficult to keep her within sight. A group of Unseelie knights passed in front of me, and when I got past them, Hazel had gone.

I elbowed my way through the crowd, cursing under my breath. Hazel was being plain stupid, and heaven knew it wasn't my responsibility to keep her safe—that honour went to her bodyguard, who I spotted standing near a frost-covered bush. Sidestepping a group of redcaps, I went to join him. "Hazel wandered off."

"I'm on it," River said in a low voice. "I can sense her. I'll pick up on it if she's in trouble, but I have to stand back here to hone in on her. There's too many people otherwise."

"Necromancers," I said. "The two who tried to kill me were right there, but they vanished."

His eyes flashed silver. "Where?"

"They disappeared. But they've been hiding here on the Ley Line. Maybe they summoned the wraith."

He shook his head. "A much stronger necromancer would be needed to cause a surge on the Ley Line. A master one."

"Greaves?" I asked uncertainly.

"No. I've spoken to him enough times to know he has very little knowledge of Faerie, the Vale included."

"Someone must know." I looked at the crowd. The sound of faerie music drifted above the mass of bodies, along with the chill breeze. Instinctively, I found myself moving closer to him, shivering. As a Summer faerie, he couldn't be particularly comfortable standing in the cold either. Perhaps it was the hint of faerie music messing with me, but I wanted to get it out in the open. "River, I didn't mean what I said to Hazel. I do like you. And I'm grateful for what you're doing for my family. I'm just… highly strung, and I shouldn't have taken it out on you."

"I don't blame you. I'd be angry in those circumstances, too. And I apologise for implying you were in any way guilty of a crime."

Words were easy in the dark, when nobody could hear and judge. "No worries. We sure look guilty. I wish…"

I wish I could tell you the truth.

Wait a moment. Agnes and Everett had known, but they'd seen the mark. River hadn't, because I'd been hiding it every time we'd been near one another. But faerie vows could be undone if a person guessed what the vow contained without being told. Maybe this one was the same. If I left the book lying around so River would see it, he'd know. If the book even let me do that.

"Yes?" He stood close. Too close. My cheeks warmed, my body remembering the downright carnal way he'd stared at me when Hazel's spell had worked its magic, and when his own magic had brushed against my shield.

I licked my lips, lost for words, and shook my head. "To be honest, I'm making this up as I go along."

"Aren't we all?" He raised his eyebrows as I gave him an incredulous stare. "I was sent to guard your sister with an absolute bare minimum of information."

"Could have fooled me."

"What I was going to say earlier," he murmured. "I meant to say… I can't think of anyone without magic who could possibly have handled today better than you did."

My mouth parted in surprise, and more than ever, I wanted to tell him the truth. When he found out, no matter what, he'd be angry with me for concealing the book from him. He'd risked everything to put himself between us and the wraiths, after all.

Cold air whipped past us, sending me stumbling on my heels. Above the house, a shadow passed overhead. A chilling breeze rose, the wind of death itself, and a grey film covered the world, muting every sound and turning each individual into a shadowy outline.

No. Not again.

Above the crowd, the wraith burned, a shock of blue-white light. Bright as Winter magic. It couldn't be a conscious being, yet somehow, it was. An empty shadow of its former self, radiating malevolence. Screams rang out as the crowd looked up, panic crashing over them, yet I couldn't move. Its power held me captive, demanding my attention.

Grab the book. Now. My hands were numb, refusing to obey my commands.

Then I saw River had gone, moving towards the wraith with determination in his stance.

I broke free of the spell, running after him—and Holly appeared in front of me, her eyes accusing.

"She did it!" Holly screamed, pointing at me. "She summoned it. Look at her!"

Screams came from the crowd, but they'd merged into a white blob amongst the grey. The spirit sight—I couldn't turn it off. Holly's soul blazed bright, but I'd lost track of River behind the wraith's dark, horrifying presence. Shadows moved, and the crowd's accusing shouts broke through the roaring in my ears.

Cold magic lifted me off my feet, slamming me onto my back on the lawn. I rolled over, wincing as icy grass clung to my bare arms, but at least the sensation had momentarily stopped the numbness which had held me captive. A redcap trod on my arm, sharp claws digging in viciously. I cried out and flung the creature aside, but another replaced it as the furious crowd surged in my direction. I threw my arms above my head, staggering, cursing the stupid dress for restricting my movements. Blood trickled down my arm from the redcap's claws. Magic skimmed over my head, a blast of icy energy veering into the sky. Looked like I was still immune to faerie magic… but the attack hadn't come from the wraith. One of the half-Sidhe in the crowd had tried to kill me.

They think I'm controlling the wraith. Like they think I'm the killer.

Fury rose within me. I tore at the dress, ripping the bottom clean off. Kicking my shoes loose, I used elbows and knees to push the crowd off me long enough to get back on my feet. Hands grabbed at me, tearing at my clothes, vicious and relentless. The image on the book's cover swam in my mind's eye, but its magic didn't come to my aid. Blood roared in my ears, and my face stung, both with cold and from the beasts which had clawed me.

"Ilsa!" Hazel's voice screamed from the bushes nearby.

I ducked into the bush's shadow, beside her, shoved my hand into the bag and my fingers closed around the book.

Sharp claws raked across my chin and I yelled, hitting out, flinging iron filings at the redcaps. Hazel ducked, her hands held above her head to protect herself. "Bloody things stole my knife," she said between her teeth, kicking out at the nearest clawed assailant.

"I've got it." I removed my knife from the bag and cut left and right, stabbing anything that came near, but there were too many of them to dispel without magic, even if I'd had the skill. The wraith hovered above the crowd like a malevolent shadow, and from the screaming, it'd revealed itself to everyone.

Maybe I needed to get closer to the wraith to banish it, but with the crowd in the way, it was impossible. *The necromancers—or Holly—did something to block my magic.* The book hadn't responded to me at all. Like it'd been switched off. It seemed impossible that Holly could even have known about it, but there was no other logical explanation. We were going to die here if someone didn't think of a plan.

"Gatekeeper," hissed the nearest redcap. "It's time for you to die."

"Like hell." I straightened upright, holding the container of iron filings. "This is your last warning: back away from my sister."

The redcaps swarmed.

16

I poured a handful of iron filings and hurled them at the oncoming redcaps. They scattered, shrieking, giving me an opportunity to help Hazel free herself from their claws.

"Hazel, climb through the bush!" I shouted at her. "Climb the fence behind it. You can run back to the house that way."

"I'm not leaving you here with these murderous faeries—"

I shoved my hand through the bush, pulling myself through. Branches scratched at my face and my bare arms, drawing blood, and abruptly, I fetched up against a solid force above the fence.

A barrier surrounded the garden. Invisible, but real enough to touch, and too solid to walk through. *Shit. How far does this thing go?*

"Hazel!" I kicked the nearest redcap away from her. Both of us were bleeding badly enough to attract a swarm. Worse, there was nowhere to run except towards them, the furious crowd, and the horrible form of the wraith floating overhead.

Hazel swore and kicked out, using her heels as weapons,

then magic exploded from her hands, through the bush, striking the fence. It didn't even budge, and the invisible barrier barely rippled.

"Their magic has sealed us in," she whispered. "I can't break it."

"Me neither." The wraith *couldn't* leave. It was trapped. And so were we. I had to hand it to Holly—she'd thoroughly duped us. It'd slipped my mind that it was possible to lock up the territory to the extent that even *ghosts* couldn't get in or out, but there was no other way she could have done it.

The redcaps swarmed again, eager for blood. They didn't seem to notice the iron shards left cruel welts in their skin and burned their feet. Even my knife barely slowed them, and they fought until they bled out.

"Fuck off," snarled Hazel, stabbing wildly with her heeled shoes. "Go and eat Holly instead."

"Hang on, I've got it." I grabbed one of the redcaps and cut its throat, grimacing as its foul blood splashed onto my hand. Then I hurled it amongst its brethren with a shout of, "You want blood? It's yours."

They fell on their fallen comrade with screams of delight, and I took the opportunity to pull Hazel out of harm's way. Magic bounced off our shields, ricocheting into the invisible barrier around the field. Even magic couldn't escape the trap encasing Winter's territory within its grasp. Holly was nowhere in sight, but below the wraith, the crowd had cleared. Shock jolted up my spine—those were the two necromancer traitors, right out in the open. I stepped towards them, and there was a flash of blazing lights—necromancer candle lights. A summoning circle, flaring around the edges. With a screaming cry, the wraith vanished in an explosion of light.

The two necromancers stepped back. Shocked silence fell… then applause. The cold breeze died down, the wraith's presence relaxing its grip. Nobody moved. All attention was on the necromancers, who stood there, basking in it. The candle lights burned bright, then went out in a dramatic flash. The wraith had disappeared entirely. More applause scattered through the crowd.

The necromancer creeps had tried to kill me, and they were being hailed as heroes. And when the crowd recovered from their shock, they'd take us apart.

Hazel gasped at my side, dropping to her knees. A knife stuck out of her chest—her own knife.

Each detail etched itself in my mind, crystal clear. Dark blood staining her dress. The knife's handle, protruding from between her ribs. Her whimper of pain snapped through my numb disbelief. I grabbed Hazel's arms, shielding her from the crowd, but I didn't dare pull out the knife in case it made the bleeding worse.

"Hang on to me," I told her, and gripped my knife tight. The writhing redcaps turned as one, entranced by the smell of the blood. The only way out was through the gate, and I'd cut down anyone who tried to stop me from getting her out of there.

And then River was there, lifting Hazel out of harm's way. "I've got her!" he said. "The barrier—it's gone. We can climb over the fence."

I nodded mutely and ran for the hedge. Of course the barrier would have disappeared now Holly had achieved what she'd planned.

She can't be dead. Hazel can't be dead.

I screamed, cutting down every redcap that crossed my path without a care for the sharp claws digging at my own arms, clawing what was left of my dress. I tore branches aside to make a human-sized gap in the hedge, grabbing the top of the fence and pulling myself out of reach.

"Hand her to me!" I said to River, who'd all but disappeared below the swarm, Hazel's limp body held above his head. I balanced on the fence, taking Hazel's arms and pulling her after me as carefully as I could manage. River vaulted the fence and took her from me before I lost my balance, dropping to my knees onto frost-coated grass.

"That way!" I pointed down the field. "The fence connects our two territories. We just have to make it to ours and they can't harm us."

River lifted Hazel's body over his shoulders, and we ran. My feet were bleeding, and the scratches on my arms and face continued to sting, but I hardly cared. *Hazel.* It was my fault. I should have confronted Holly or at least argued that we stay behind, but I could hardly have predicted she'd know about my magic, much less be able to stop it. I didn't give a crap what the rest of the town thought of us. I just wanted to save Hazel.

Holly... she'd betrayed the peace treaty with our family. But unlike the faerie Courts, we'd never been to war with one another. After all, our own needs came second to Faerie. Always.

Never again. Ever.

On our right, Winter territory ended, its dark forests merging with Summer's on the territory divide. My heart drummed against my ribcage and my palms were slick with sweat. As we passed by the forest, the icy breeze turned to thick, humid air. But even now, close to home, Hazel didn't stir. *Please don't let us be too late.*

The forest came to an end, revealing our own garden. Rather than circling the house to use the front gate, I climbed over our own back fence, taking Hazel from River so he could climb and join me. Her arm draped over mine, and she didn't respond when I whispered her name. I swallowed, my throat dry. *She'll live. She has to.* She was so pale... and I'd never seen the mark on her forehead so faint. The territory was deathly silent, more so than I'd ever seen it. There was no hint of shimmering magic around the fields or house, no faint humming noises, and even the piskies had gone.

I led the way towards a narrow opening between hedges beside the Summer Gate, to the Inner Garden. As we passed, I couldn't help scanning the gate in case Sidhe warriors rode through it, but it was as rusty and overgrown with ivy as ever. More of an ornament than a gateway to Faerie. Still, I sent a silent plea to the Summer Sidhe all the same. *Please. If anyone can help her, you can.*

There I was, praying to the monsters who'd ruined our lives. But what choice did I have? The heart of our family's magic might lie in the bloodline, but its central point was at the right of the gate, where Summer directly overlapped with the Ley Line. I'd never been through before, because only the Gatekeeper and heir were allowed to get that close to Faerie. My heart thudded as we drew closer—my blood might allow me passage, but River's probably wouldn't.

"I have to carry her," I whispered to River, my voice hoarse. His wide eyes met mine, and he nodded.

I inched towards the Inner Garden, Hazel draped in my arms. I tried not to jostle the knife, but it took everything I had to carry her through the entryway. The space was hardly bigger than our living room, a grassy clearing surrounded by hedges with a pool in the centre. Those waters could heal any injury, Mum said. I'd heard the rumours, but I'd never been allowed in. Shakily, I laid my sister's inert form down in the pool. Immediately, cool water washed over my hands and covered Hazel's body. I propped my sister's head up so she'd be able to breathe, but instinct told me the faerie waters weren't like a regular pond. I just hoped it'd work.

"What now?" asked River, from the opening to the grove.

"We wait." I swallowed. "The waters have brought people back from the edge of death before, Mum said. This is where our power comes from." I'd said *our*, but it wasn't true. My power was different. Unknown. And this evening, it hadn't helped us one bit.

"I don't understand," I said, my voice shaking with the tears threatening to burst free. "Even if Holly was happy to break the truce between our families, no Lynn can harm another. Who did this to her? The redcaps?"

"I didn't see," he said. "But that weapon—" He dropped the knife to the ground. Carved with precision, stained in Hazel's blood.

I picked it up, stepping backwards towards River. "It was her own weapon. They tried to—" Tears were streaming down my face, and I couldn't stop. "This is my fault."

River's arm drew around my shoulders. "You couldn't have known."

"I knew Holly was a traitor." I took in a shaky breath. "I didn't know she'd go to these lengths. And you know what's really fucked up? The Sidhe won't punish her for this. They'll say it's the product of a family feud. I mean, if one of them —*died*, it might be a different story. Because there'd be no heir." In all these years, the heir had always been a Gatekeeper. What Holly had done had trampled on years of history, wrecked the fragile peace between our families, and possibly turned the Courts on one another, too. Hazel had placed herself in harm's way out of desperation to maintain that peace, not just because it was her job, but to protect me. I'd never considered she might have stuck with the job out of choice rather than resignation.

I stole another painful glance at Hazel. Her eyes were closed, and now the blood had dissipated in the water, she looked like she was sleeping. When I crouched down beside her, I heard my sister's quiet breathing. The knot in my chest loosened.

"She's alive," I whispered.

I climbed to my feet, my body swaying with relief and exhaustion.

"It's okay," River murmured. "She's okay."

"Yeah." I wiped my eyes with the back of my hand, shuddering when my gaze caught the redcap's blood staining it. "It only works on life-threatening injuries. I need to find a first aid kit."

"Don't you keep witch healing spells?"

I tilted my head to look at him. "I thought you hated witch spells."

"I don't hate them. I distrust their creators, and I think there's a strong chance one of them was involved in the operation tonight. It was too well put together."

"There weren't any witches there." I attempted to wipe my hand on what was left of my dress, except it'd turned back into my hoody and jeans. As Hazel had promised. "Those necromancers, though…"

"I'll report them," he said in a low voice. "I've already contacted Greaves with their descriptions, but he still seems convinced the three of us were wandering around the village committing crimes."

"Great. Add that to summoning wraiths. I can't believe the crowd fell for that one."

He frowned at me. "No. What was she thinking with that?"

That I have the book. She knows about Grandma's magic. But then, why not confront me directly? She'd cut off my power without even trying.

My burning eyes met River's. "They're going to pay for this," I whispered. "I'll make sure Holly never ascends to Gatekeeper. I'll ruin her."

"She can prove she didn't deal any damage to your sister herself," he said. "I wish there was proof, believe me, but that performance of hers was calculated to divert the blame away."

"It was deliberate," I said. "The wraith didn't actually attack anyone, did it? But it scared the living hell out of the crowd. Now her necromancer friends look like heroes."

"Not to me," River said tightly. "I saw through the veil. They didn't banish it. The wraith vanished… which means someone close to the house was commanding and controlling it. I don't think it'll come here yet," he added. "There might still be guests in the vicinity. She'll want to make sure nobody is around when she calls it back."

"But it makes no sense that she managed to keep it contained. I don't get it."

"Because it's not a physical barrier they used," he said. "It was a spirit barrier. Essentially, it's like a summoning circle that covers a wide area—in this case, the grounds of the Winter house. It kept all the spirits inside imprisoned, and prevented anything else from getting in or out. The spirit barrier locks out the veil entirely. Very powerful, dangerous magic."

But that—that must be why I couldn't use my magic.

Arden appeared besides us in a flurry of feathers.

"Where the hell were you?" I all but screamed at him. The raven had completely slipped my mind—which made me angrier at myself than at him. "Hazel nearly *died.*"

"I got caught in that Winter girl's spell." The raven's eyes gleamed with fury. "First it stripped away my glamour, then it trapped me in this form. It's lucky nobody saw me transform."

I threw up my hands. "She didn't care if Mum was there or not, did she? You're supposed to help us, not fly away."

"I thought you would have liked me to spy on the enemy," said Arden. "As it happens, I gleaned some *very* interesting information. Did you not wonder where the Winter Gate-keeper was?"

"Yeah, for the brief moment before all hell broke loose. Why?"

"She wasn't at the ball," Arden said. "In fact, she didn't appear to be in the house at all."

"What? She wasn't there?"

Had Holly gone rogue? Or was her mother in Faerie?

"The spell on the grounds was unmistakably necromantic in nature. It appears we have a traitor." His eyes were on River.

"I wouldn't be foolish enough to set up a spirit barrier on the Ley Line," River said. "If it broke or went wrong, it might have been catastrophic."

"Like that wasn't catastrophic?" said Hazel, sitting up without warning. "I feel like shit."

"You're okay." My voice cracked. "Thank Summer. I thought—"

"Like I'd die that easily." Hazel coughed, dripping water everywhere. "Can I get out of this pond now?"

"Only if your wounds are healed." They had. Even the cuts on her hands and arms had healed up.

Hazel climbed to her feet. Her dress had transformed into regular clothes, too. "I want to sleep for a century. Then I want to kill those redcaps."

"It was the redcaps, then?"

She grimaced. "They stole my knife, the bastards." She took it from me, wiping the blood on her sleeve.

"Were they Unseelie, or outcasts?" River wanted to know.

"They stabbed me," Hazel said. "I didn't exactly have chance to ask for their names and addresses, did I?"

"Hazel," I cut in. "You're soaking wet and you nearly bled to death. We can talk about this tomorrow."

Hazel stumbled. "God. Does that pond make hangovers worse?"

"Probably," I said, taking her arm to help her cross the lawn to the house. Hazel stumbled a few times, but she made it upstairs with a little assistance.

"I'll be fine," she said, her voice slurring, "but I meant it about the redcaps."

Then she walked into her room and collapsed face-first onto her bed.

Stepping back, I closed the door behind her. Fresh tears pricked my eyes, and I shook them away angrily. Some use this new power was when it disappeared in times of crisis.

A warm hand on my arm made me turn around, startled. River had crept up on me in the dark.

"Sorry," he whispered. "She'll be fine when she wakes up. The magic in that pond is powerful. I've never seen anything like it."

"It's not exactly something Mum broadcasts," I said. "But —Holly has to pay for this. She and her necromancers set that wraith loose, and she can use it to attack other people and claim I was responsible."

"Exactly," he said. "I'd go after it, if not for this blasted vow."

I frowned at him, unable to see his expression in the dark. "I thought you volunteered for the job."

"I did," he said tightly. "That doesn't mean I agree with the way the Sidhe run things, nor did I know that the wraiths would target a village where not a single person has the skills to banish them."

"They don't? Not even Greaves?"

"As far as necromancers go, he's barely above junior level. They're going to get killed."

"Seriously? I know wraiths are rare, but it's a stretch to

assume nobody in this realm has ever dealt with them aside from you."

"In cities, certainly," he said. "This is a small village in the middle of nowhere. Many others have dropped off the map for this precise reason. The rogue Sidhe will leave nothing behind."

"Agnes and Everett would beg to differ." But they weren't necromancers. And if Holly really did know about the book, enough to safeguard the wraith against it, then everyone in town might be collateral damage.

River said, "I'm going to try and lure the wraith into a trap and confront it without breaking the terms of the vow. If I manage to do so, I'll face it alone. Neither you nor your sister will be placed in harm's way."

"You'd die," I said before I could stop myself. Words caught in my throat, tangling together, and I cursed whoever had bespelled the book to the heavens.

"You seem certain of that," he said. "Is there anything you want to tell me?"

"Yes." I just couldn't speak the words aloud, and when he found out, I'd doubtless take the heat for whoever's spell had bound the book. "I don't want you to get hurt."

"This is my job," he said in a low voice. "I can't afford to fail. There's… I've suspected for a while that there's a conspiracy in the Grey Vale against the Courts, and I think the wraiths are part of that threat. I found evidence during my missions in the borderlands that more wraiths are slipping into the faerie realms. So when word of this mission reached my father, I was immediately suspicious that there was a connection."

I stared at him for a moment. "So you didn't come to guard my family?"

"I was contacted about this job because of my knowledge of the wraiths, but I have a suspicion that these events are all connected," he said. "Attacks from the Vale have become more frequent in the last few years, but the mage councils in the human realm, even Edinburgh's necromancer guild... they aren't going to investigate a village in the middle of nowhere. Especially as it's generally the Gatekeeper's job to keep the peace in this region."

Indignation rose within me on Hazel's behalf. "She's trying. Both of us are. We aren't trained for this, and it's not our job to deal with wraiths."

"I'm not blaming you. I'm saying you're being targeted as part of the Vale outcasts' plan to work against the Summer Court."

"I find that hard to believe." I knew barely anything about current faerie relations, but my family had given their lives to preserve the peace, for generations. Surely someone would have known if they faced a threat on that scale. "Do the Sidhe know your wild conspiracy theories?"

His mouth flattened. "The Sidhe and I aren't exactly on good terms."

"Wait, seriously? Why?"

A moment passed. "The last Seelie client I worked for turned out to be keeping and torturing humans in his home. I managed to set them free, but the Sidhe found out. I took on this job as a last chance." He was breathing heavily, his fists clenched. "And I apologise for taking it out on you and your sister, but she was deliberately negligent tonight without a care for the consequences."

"She was," I said, "but because she's terrified. How many times have we nearly died over the last week? It was me she was worried about, because I don't have magic. That's how they got her."

"Exactly." His eyes glittered in the dark. "I was preoccupied with you, too. If I hadn't been watching you more closely than her, I wouldn't have lost sight of her and let those redcaps sneak up on her."

I stared. What in hell was I supposed to say to that?

He didn't give me the chance to reply. Just turned and walked downstairs, leaving me standing in darkness.

Tomorrow, I thought as a wave of tiredness crashed over me. Tomorrow, Holly would pay for what she'd done. Tomorrow, we'd get answers.

17

I woke with a new sense of clarity. And as much as I wanted to find a way to make Holly pay for what she'd done, I had the means of conquering the wraith and stopping her in my own hands. Maybe I needed to coax obedience out of the book in my own way rather than chasing Grandma's ghost. I already knew the theory of necromantic magic even if I'd never had reason to learn it in detail.

I found out pretty quickly that I'd skipped to the top level of necromancy without even trying. As low-level necromancers, the ones in the village could use their spirit sight to track and speak to ghosts in both the veil and the living world, as well as banishing and binding them in spirit circles. Basic stuff. River's veil tricks were way up on the top level. And me? Nothing I read told me how the book had come into existence, and I found no references to the symbol on the cover, either. There were a few variations of faerie languages, but none matched the rune on the book, even closely. I was an academic, for the Sidhe's sakes, but there were no primary texts from Faerie itself. Not in this realm.

I drummed my fingers on the desk, adding the latest book to the ever-growing stack on my desk. If anything, the spell-book itself ought to be a source, if I could trick it into revealing its contents...

Wait. Our family tree. It was there, on the wall. If Grandma had been given the book, she must have inherited it, right? I crossed the room to the tree, traced the line with my fingertips back to old Thomas Lynn himself. Two daughters. One bound to Summer, one to Winter. Their children were the same. So had this book fallen into our line's possession after the split—or before? Had Thomas Lynn himself brought it back from Faerie, or had it wound up in the family another way? The records were gone. Buried. Only Gatekeepers were listed on the family tree. The others were... gone.

I swore as the book pile teetered and toppled over, scattering on the carpet. But that wasn't what I saw in my mind's eye. The graves. All Lynns. The Gatekeepers *and* non-Gatekeepers were buried in that graveyard. And Grandma had implied that the Gatekeepers couldn't use the book's magic. But someone of the bloodline could.

Grandma had had a sister. Like me. Great-Aunt Enid...

Her grave was recently disturbed. And her spirit would be long gone. But I couldn't help wondering if Grandma hadn't given me instructions because the magic had never been hers to begin with. But if I was right, who'd given it to my Great-Aunt Enid?

I pulled more books from the shelves, my heart racing. This place might be a shrine to the Lynns, but plenty of non-Gatekeepers had lived in this house. If Great-Aunt Enid had intended someone else to wield her power after her death, she must have left some information behind. But I'd been away from home when she'd died four years ago. Some detective I was. Surely she at least knew that the book couldn't be read unless it wanted to be. Right?

"Grandma," I said, aloud. "You can't just show up whenever a wraith does and then vanish the rest of the time."

But come to think of it—the barriers on Unseelie territory would have affected her, too. They'd come down specifically when the wraith had shown up, thanks to someone inside their territory. But how had they known I had the book? Maybe Holly had all the information, and that's why I couldn't find anything here in the house.

Frustrated, I went outside to clear my head, and found River laying out candles on the lawn.

"Hey," I said awkwardly. We'd barely exchanged two words since our encounter last night. Luckily, Hazel had seemed too out of it to notice. "You're not luring the wraith here, are you?"

"No, but if it comes back, we'll be ready." So he was back in professional bodyguard mode. Maybe it was for the best.

"I was wondering—what do those symbols on your sword mean?"

"My sword?" he said in surprise. "Any reason?"

"It sort of looks the same as the spell signature, the one they thought was ours." I willed him to take the bait.

"Not exactly." He drew the sword, turning it over in his hands. Green magic shimmered along its hilt to his hands. "They're Sidhe symbols... not human spell signatures. Faerie magic doesn't leave a specific signature, not in the way your family's does."

"No, but it *looks* similar."

He flipped the sword over. "Maybe." The runes shimmered with green Summer magic, and his hands shimmered at the same time. The weapon was perfectly attuned to him. He owned it. And if he failed in his mission to protect Hazel, the Sidhe would take it away—and his magic along with it.

He sheathed the weapon again. "I've been wondering since I got here why the Sidhe would put that mark on a human to begin with."

"You know our family's history," I said. "Thomas Lynn got his whole family cursed. The mark is the manifestation of the curse."

"It's no curse," he said. "It's a vow."

I blinked, disarmed. "What?"

"This… binding you're under is a faerie vow. You're obligated to serve the Court, on pain of death. If you disobey, what happens?"

"The Sidhe turn up and haul you into Faerie," I said automatically. "I've been looking into ways to get out of the damn thing for years, but there's nothing. Not only has no human ever escaped a faerie vow, they usually don't span multiple generations. And—"

"And you don't know the original vow's meaning."

"Obviously not. What does this have to do with anything? I can't break the vow, and if I could, it wouldn't stop the village from thinking we're murderers and the wraith from coming after us."

"I agree," he said. "I was trying to think of reasons Holly would have turned on the Courts. But I don't know her."

"Neither do I. We haven't spoken in years, but she's self-centred… arrogant… basically like her mother. And I guess she might have resented the Courts' hold over her. Or wanted more power." From the outcast faeries? Maybe. But that didn't explain why she wanted to bring *us* down.

She'd known about my magic. Who could have delivered that information into her hands? Who knew? Only Hazel and River… Agnes and Everett… even old Mr Greaves. Any of them might have betrayed us.

River paced around the spell circle. "That will draw in the wraith, if it enters the grounds. I presume Holly's keeping it under control, or one of her necromancer companions is. That limits the places it might be hiding, because at least a few of the other necromancers in the village would be able to detect wayward spiritual activity."

"You're saying it's still hidden on the Ley Line somewhere?" Or in the Vale? Perhaps it was. If Holly had made a deal with the Vale Sidhe, that was grounds enough for execution. "I wish we could run right to the Sidhe and report Holly directly to the Court itself."

"Wait," River said softly. "Who else has permission to travel between the Court and here? Your messenger was conveniently absent during the battle yesterday."

"What, Arden?" I frowned. "He had to be. He was pretending to be Mum, and they'd have quickly figured out he wasn't if he'd used magic."

"He has free run of your house, and you said yourself that he's the one who first removed the bindings. He's also not obligated to obey either of you."

"He obeys the Gatekeeper," I said. "He also attacked Holly on our behalf."

"And delivered the false message about finding the heir."

He was right. "Maybe, but his magic is tied up with ours. The family's. He's bound to serve us, not to betray us. All he does is carry messages."

And information. *He* knew about the book, and my magic.

"But he *can* use glamour and transform," said River. "Those reports of you wandering around the village…"

I shook my head. "Not away from the Ley Line."

Unless he was the one who'd put the spell on my house in Edinburgh. I never had seen who'd cast the spell, and the note had been unsigned.

"I can't detect him in the spirit realm at all," River said. "When he sneaked up on me the other day—the reason he startled me is because I use my spirit sight to watch for intruders, and I didn't sense him. And his magic gives me a similar feeling to that spell signature. It's not so difficult to copy a mark if you're a highly gifted magical being infused with the family's own magic."

"But the signature isn't our family's," I said.

No. It was mine… and it was *me* they wanted to frame. Not my sister. Hazel, they wanted dead. Maybe they'd thrown me into that grave because they'd thought I was her. The only reason we'd survived was because of my magic combined with River's presence. The enemy hadn't predicted we'd have help from the Court. But whoever had sent him after us had known. Did that mean they knew Arden might betray us? Why did I find it so easy to believe?

Maybe because I'd seen him in the village, outside Agnes's shop. The Gatekeeper's messenger. It made no sense for him to turn on us… but I never did figure out whether he had his own motives. He was tied to the Court, and through them, to us. Who knew where his real allegiances lay? Maybe even Agnes—

Wait. Agnes hadn't directly said Grandma had used the book herself. I'd just assumed it. And she was old enough to have known Great-Aunt Enid, too.

"I'll call Agnes," I said to River. "I saw—I'm positive I saw Arden flying outside her shop when we were in the village, but I need to be sure before I confront him. He might be tied to the Courts, but he has more magic than I do."

Or maybe he didn't. Not now I had the book.

I left River to his summoning circle and walked back to the house to call Agnes. Luck was with me and I found a signal. The phone rang a couple of times, and then she picked up.

"Hey," I said. "It's Ilsa, and it's urgent."

"Ilsa," said Agnes. "You're in trouble, aren't you? Half the village is calling for your arrest."

I closed my eyes. "It's—someone's framing me, and trying to kill my sister. I think they might be using witch spells to disguise themselves as us. I wondered if you'd lost any recently. Or sold any of those disguise charms to anyone else."

There was a pause. "No, I haven't sold them to anyone else. But—Everett—"

I heard her whisper something to her husband, then she spoke again. "Yes. Two went missing yesterday. They were in a locked box in the back room, but frankly, that's the *least* alarming thing I've heard in the last week—"

"If you see Arden, the family's messenger, don't let him in," I said. "I'm almost certain he's working against us. And there's a wraith on the loose somewhere in town."

"Your messenger? Are you sure?"

"River is. I'm *not* sure, but I don't think he'd make that accusation without reason. But I wanted to ask something else—did you ever meet my Great-Aunt Enid?"

"A couple of times," she said. "Why?"

"It was her," I whispered. "She gave me the book. Her ghost isn't here, she moved on when she died, but it wasn't Grandma who had this power. Because it's not the Gatekeeper's. I can't think of any other way it could have survived in the family without anyone finding out. If it didn't belong to the Gatekeeper, it won't have been recorded in the usual way."

Agnes sucked in a breath. "Now that you mention it, when we met, she used to go everywhere with that bird. Arden."

"What—seriously?" Then he knew... he'd always known. He'd passed on the information to the enemy, and the only reason they hadn't tried to kill me was because they'd thought I knew nothing at all. I was no danger to anyone as long as I couldn't read the book.

"Yes. Why did you go to the ball, you foolish girl? I even sent you a warning, and called your house. But the connection cut out."

"Maybe Arden did that, too," I muttered. "I have to tell Hazel. And—it wouldn't surprise me if they planned to take you out of the picture, too."

She gave a short laugh. "Nobody gets *me* that easily. I'll be ready."

"I hope so. He fooled us—and Mum, I guess, unless he only recently went double agent—"

There was a buzzing noise, and the connection died. The lights went out in the house behind me, and a blast of icy air slammed into me. I braced myself, hand on the wall for balance, alarm ringing in my head.

It's the wraith. It's back.

The chill wind blew in from over the fence. I ran in that direction, reaching for the book. On the garden's other side, the air shimmered above the fence dividing our house from the field alongside it.

"Ilsa!" River shouted from behind me, but I'd already started climbing the fence. My clothes snagged on the wooden planks, but I pulled them free and leapt down on the other side. River climbed over the fence behind me.

I gripped the book in my pocket, prepared to reveal it to him, but no sign of the wraith appeared. Just bitterly cold, icy air, from the direction of Winter territory. I ran alongside the fence, past the blurred forests that masked the end of our garden, at the point where they abruptly changed from magnificent evergreens to a mass of oppressive, frost-coated branches.

"That wasn't a wraith," River said quietly.

Another gust of ice-cold wind whipped at me. I caught

my balance, my gaze catching on the shape of Winter's house ahead. But the blast of wind hadn't come from that direction. No—the source was inside the forest, somewhere in the mass of trees on our left that covered the ends of both territories where they merged.

At the gates.

I stood on tip-toe to see over the fence. Holly stood in the centre of the lawn, the silvery mark on her forehead glowing bright blue. Her hair streamed backwards as a breeze blew in the opposite direction from us, out of the gate.

Winter's gate was opening—a path directly into the Unseelie Court.

I kept still, watching her. Holly wasn't looking at me, but at the steel-looking sharp points of the gate, the only place in the mortal realm that led directly into the heart of the Winter Court. And someone was coming out.

I hardly dared breathe. A voice in the back of my head— maybe the human part—told me to run. *They're coming. They'll kill you. Run.*

I pushed those instincts aside, standing my ground. Immunity to faerie magic didn't take away the raw fear that came from facing something as inhuman as the Sidhe, but part of me was in stark denial that she'd had the audacity to open the gate at all. Numbness flooded my body, giving way to a fresh wave of fear when three figures rode through the gate on horses white as the snow beneath their hooves.

Sidhe. There really are Sidhe involved in this. This was worse than I'd feared. Even knowing necromancers had teamed up with Holly to summon evil Vale fae, part of me had hoped the culprits were human.

Looking at the Sidhe was like trying to keep an eye on the horizon while on a rocking ship. Everyone saw something slightly different, depending on their definition of "out of this world scary". Beauty and horror, though some mortals confused terror for rapture. It was the recognition of a being which was utterly alien, and didn't belong on Earth.

The three figures on horseback wore gleaming silver armour, and though they weren't looking at me, I knew they all had the bright blue eyes of powerful Winter Sidhe. A glow surrounded the three of them like the moon on a winter's night, and I didn't blame the first humans who'd set eyes on the Sidhe for thinking they were angels. Devils, more like. Who'd said that? Agnes?

They're poison to mortals, even if they don't mean to be. An eternity is nothing to them. You're just curious insects.

Except for the Lynns. They were definitely delegates from Winter, from the rippling blue and silver banners they carried… so did that mean Holly wasn't working with the Vale outcasts, after all? Holly shouldn't have been able to open the gate. Not when she'd broken the treaty and nearly got Hazel killed. They should be punishing her for her crimes. More to the point—she was heir, not the Gatekeeper.

"You called us?" said a soft female voice that caressed the skin like a kiss. Leaving a sting in its wake. The part of me not immune to the Sidhe's magic longed to see the speaker, yearned to see the beauty that went with the voice, but I knew better than to move any closer. Holly was the focus of their attention. She should by rights be scared out of her mind. These were the beings that snapped humans in two like children playing rough with old toys.

"Yes," Holly said, with a low curtsy. "I hope you don't mind if I ask you for a favour."

I sucked in a breath, wincing. Nobody willingly made a bargain with the Sidhe if they knew all the potential consequences. And Holly sure as hell would. She was the Gatekeeper's heir. What could possibly have happened to make her that desperate?

"I need…" She paused. "I need to be freed from the binding. My mother—she—"

"You ask for the impossible," said the female voice. "No vow can be broken, yours least of all."

"I—" Holly's body was rigid. Terrified, as she rightly should be, considering the beings casting judgement down on her. Either they'd tongue-tied her, or she had nothing to say.

Holly had always struck me as a rule-follower, not a rebel. She'd *liked* the power. And from the pact she'd made with the necromancers, she wanted to use it.

"I cannot accept the offer," said the Winter delegate coldly. "Even from the heir. Are you truly so indifferent to your own life?" She moved her own hand, and Holly was sent flying head over heels in the snow. "When you ascend to the position of Gatekeeper, you will never set foot in this world again."

A gasp escaped Holly, then she flopped onto the grass. I stared at the Sidhe and her steed, completely stunned. One of the few consolations to being the Gatekeeper was being able to live in both worlds. Now the Winter Sidhe had taken that away. She'd never survive in Faerie, regardless of her magic. They'd effectively given her a death sentence.

The Sidhe's magnificent white steed turned around, and she rode away without a final word. The two other Sidhe knights followed her, and nobody looked away from the gate until it had closed.

18

River tugged on my arm. "We need to move. Now."

Holly crouched in the snow-covered lawn as though the gallows waited ahead of her, and I hated the rush of pity that momentarily drowned out my fury at what she'd done to Hazel.

"I'm not leaving until I get some answers," I said.

The hedge rustled, and several redcaps ran out with gleeful cries. "Trespassers get eaten," one of them growled.

Blazing anger rose, quelling my disbelief. I didn't care if Holly saw or heard us. *You'll pay for what you did to my sister.*

I whipped out my iron filings and flung them into the nearest redcap's face, then grabbed my knife. River's sword gleamed silver, and magic burst from his free hand, sending a dozen redcaps sprawling into the dirt. I found one who looked alert, and rested my foot on the redcap's chest. His eyes bulged.

"Not Lynn... not you."

"Oh, you'd better believe I'll end you. Who told you to murder my sister?"

He sank his teeth into my foot. I swore and kicked out,

182

glad I'd worn my thickest boots. Those teeth were razor sharp and hung on tenaciously. It took three kicks to shake it loose, sending the creature flying into the hedge. Iron shards spilled carefully from my hands, forming a barrier between me and them. River's sword cut down, severing hands and limbs, but they kept swarming, drawn by the smell of fresh blood. Over the fence, I'd lost sight of Holly altogether.

Well, it worked last time. As a redcap tackled my legs, I grabbed it by the back of its neck, hoisting it into the air, and stabbed it in the neck. The redcap moved at the last second so the blade sank into its shoulder instead, and it wailed.

"Quiet," I snapped. "You tried to kill my sister. *Who* gave you the orders? Holly Lynn?"

"Lynn… no. Not that one."

"Arden?" The redcap wriggled free, dripping blood everywhere, and fell shrieking beneath his companions as they pounced on the source of fresh blood.

"Ilsa," River said urgently. "We have to leave."

"No, we don't," I said. "A Lynn gave them the orders. Not Holly. There's only one other Lynn here."

The Winter Gatekeeper. Who could command Arden? *I only obey the Gatekeeper,* he said. He didn't say *which* Gatekeeper.

River's expression darkened. "I don't think I can go much further from Hazel without surpassing the limits of my vow —frankly, I'm surprised I got this far."

"Are you really." My thoughts were clear—sharply so, and it hit me exactly how screwed up the situation was. "Did your vow by any chance to say *Guard the Gatekeeper's heir?* In those exact words?"

His mouth parted, surprise furrowing his brow. "Yes. Why—?"

I marched towards the fence. *So that's how it is. She knew. They all knew, except me.*

Holly had been behind the house and I hadn't seen her pass by, so I aimed for the section of fence hidden by hedge, where I'd climbed over the day before. The house's sheer wall rose opposite, stark and ice-coloured.

"Are you seriously climbing over there?" River demanded. "Ilsa! You're—"

"She did it," I said. "The Winter Gatekeeper ordered my sister's death, and she's in there somewhere. But Holly just argued for the Sidhe to free her from the bargain. Aren't you a little curious as to what it all means?"

"Of course I am, but—"

"But nothing. Is there a spirit barrier on the place?"

"No, there isn't. But…" He paused. "I sense *something*."

"Necromantic?" I rested one foot on the fence.

"Possibly. I can't get a reading on it." He pulled himself over the fence easily and reached out a hand to help me climb down. His hands were warm in contrast to the chill coming from the direction of Winter's gate. A thick coating of snow covered the grass and the house's roof, and icicles fringed the blacked-out windows. All the curtains appeared to be drawn, and there were no other signs of life… or death.

"Ready?" he asked, his eyes wary.

"Yeah. Just watch out for those redcaps."

We ran from bush to bush like spies in an action movie. Coldness poured from the house in waves, making my teeth chatter.

I raised my head, trying to see through the window without moving within view. "Are you sure she's not in there? The Gatekeeper?"

River swore under his breath. "I sense something… it's inside the house."

I ran the last metre to the row of thorny, frost-coated bushes directly beneath the house, and before I could question whether I was making a stupid mistake, I put my hand on the book in my pocket and almost unconsciously, let its power flow through my skin.

Greyness seeped across my vision, blotting out the world. River was a steady glowing presence beside me, but other than that—*ow*. I'd tried to push my awareness outwards to the house in front of me, and it was like I'd hit an invisible shield. Was there a spirit barrier on the house? If I went inside, I'd know, but that'd put me at the mercy of any tricks Holly had devised.

But where's the Gatekeeper?

"It's locked," River said. "I'd almost say there's a spirit circle, or something similar, around the house itself."

"Shit. Is the wraith *inside* the house?" Holly really had lost her mind. I crouched beneath the window, extending my awareness again the way I'd known which direction old Greaves's ghost had been in by the graveyard. Holly must be behind the house, but I couldn't sense her spirit at all. Whatever spell was on the house entirely blocked my awareness. *Spirit circle...* now I knew what to look for, I picked up on the lights buried beneath the snow, surrounding the house in a perfect circle.

I grabbed River's arm, pointing. His attention sharpened as he saw what I'd sensed with my spirit sight—a candle, burning even beneath the snow, encased in ice below the window.

"Good catch," he murmured. "I wouldn't move it without knowing what the circle contains, but here..." He stepped to the door, running his hands over the wood. "The circle contains the whole house. Opening the door won't let the spirit—whatever it is—escape."

I nodded. He hissed out a breath, withdrawing his hands. "Winter magic. A spell."

"The window?" I suggested. But the house was doctored with the same type of spell that Mum had put on our own territory, governed by whichever rules the Winter Gate-keeper chose. It was entirely possible one of us would end up turned into an ice statue the instant we stepped inside. If not me, because of the truce, then certainly River. And he was Seelie, so he'd probably get hit twice as hard.

Think, Ilsa. If I'd been attempting to break into Summer's house… but I was a Lynn. The normal rules didn't apply. This might not be my house, but I knew the magic that sustained it as intimately as my own. And it'd never harm another Lynn.

"Step back," I said to River out of the corner of my mouth. "This is gonna set off the defences, but they can't hit me."

"You'll draw Holly's attention."

"I don't care. Whatever's in that house must be what's screwing with the spirit line."

"Wait—how are you so certain about that?"

I shook my head. There was no time to explain—and I wasn't about to let that wraith attack anyone else.

I slammed the heel of my boot into the door. It might be magic, but I'd seen my own house crumble under an onslaught of debris. It wasn't invulnerable. River's sword could probably cut it down, but that would trigger the defences. I, on the other hand, wouldn't.

Bang. Bang. The door rattled in its frame. I knew where the lock was, thanks to it being a mirror of the one on our own house, and I vividly recalled the time Mum had knocked it clean off its hinges in a temper. Not to mention when River himself had done it… using necromantic magic.

Greyness dampened my vision, and the echo of that cold, binding power passed over my skin. I gripped it, hard, and *shoved.*

Icy wind blew the door inward, and I grabbed the door before I lost my balance. River exclaimed behind me, and I knew *he'd* seen what I'd done—but he'd disappeared. So had the house. All that remained was a screaming void of grey, and a… thing trapped within it. My consciousness crept outwards, pinpointing the shadow to where the Lynns' living room was in the waking world.

A spirit was trapped inside. A powerful one. The whole house trembled with energy, making my own power feel muted by comparison. *A wraith? No way.* It shone too bright, a blinding presence, somehow familiar…

No. It can't be.

The Winter Gatekeeper was already dead. It was *her* spirit tethered to the house, trapped in what must be a giant summoning circle.

Damn the Sidhe, now I knew why Holly was so desperate to free herself from the curse. With the Gatekeeper dead, she'd be the next one. So she'd… bound her. If the Gatekeeper continued to exist, that meant Holly herself wouldn't ascend to the position of Gatekeeper. She'd found a way around the vow. And the necromancers had obviously helped her preserve her mother's life, tethering it to this realm. Which meant she wasn't dead, she was somewhere in between, caught in the veil.

Oh my God. It was *her* magic that had raised the dead, the wraiths, and caused chaos up and down the Ley Line.

River moved to my side. "She's going to mess up the whole spirit realm."

I blinked the greyness away, stumbling backwards beside him.

"She's dead," I whispered. "I don't understand. She was alive—she was absolutely fine the last time I saw her. She's only Mum's age."

"I think that's the least of our concerns."

No kidding. This was some secret and a half. How long had she been like this? Could she even be banished?

I have to try. "River, could you… banish her?"

"Not while the circle's locked," he whispered. "It has some power source I can't detect."

"Of course. It must be the necromancers. They're still here somewhere. We have to kill them."

"I can't let you do that, Ilsa," said Holly. She stepped into the hallway, a gleaming icy dagger in her hand. "You're trespassing."

The knife left her hand as she threw it at River. He deflected it with the side of his blade, sending it clattering against the family portraits on the wall. Despite the horrible presence within, the house looked exactly the same. How had neither of us picked up on this yesterday? She must have had the spirit barrier set up all along.

I waited, my body tense. I couldn't harm her, after all. But there was no way I was letting her keep that *thing* imprisoned here, barely contained, with enough power to shake up the Ley Line itself.

Holly's mouth twisted. "You people don't know when to quit."

"We're tethered to the Sidhe, same as you," I retaliated. "Not that it means anything to you, seeing as you tried to have my sister killed."

My hand crept towards my own knife. I knew how powerful, how devastating her magic was—and that River had no defence against it.

"I didn't try to have your sister killed. Him, though—I don't care."

Icy shards materialised in the air, daggers aimed directly at River. If I got in the way, my magic wouldn't save me. River's sword sliced diagonally, severing a dozen of them at once. *Whoa.* I'd forgotten, given the power we were faced with, just how strong a faerie talisman was. Maybe enough to outdo a Gatekeeper. But that spirit—

Icy air blasted down the hallway, rattling the portraits,

causing both River and I to stumble backwards in the direction of the doorstep. Death energy. I wasn't immune to necromancy.

Holly raised her palms, the circlet on her forehead glowing with silver-blue light. The same power Hazel had used to blast those Vale faeries to pieces.

I shoved River out the way and tackled her. We slammed into the wall, the magical assault bouncing off my shield and leaving River unharmed. He swore, and the house *moved*, its magic rattling my teeth in my skull. The house's magic must have picked up on the intruders and now it wanted to throw us out.

River stepped backwards off the doorstep and I moved in that direction as well. The spirit circle was outside. We needed to break it to free the spirit. And then… presumably, she'd move on, through the gates to the afterlife. Beyond. Right? That coldness I'd felt from her, though… she still retained some kind of awareness. A person as powerful as she'd been in life probably did keep her mental functions after death. What Holly was doing was sick, twisted and cruel… but I couldn't forget that it was the Gatekeeper who had the authority to give Arden orders, and had supposedly set those redcaps on us. If I believed them.

Icicles rose from the windows to throw themselves at River. He cut them down, driven backwards away from the house. We could theoretically make a run for it from here, but that was the coward's way out.

"You've lost it," I told Holly. "The veil… the whole Ley Line might crack open again if you keep that spirit caged here. Let her go. Move on. You didn't have to—"

"Please." She laughed harshly. "Like your sister wouldn't do the same."

"No. Hazel wouldn't do that. And even if she would, we have to stop you."

"Is it worth tearing the realms apart for?" River cut in. "Your mother's spirit's a powerful one. It's sending shock-waves across the whole veil."

"Not my problem," said Holly. "You don't know *anything* about me, or about our family."

Coldness rolled through me—not from the wind, but from the book stirring in my pocket. A film of grey surrounded my vision again. One blink and the spirit world overlaid the realm of ordinary sight. I could still see River and Holly, and the bright shapes of their souls—but beyond that was a brighter shape, an orb of light like a second sun. The Winter Gatekeeper's soul. If I freed and banished her, I'd be able to send her Beyond the gate for good.

Ice exploded from Holly's fingertips. I screamed a warning to River, but he moved swiftly, dodging her attacks. Summer magic swirled around him, breaking the icicles, and coalescing into a whirlwind of energy aimed at Holly. She waved a hand and an icy shield deflected his attack. *Dammit.* If we could both fight her at once, we might stand a chance, but that truce—

Wait. I crouched, grabbed a handful of snow, and flung it into Holly's face. She gave a startled hiss, and River took the opportunity to strike, blasting her with necromantic power, driving her backwards towards the house.

I reached into my pocket with numb fingers, cursing the icy wind still rolling from the mansion. Snowflakes drifted around, stinging my face and hands, but I pulled the book free and willed its cold magic to fill my veins.

The house and garden trembled as a shadowy form descended, bringing a blast of icy cold energy that felt like the depths of hell itself. The chill breeze struck me head-on, and my back hit the wall. The wraith must have been hiding behind the house—and unlike the Winter Gatekeeper's ghost, it wasn't bound by the spirit circle.

Holly stepped into the hallway, a smirk on her face. So she'd decided to back out and set her pet monster on us instead. Winded, I clutched the book by sheer reflex, its pages spinning, words passing over them. Banishing words. They rose to my tongue—but River spoke first, advancing on the wraith as it descended beside the house. *Dammit, he's going to get himself killed.*

"Hey!" I screamed at the monster, brandishing the book. "Get over here." I grabbed the salt canister with my free hand and threw the contents down in front of me. "River, get back here. We don't need the—"

Holly lunged at River, tackling him to the ground. He flung her off, but the wraith bore down on him. His sword came up, piercing the wraith's shadowy form, and it shuddered, fury rolling off it. The weapon did hurt it—maybe because it was forged in faerie magic—but it wasn't enough to kill.

The words in my mouth and the power in my hands were.

I spoke deliberately, like remembering a language half-forgotten. Grey light spun from my fingers almost like magic itself, slamming into the beast. It continued to sweep across the ground, and alarm sang through me—*it's not enough. The book isn't enough.*

The spirit realm remained, a monochrome plane covering everything. Holly's soul shone in the gloom—and River's, alight with necromantic magic. *Wait.*

"You know the words," I said to him. "Speak them."

"How do you—"

"Come on!" I shouted the line again, and River spoke, too. Cold magic rose to my hands, mingling with his, and the combined force of our power struck the wraith directly. It fell back, writhing, screeching, and its body exploded into fragments.

Silence descended. Then River turned to me, betrayal and disbelief etched on his face. "You're—"

"How *dare* you," snarled Holly. "Have you any idea what I've done to get my hands on the Gatekeeper's book?"

Somehow, I found my voice. "I think the evidence is right behind me. Too bad you couldn't bribe Arden to steal that, huh." The book glowed, its grey sheen shimmering up my arms. Magic. Could I hurt even Holly with that power?

Let's find out.

"I didn't want to do this, Ilsa," she said.

Two figures came out behind her. Necromancers. The henchmen from before. Their hands glowed, too, their souls shining bright in the greyness.

River ran to meet them, his sword slashing. I ran to join him, but cold hands reached and locked around my throat, pushing me backwards. *What—?* The two of them weren't anywhere near me. One fought River, the other stood behind —yet his hands were at my throat, and his face swam before my eyes.

His spirit had detached from his body. I gasped and raised my hands to pull him off me, but my hands passed straight through his indistinct form. I could breathe just fine, but his hands weren't on my physical body at all. He was trying to pull my spirit *out* of my body, and the horrible chill that froze my blood was the sensation of death calling me.

But I held the means of using death's magic against them in my hands, and I had no intention of letting another soul get hold of it.

Grey light shone from my hands, the book's cold magic rushing through my veins. I grabbed his hands in mine, hard, pulling them from my throat. I might not be as versed in necromancy as I liked, but I knew that physical strength in the waking world meant nothing in the realm of spirits. What mattered above all else was *will*—the iron determination to cling to life. That's what made the most persistent ghosts. And that's what fuelled my power. I grabbed his hands, pulling them from my neck, and *pushed.*

His spirit flew backwards, in the direction of his body. Exhilaration filled my blood. *Finally.* If I could manipulate the dead, maybe I could do the same for Holly. I turned, seeking the familiar glow of her spirit—and saw her living form, holding River's sword.

The grey light switched off and I gasped. River lay on the grass, completely still, snow already piling onto him.

"Bastard cut me," said the necromancer. "I got him, though."

No. River wasn't visibly injured. But he didn't seem to be breathing or moving.

I switched on my spirit sight again, greyness flooding my vision. Showing the two necromancers, Holly… and no sign of River.

"Don't worry," said the second necromancer. "He's not dead. Ilsa Lynn, is it? You're not the one I'm supposed to kill. You'll be more valuable to us alive."

Horror coursed through me. They'd ripped River's spirit out of his body, and if it wasn't here, there was only one place it could be—the afterlife. He was as good as dead.

"Throw him out," Holly told the necromancers, indicating River's prone body. "And take her."

He can't be dead. No way. His spirit wouldn't have just —vanished.

One of the necromancers lunged for me. I kicked out, catching him in the kneecap, but that didn't slow him down. He aimed a punch, which I tried to block, but missed. His fist caught me in the cheekbone and knocked me back into the wall. My head rung with pain, my vision swimming, made worse by the glowing spirits behind him and Holly—

Wait a second. His spirit… it didn't match the person who

faced me. He looked human in the waking world, but from what I'd seen of spirits through the veil…

He was half-faerie, and spinning a glamour.

I dived down, scraped the scattered iron filings from the earth, and threw them in his face. He fell back, screaming in pain as the iron burned his skin, burned away his disguise. I drew back, prepared to fight—then saw the second necromancer leaving, carrying River's body.

Sorry, River. I'm so sorry.

I threw the last of the iron fragments at the necromancer, and ran.

19

I kept running, breathing sharply, inhaling cold air carrying the scent of death. Anger rolled through me, but my powers only worked on the dead, not the living. And it wasn't enough. It was never enough.

And now River was gone, somewhere in Death, where I couldn't reach him.

It's my fault. I dragged him onto their territory.

I caught up to the necromancer with a hoarse scream, throwing myself at him from behind. He hit the fence, and I fumbled for my knife, stabbing wildly. He threw me off him, hands grabbing at me, but I kicked him full in the face, feeling cartilage break beneath my boot. He must have thrown River's body over the fence—right into that redcap nest.

I threw what was left of the iron at the necromancer's bleeding nose and trod on him to climb the fence. River lay several feet away. I dropped to my knees, feeling for a pulse. It was there, but faint. So he still lived... but his spirit had disappeared. Without it, his body would eventually die. Like the Winter Gatekeeper's must have, by now.

"River. *River.*"

My grey-tinted vision showed nothing but a blur, and even the Gatekeeper's spirit behind me had disappeared from view. I grabbed his arm, looped it over my shoulder, and half-dragged him down the field. My arms screamed, protesting at the exertion. Coldness dragged at my limbs, threatening to pull me down, but I stayed upright—somehow. *I can't let him die here. I can't... I can't.*

The field on my right became forest, thick forest with frosty trees masking the gate from view... the gate where the Sidhe had rode through and cast judgement down on Holly... the Sidhe, who would never come and save us...

Frosty trees slowly began to merge into evergreens. River's dead weight leaned on my shoulder. My arms were numb.

Greyness folded over my vision. I felt my knees give way, River slipped from my grasp, and the grey was relentless. Never-ending. Like the veil.

"Get up," whispered a voice. Grandma. "Ilsa."

"Damn you," I croaked. "You're too late. You could have..."

But there was nothing any of us could have done. River was trapped beyond life or death, and even necromancers couldn't...

"Ilsa."

I looked up, anger melting the ice freezing my hands and momentarily restoring my energy. "Thanks for telling me it was Great-Aunt Enid who did this," I growled at her. "And for vanishing when I needed your help. Why is the book working for me now when it wouldn't before?"

"The book only obeys the Gatekeeper," Grandma's spirit said. "I apologise... I hoped the book would not surface again during your lifetime, and that you wouldn't have need of it."

"You were wrong." I crawled to my knees and pulled the

book from my pocket. The symbol on the cover glowed with incomprehensible power. *The book only obeys the Gatekeeper.* When I'd told River the words of the vow... I'd acknowledged that this was what I was. But Gatekeeper of what, exactly? "How in hell did this book end up in the family in the first place?"

"The same way anything came to our family," said Grandma. "The Sidhe."

An icy pit opened inside me that had nothing to do with the lingering chill from Winter's territory.

"Thomas Lynn was lucky enough to escape their clutches with his mortal lover," she said, "but the taint of their magic remained. Even after his death, the contract he made in Faerie didn't cease to exist. Both Summer and Winter had their claim on his daughters' souls, and when both Courts were embroiled in a vicious conflict, it might have been the final straw that caused the Courts to destroy one another."

"So they sacrificed themselves?" I asked quietly. "That's what happened—right? One Court claimed each."

"They did, and the result was decades of peace across the realms. And because of that very same contract, the Sidhe were tied to this realm and were obliged to step in and assist us against the outcasts when they attacked. But the book you hold in your hands is from a pact just as ancient. The family has necromancer blood running through it as surely as the faerie magic in our veins, but only one who is not heir to either Court can wield it. The book gives one power over death itself, even those who are beyond life and death."

My mouth fell open. "So... that must be why it came to the surface now."

Puzzlement flashed across her face. "What do you mean?"

"I—oh, screw it, it's not like the Sidhe can come after you in Death. The Sidhe's source of immortality was apparently destroyed."

She gave me a sharp look. "Who told you that?"

"A ghost," I said. "Why? It makes sense."

"The book awakens when the peace is threatened," she said. "That must be why. That Holly... I knew she was searching for the book, but not why. She wanted that magic you wield, but she didn't know where it came from."

Of course. Holly thought I'd picked it up by accident. She'd been furious, because it held the exact type of magic she needed to preserve her mother's spirit and prevent the Winter Court from claiming her.

"I guess you don't know how to banish that spirit, if Great-Aunt Enid was the one with the power."

"No," she said gently. "But I can help you find your friend."

"You can help me find River?" My voice rose. "But—he's gone."

Her hands gripped my arms, tight—too solid for a ghost. I yelped as a horribly cold feeling spread down my spine, like someone had poured icy water down my back. The sensation crept up my arms to my fingertips.

"What the—?"

"You only have a short time," she said, her voice faint. "Run."

I spun on the spot, but Grandma had disappeared. The noise ahead grew louder. My hands shimmered oddly under the dim light. Had Grandma given me some new kind of power? My body felt... light. Floaty.

She hadn't given me magic. She'd pulled me out of my body entirely.

River was here somewhere. In Death. Together, we might be able to banish the Winter Gatekeeper's spirit before Holly doomed us all.

I'll make it right. I promise.

Greyness blanketed the world, and the field had entirely

disappeared. Presumably my body still lay there on the grass at the boundary of my own territory, but all around were shades and little more. As a ghost, I could move anywhere—even find the necromancers, and warn them that they were needed. But how did the waking world relate to this grey haze? I hadn't a clue.

After floating a little, it occurred to me that while I hadn't consciously been moving in any particular direction, something drew me forwards. The outline of a long, endless shape appeared in the distant haze. Sort of like—a gate.

The gates of death. Everyone was drawn to the gates when they died, and while I might not actually be dead, the tugging sensation was clear—the gates would take me anyway.

I floated some more, through greyness so complete, I forgot there was another world beneath entirely. My thoughts became sluggish, drifting away on the breeze, and I halted in alarm when I found myself drifting towards the mass of greyish spirits, in front of the vague transparent shape of the gates.

"Nope." I stopped, fighting the tug with everything I had. "Not happening. River!"

Nobody responded. Sad spirits drifted around, some of them muttering to themselves. I caught enough words to know most of them had forgotten who they were and what they were doing here. Some called after family members, others blankly stared until the crowd's momentum carried them towards the seemingly endless stretch of spear-topped, towering gates. Worse, my own name began to slip through my fingers, too.

"I'm Ilsa Lynn. I won't forget who I am. I'm not dead. And I need to find River." I repeated the words over and over again, grasping for the surety I'd felt when I'd sensed his spirit as I'd stood in that grave…

And then—I saw him. His spirit glowed brighter than the

other ghosts, perhaps because he wasn't actually dead. He floated apart from the others, wearing the same distant expression as all of them. I directed myself towards him, hovering above the grey. The spirits weren't solid so I floated straight through them, my gaze fixated on River's blurred form. Indistinct. Fading.

Not if I can help it.

"River," I gasped. "You need to come with me right now."

He looked past me, muttering something unintelligible.

"Don't you start talking to dead people as well," I snapped. "I'm Ilsa. You're River. And we're both alive."

I grabbed his hand, which slipped through my fingers. Dammit. How was I supposed to grab hold of a ghost?

He drifted to the left, towards the relentless crowd borne through the gates. I couldn't see anything more than that. The world of Beyond was unknown to everyone except the necromancers.

"I have to find them," he said.

Was this what necromancers had to put up with all the time? No wonder they were so bad-tempered. Ghosts were more unreliable than even the Sidhe.

"In case you've forgotten, River, you're bound by a vow to protect my family with your life. Which means your life is tethered to ours. Like the Lynn family curse."

"Family curse," he repeated.

"Yes, I told you about it." I looked him in the eyes, which gleamed with green Summer magic even in death. "Don't you remember?

Remember...

The vow that bound me only worked on the living. Even if he hadn't seen what I'd done, I'd be able to tell him all of it now. The book, as far as I knew, hadn't followed me into death. *But maybe it can.* Necromancers seemed to be the exception to every rule. The fact that neither of us had floated through the gates yet was proof of that.

"I have something really important to tell you, River, and I hope you remember it when you wake up. I'm the one who banished the wraith. Grandma—well, Great-Aunt Enid—she gave me this book with necromantic magic that's been in our family forever, and it bound itself to me. I can't tell anyone about it, but I got around the vow."

"You banished the wraith?"

"Yes." I grabbed his wrist. To my surprise, his hand felt solid this time. So did mine. "I did. And I think *I'm* the Gate-keeper you're supposed to protect. Somehow…"

He looked at the gates, then back at me, his expression clearing. "You're the Gatekeeper. You're… Ilsa."

"At least you didn't call me Hazel. Tell me you remember who you are now."

He looked down at our entwined hands and shook his head. "I'm too far gone. Maybe my vow kept me alive this long, but I don't think I can—"

The breeze tore at him, threatening to break my grip on his hand. I wasn't strong enough to fight the pull from Death's gates. No matter what I did—

"Think about your family," I said desperately. "Think about something real. Anything." Strong emotions attached ghosts to the waking world, I knew *that*, but I didn't know him well enough to make an educated guess as to what would work in this particular case. All I knew was that I wasn't letting go of his hand.

"My father didn't believe my reports on the wraiths." His hand solidified as anger and pain flashed in his eyes. "Nobody would take the word of a half-blood seriously in the Courts, even on matters that threaten their lives."

"Oh." Suddenly his initial interest in the wraiths made a lot of sense. "I'm sorry. He's wrong. You were right, and you have to tell the Courts that. You'll finish your job and they'll forgive you for helping humans…" Dammit. His hand had gone transparent again, his expression clouded.

"River," I said. "I want you to think very clearly. What exactly were you thinking when you saw me step out of Hazel's spell circle?" Maybe I needed something more powerful—but I didn't know what he cared about most of all, in this world or Faerie. Hadn't had the chance to ask.

I dug my nails into his palm, grabbing his shoulder with my free hand. Death's cold embrace tugged at us, but I planted myself right there and refused to budge.

"I was thinking…" His gaze cleared. "I was thinking that if I could break my vow and spend the night with you instead, I'd do it in a heartbeat."

Shock filtered through. For all the restless spirits floating past, we might have been alone. "What? I thought you were mad at me at the time."

He shook his head. "I was mad at your sister for not taking the threat seriously, but you… I wished it'd been you I'd been asked to guard."

"Well, you got your wish." Maybe being a ghost did away with my reservations, but I had to try. "If you go through those gates, you'll never get to spend any more time with me in the waking world." I placed my hands on his shoulders. "Don't you want to see what that would be like?"

I closed the last inches between us and kissed him. I wish I could say I felt the whole thing, but with little left of my senses, all I got was the whisper of his lips on mine and the barest hint of the earthy scent of his magic.

I looked up to find the gates had disappeared, to be replaced by more endless grey. The fog cleared, revealing my house, and we dropped through the roof as though it wasn't there at all. Down, down into the living room, where Hazel slumped beside the sofa, her head bowed. Two bodies lay there, one on the armchair, the other on the sofa.

"Oh god, she's going to kill me. She must have found our bodies out in the field," I said. It was weird as hell to speak while looking down at my own lifeless body. *Shit. Hope it's not too late.*

I looked for River, but he'd disappeared. Below, on the armchair, he stirred, his eyes opening. Alive. We'd made it.

I closed my eyes, concentrating on the solid sensation of the book in my hands—*wait. Am I holding the book?*

My eyes flew open and I sat up. I *was* holding the book— and text covered every page in swirling lines.

20

Hazel screamed. I lowered the book and shook my head, my mind spinning from the weird sensation of suddenly *having* senses again. Like the ability to feel freezing bloody cold, and the sting of the cuts on my face and arms where the redcaps had attacked me. At least my clothes were dry and dirt-free, thanks to the house.

River groaned, sitting up, running a hand over his forehead.

"What the fuck?" Hazel croaked. Her eyes were puffy with tears. "You're—you're alive."

"Sorry," I said. "Didn't know it'd take that long."

"You were *dead.* I mean, you were breathing, but I couldn't wake you up. Either of you. What *happened?*"

No excuses presented themselves. I'd failed, totally failed to best Holly, and almost got both of us killed. And yet—the book. I'd finally unlocked it.

"Holly," I said. "Turns out those creepy necromancers were half-faeries using glamour, and they trapped River in Death. So I had to get him out."

"I can't believe you went there without me." She scrubbed a hand over her forehead. "I'm the freaking Gatekeeper."

"There was no time," I said. "Holly—she was up to something bad over there. Really bad. The Winter Gatekeeper… she's dead."

I ran through what we'd seen, with River's input. Hazel looked between us as though expecting me to admit it was all a joke. By the time I'd finished explaining my encounter with Grandma's ghost and my trip over the veil, Hazel and River were both gaping at me.

"Necromancers—in our family?" said Hazel.

"Yep," I said. "Great-Aunt Enid. Supposedly, I'm the first in a while, and the book only awakens when it's desperately needed."

"And you decided not to tell anyone," River said.

I shook my head. "The *book* decided not to tell anyone. Or whoever put that spell on it did. Every single time I've tried to bring up the subject, it's stopped me."

"Until you used it to break into Holly's house," he said. I didn't miss the accusing note in his tone.

"I was improvising," I admitted. "I've been playing it by ear the whole time because up until now, I couldn't even read the damn thing. When I banished the first wraith—"

"I knew something wasn't right," said River. "That beast was too powerful for my first spell to have been enough."

"I thought it'd killed you," I retaliated. "Believe me, I'd have liked to talk to someone living about this crap. I wasn't trying to be deceptive. Blame my Great-Aunt Enid, who didn't have the decency to stick around as a ghost and explain all this. If it'd worked yesterday at the ball, you'd have seen it for sure."

"But the spirit barriers blocked your magic."

Your magic. The words sent a weird thrill through me

which almost caused me to forget the mire of shit we'd landed in.

"I guess they did. I really *don't* understand how to use this power, though. I just spoke the words… heaven knows where *they* came from. I wasn't trying to deceive you, River, honestly. If anything, I think you could have helped me."

He nodded, not looking too happy. Maybe he was remembering our kiss. Whether he'd meant what he said or not, I didn't blame him for being angry with me. He'd helped us, even at the risk of being accused himself, and now…

"So you know all the binding words?" he asked.

"Apparently," I said. "So far I've only been able to use any magic when my spirit sight's switched on, and I only just figured out how to do *that* on command. But Holly… she knew about it. I think Arden told her, or gave her the information. She was looking for the book before she even knew I had it."

"What—*Arden?*" said Hazel. "How could he have told her?"

"We're sure he's a double agent," I explained. "He stole the spells from Agnes, so people could walk around pretending to be us."

Her mouth fell open. "But—he's the Gatekeeper's."

"Not just our Gatekeeper's," I said. "She—I don't know how, considering her spirit's trapped within that house, but she's the one who set the redcaps on us last night, too. Unless Holly's somehow wrangled obedience from him when she's not technically Gatekeeper yet."

Hazel swore. "The snake. He… you're saying he left the mark, too, right?"

"This mark," said River, indicating the book. "It *was* yours. Can I take a closer look at that book?"

I handed it to him. To my surprise, the book didn't resist. "The pages are blank, usually," I said. "But they turn up with the right words if I need them. I guess it's programmed to do that. With magic... whatever spell was put on it to begin with."

River swore under his breath. "That's why you were asking about my sword. The mark... I don't know this one, but I think it's an Invocation mark."

Hazel gasped. "Of course. I should have known."

I cast about for the definition—"Invocations. The original faerie language, all-powerful, can't be spoken aloud by anyone who isn't a Sidhe without their mind falling to pieces... right? Those are the symbols on your sword."

"Got it," said River grimly. "If I'd seen the book before, I might have guessed, but I can't say I know what that symbol actually says. There's no dictionary of the language. And when that spell signature appeared... I should have put two and two together. But humans aren't supposed to know the language. I've seen those symbols on other talismans—"

"Talismans." I looked up. "That's what it is—right? It's a faerie talisman."

"Possibly." A furrow appeared between his brows. "But it's not the usual sort, at all. Most are weapons, bonded to their owners. The book appears to have chosen you in the same way, but the magic inside it isn't typical of Faerie at all. It's neither Summer nor Winter. I'd almost say it's... a man-made talisman."

"Wow," said Hazel. "Well, never mind where it came from. Can you use the book to banish the Winter Gatekeeper?"

"Possibly," I said. "But she's sealed within the house with some kind of binding. If it's anything like the other spirit barrier, then we'd need to destroy it before banishing her."

"But wouldn't destroying it set her free?" asked Hazel.

"She has a point," said River. "The Gatekeeper ordered the attack on your life..."

"She's conscious." Chills ran down my arms. "She... oh

god. She's still Gatekeeper, which means she must still have her magic, even as a ghost. Like a wraith… but human."

I hadn't got close enough to sense her, but if she was in any way like the other wraiths, she'd be little more than contained emotion, trapped… and probably not happy about the situation. Freeing her would unleash the entirety of the Winter Gatekeeper's wildly uncontained magic into the already-volatile Ley Line. At best, everywhere on the Ley Line up and down the country would experience wild bursts of dangerous spiritual activity. At worst… the barrier between earth and the Grey Vale would tear open again, potentially triggering another invasion.

"Shit," said Hazel quietly. "We can't set her free."

But I can't banish her as she is. Think, Ilsa. "River… is it possible to set up two spirit circles at once? If, say, we put our own circle around the territory, and *then* switched off the one binding her to the house, she'd still be trapped."

"Yes, she would," River said. "Then we'd be able to banish her. But Holly has those two faerie-necromancers on her side. I suspect they're the ones who set it up. We need to strike first. Take them out of the equation."

It took me a split second to grasp that he meant killing them. And quickly. After the last few days, I had no doubt that I was capable of it, and that they deserved it, but Hazel's face had paled and she shook her head. "I can try… but my power is intended to be used to keep the peace, not destroy."

"So is Holly's," I reminded her. "We can't kill her—there has to be a Gatekeeper, otherwise the Courts will turn on one another."

"That's it," Hazel said, leaping to her feet. "The Sidhe. If they find out the Winter Gatekeeper is dead… you said Holly didn't mention it to them?"

"No. I can't figure out why," I admitted. "But you're right —if they find out she's dead, then Holly will inherit the power. The Gatekeeper will lose her magic and I'll be able to free her without setting her magic loose."

Hazel slumped back onto her chair. "Great idea, but there's one small problem. I can't call the Sidhe. Believe me, if I could, I would already have."

There was an explosion of feathers, and Arden appeared in the middle of the room. "I can assist with that."

"You knew how to get into the Courts the whole time?" Hazel all but screamed at him.

"You're a traitor," I said, jumping to my feet. "You said I had to find the heir to Summer. That whole thing was a setup to lure me here so Holly could steal my magic."

"And you framed us," Hazel added. "Using our mark. On the graves."

The raven perched on the chair. "Unfortunately, I am unable to disobey a command from either of the Gatekeepers."

"So it was definitely her." I glared at him. "Is the Winter Gatekeeper pulling the strings, or Holly? Or both? You know what, I can't trust a word you say. You've played us too many times, and you said yourself you only obey Mum or the Winter Gatekeeper."

"I am a Lynn," the raven said. "That means I cannot harm any of you. I can't say I'm a fan of war, either. The last one was an inconvenience."

"You're such a colossal piece of shit," Hazel said. "If you really want to do your job, I'm giving you a message. Fly through the gates, find the nearest available Sidhe, and inform them that the Lynn treaty is being breached. Oh yeah, and it might be the end of the world as we know it. Not that they give a flying fuck. It'll probably take them twelve years to show up."

"Caw," said Arden. "I will always protect the Lynn bloodline. They will come."

And he soared out the window, scattering black feathers in his wake.

Hazel and I looked at one another. "I don't trust him," she said.

"Nor me, but the Winter Sidhe were right there. By the gate. I wish they'd stayed long enough to see what Holly did."

"Yeah… I just don't understand why Mum didn't know about any of this."

"Maybe she did," I said. "If she's stuck in Faerie, her options are limited."

Maybe she knew, maybe not… but River had been sent to guard the Gatekeeper.

Me.

Someone in Faerie knew about the book… I just had to hope they were on my side. And that I'd find out the truth, if I survived this.

A blast of icy cold air shook the room. The lights flickered and went out, plunging us into darkness.

"Damn," said Hazel. "Another wraith?"

"I don't think so," River said. "Look at that."

Green light shone from his palms, lighting up the room. Frost crept across the windows, icicles forming before our eyes. My arms broke out in goosebumps, a chill breeze sweeping through the room as though someone had left a window open. Like inside the Winter estate.

Hazel made a choked noise. "I—I think the house's magic has switched off."

"Winter," I said. "Holly. Or—"

"I worried about this." River took a step towards the door. "The Gatekeeper—she's far stronger than a regular spirit, and she has her magic. I think she's trying to break out."

"Oh hell." I turned to Hazel. "Are you ready? If the house's magic's fading, the barriers…"

"They've already fallen." She swore and ran from the room, into Mum's workshop. "Need any weapons?"

"Yeah, I threw all my iron at those necromancers. They're part faerie, if it helps." I ran to join her, replacing the iron and salt containers in my pockets, and finally sticking the book in my coat's upper pocket within easy reach.

River appeared behind me, a bag slung over his shoulder. "The candles," he said in explanation. "We need to move fast. Holly's doubtless trying to drive us off the territory."

"Yeah. I hope she thinks we'll run to hide in the village rather than attacking the house directly. She probably thinks Hazel's alone in here, and that you and I are dead."

It'd been close. Too close. And more would die if we didn't stop her. Maybe even the Sidhe. Whether there'd ever been a Summer heir at all—one thing was clear. The Sidhe could die. And Holly Lynn and her half-dead mother might be the end of them.

I put the last of my weapons into my coat pocket. "That'll have to do. I can't take any of them with me if I end up in Death again…"

"Try not to," Hazel said. "You scared the living crap out of me, Ilsa."

"I might not have a choice," I admitted. "This is what I am. The Gatekeeper."

Hazel nodded. I saw my own fear in her eyes—the fear that we'd never see Mum again. But that determined glint was still there, and her face was set.

"Let's go show them why you never mess with the Lynn family."

21

We walked in silence, approaching the fence. I'd never known the estate so quiet. It felt *wrong*, like something was missing that went beyond the Gatekeeper. I found myself shivering, and the temperature seemed to have dropped ten degrees since our return from Death. Already, snow settled on our own yard. The sky was murky grey, the air chilly and biting, and the field beyond was blanketed in snow. I tugged on thick gloves and climbed the fence for the third time in the last twenty-four hours, the others on my heels.

The Winter estate remained shrouded in darkness, an icy blizzard sweeping across the garden. It was impossible to see if Holly or the necromancers were nearby, but they must think River was still trapped in Death. Unless Holly had guessed the extent of my powers. I never had asked Arden how much information he'd given her.

But one thing was for certain—the Sidhe in all likelihood weren't coming. The rest was up to us.

We reached the division between the other Lynns' fence and ours.

"Start the iron barrier here," I said, pointing. "Once we've covered the part outside the grounds, one of us can jump the fence and complete the circle inside the garden." That was the risky bit. The Winter gate was at the garden's end, and because of the magic surrounding it, we'd need to put the candles at a safe enough distance that its constant pulsing Winter magic wouldn't put them out. The snow was bad enough.

Hazel nodded grimly, and ran alongside the fence, scattering iron filings. River's idea. The necromancers would be entirely caged in the territory, and perhaps the iron would make the Winter Gatekeeper hesitate to break free. Or at least slow her down. River, meanwhile, started passing candles to me.

"They're set to come on at the same time if they form a complete circle," he explained. "I can activate them from a distance."

"Good," I said. "I don't think much of our chances of lighting matches in this wind."

My hands were numb even with gloves on, and I wished I'd worn a thick coat, but I'd opted for my lighter jacket for ease of movement. I surveyed the line of iron etched in the snow, and the candles placed at intervals. Twelve candles was the key, apparently.

"This is the wonkiest circle I've ever seen," I admitted.

"'Spirit hexagon' doesn't have the same ring to it," Hazel said wryly. "Just as long as it works…"

"It'll work," River confirmed, laying down another candle carefully and brushing snow from its top. "That the candles are close enough together is more important than the shape. But those necromancers—I can't sense them."

"Can you sense anything beyond the fence?" I continued sprinkling down iron—alternating with salt, though I suspected it'd do little to deter that particular spirit.

He shook his head. "I wish I could. From what I saw, her body is dead, but her spirit is alive. Once the body and spirit have spent too long apart, the soul decays and so does the body. The link is severed, permanently."

Almost without thinking, I willed the grey film to cover the world, showing me the spirits beneath. I sensed the three of us right away—three bright sparks in the grey haze—but beyond… nothing. I'd only been able to sense the Gatekeeper's spirit when I'd more or less been standing on top of it.

The clouds over the Winter estate were so dark, it was impossible to make out what was going on over there. I blinked the grey away, disarmed by how easily my vision shifted between spirit sight and normal sight. I wished I'd had the chance to practise. Odds were, we'd have only one chance.

And I'd never let them drag River into Death again.

I put down the next candle. The snow became a blizzard, and it seemed to take twice as long to reach the next part of the fence. Hazel fell behind, and a strange humming noise kicked up. Greyness filtered over my vision, and a gleaming shape passed behind the fence.

I froze. *They're here. They know we're here.* The necromancers must know we were outside. They might not know *what* we were doing, but they were ready.

So was River. He crouched in front of the gate, laying down three candles. Not part of the circle. Rising to his feet, he drew his sword.

"Don't," I whispered, putting a gloved hand on his shoulder. "They got you last time."

"It won't happen again." His jaw was set. "I still haven't got them back for attacking you."

"If it's any consolation, I think they thought I was Hazel." I pulled out my knife. The quietness was a distraction. The grey film on my vision told me what they were really doing. The necromancers' spirits shifted on the other side of the fence, and I stepped back into a defensive stance.

The two necromancers leaped the fence, one of them colliding with me at speed. We fell into a heap in the snow, candles flaring around us—but we'd missed River's trap. River himself traded blows with the second one, who wielded a short knife of some type. The one pinned beneath me shifted, but I sank my knife into his arm.

He yelled aloud, eyes widening as the iron poisoning hit. Rolling to the side, he displaced me onto the snow, hurling Winter magic into my face. I anticipated the move and let the attack bounce off my shield. Summer magic sprang from the palms of the second, and it hit me that they'd entirely dropped their disguises, unmasking themselves as faeries. *And one of them's from Summer. He left the traces at the crime scene.*

The bigger necromancer wielded Winter magic in one hand, a knife in his other, driving me backwards. I was far outmatched skill-wise, but we'd bested them once already, and despite the viciousness of his strikes, he wasn't aiming to deal a fatal blow.

They need me alive.

I lunged forwards, tackling him into the snow. Magic blasted me again, making my teeth rattle, but ricocheted off the shield. My grip on the knife slipped, my hands numb, but I held on, punching him with my free hand. He screamed, writhing—I'd kept my fist clenched on a handful of iron filings. The iron left angry welt marks on his face, but before I could stick the knife in, he threw me off him. My back hit the dirt, and he lunged, grabbing my legs. I kicked out wildly, missed—and Hazel pounced.

Magic exploded from her palms, knocking him forwards. I kicked him again, and the headless body of the second necromancer fell across our path. River stood over him, his sword gleaming with blood.

"Get him in the trap, River!" I shouted.

He grabbed the surviving necromancer and threw him into the candle trap. Binding lights shot up around him, caging him in. At the same time, River's blade came down, sinking into his arm.

The faerie-necromancer spat. "Let me go."

"Not until you tell me your allegiance," River said. "I killed your friend. Don't think I won't do the same to you."

"Not to your Courts, scum."

"Vale outcast, then," he said. "Necromancer for hire... I imagine your skills are in high demand, but not amongst your own kind."

He laughed. "You'd be surprised. I don't fear death."

From a half-faerie, that was like hearing 'I don't fear cars' from a small woodland creature. It didn't compute.

"How did Holly find you?" I asked.

He coughed, spitting blood. Iron poisoning. Already his face was turning grey as the impact of the stab wounds spread through his body. "You really think you've trapped me?"

Icy hands grabbed my throat, throwing me into the air. Greyness seeped across my vision, and the bared teeth of the first, dead, necromancer floated before my eyes. *Not again.*

If I didn't get him off me, fast, I'd be joining him in Death. Greyness smothered the others entirely, locking the pair of us into a hazy space, his hands gripping my all-too-mortal throat. Tugging me forwards. A horribly familiar pulling sensation gripped my soul, pulling me towards the gates. I braced my feet, raised my numb hands to my throat, but grasped only empty air. His hands weren't gripping my physical body, and I couldn't—

I grabbed River as a ghost.

I dug down for the sensation I'd had then—the realisation that I was the Gatekeeper. I could walk between the realms of death and the living. This guy was dead, permanently, and when the veil took his soul, there'd be nothing of him left.

Cold, solid hands appeared beneath mine as I tightened my hold on him, even as my own arms dropped to my sides. Ghostly hands, my spirit detaching itself from my body, grabbed him, pulling him off my earthly form. His grip slipped—and I grabbed his hand in mine and squeezed. Hard. He was physically stronger than me in the mortal realm, but as ghosts, such things didn't matter anymore.

I yanked him towards me, hard, and he stumbled—or rather, floated, dropping in mid-air. I probably couldn't cause him any physical damage, but instinctively, I knew what to do.

Grabbing his wrists again, I envisioned the towering gates, fiercely, intently. The gates weren't bound to a particular place. No matter where you died, they always found you.

A flickering came from behind him. Then the gates appeared, towering, endless, paradoxically going on forever and everywhere at once.

"No!" he screamed, but I shoved him, with everything I had, in the direction of the gates. The tide of spirits swallowed him up, and he was gone.

The gates' pull caught me, insistent. I spun on the spot, my heart sinking. I'd disconnected from my body again. How—

"Ilsa!" River's voice shouted in my ears. There was a flash of light, a hand caught mine, and the fog cleared. I lay on the grass on my back, a candle burning at my head.

"I sent him over the veil," I said, unnecessarily. "Let him try coming back to make trouble now."

River nodded. "The other died—but you shouldn't do that

without training. If you're not careful, the gates will sweep you away."

"Yeah, I got that." I got to my feet, my hands still numb with cold, yet warm in the spot where he'd touched me. "Where's Hazel?"

"Finishing the iron barrier. Holly must know, but she's still inside the house. We need to get onto her territory in order to finish the spirit circle."

Greyness covered the world, so suddenly that I floated right out of my body, the gates' siren song pulling, pulling. There was another jolt, and I came to awareness, face-down in the snow. I lifted my head, shakily, seeing River braced against the fence. "What happened?"

"That was a huge disturbance in the spirit realm," he said, his face ashen. "Someone is dead."

22

River staggered back from the fence and began to run, following some sixth sense I couldn't detect.

"Is she breaking out?" The circle was only half complete, and the second half needed to be inside the grounds of the Winter estate.

River stopped. So did I. The prone form of a piskie lay in the dirt. In fact, there were several, all coated in a thin layer of ice. I took two steps towards the nearest, which appeared to still be breathing, though its form was almost see-through. Dying. I turned back to the Winter estate. The blizzard had worsened since we'd left, a thick curtain of snowflakes blanketing the whole house, and its terrible magic was infiltrating the world outside, killing any Summer faeries which came near. Even on our territory.

"They're harnessing death energy," River said quietly. "It's more than necromancy. Something is sending out a wave of death energy. Anyone who comes near..."

"Might die?" I stared at him. "But we're—"

"It's not enough to affect humans... yet. We need to..." He trailed off.

Old Mr Greaves's ghost had appeared in the middle of the road.

"Stop them," he said. "They've taken him." The spirit was barely there, his voice more like the whisper of leaves on pavement than an actual, human voice. But it was definitely him.

"Damn." River's sharp voice broke the silence. "I knew it felt like a necromancer. They have Greaves."

My stomach lurched. "The living one?"

The spirit vanished into the fog. River gritted his teeth and walked against the driving blizzard, towards the gate.

I grabbed his arm. "You can't—if they have him, they'll take you, too. They're after necromancers, aren't they? We're affected worse."

River shot me a look. "That includes you, Ilsa. I'm bound to protect the Gatekeeper."

The Gatekeeper. The gates of Faerie... or death? Both, maybe. Both were in danger today, and both depended on the two of us to save them.

River halted. "There's someone moving over there."

"Holly?"

His breath hissed out. "Undead. I can sense them."

Like we needed any more enemies. "Damn," I said. "I'll get the salt—"

Two short figures jumped out of the hedge. Pointy-eared and about level with my knees, they leaped at us, claws aiming for my face. I struck back, the knife cutting a line down the nearest redcap's arm. Its screech threatened to burst my eardrums, but this time, my knife found its home in its throat. Crimson stained the snow, and River tossed the body of the second one aside.

Then the dead redcaps stood up.

"Oh shit." I backed up, fumbling in my pocket for the salt

shaker, cursing the coldness for numbing my hands. As I flung salt at it, the redcap's face dissolved. *Ugh.*

"It's a knock-on effect," River said. "The veil—anything that died recently will come back."

"Think I worked that much out," I responded. "That means—the undead will *keep* coming back unless we take them to pieces."

"I'll hold them off," he said. "You're the one who needs to finish the circle."

I didn't argue. He was a better fighter than I was, and one of us needed to secure the rest of the spirit circle. Fast. If the dead were rising of their own accord, it meant the Winter Gatekeeper was moments from breaking free.

I reached the front gate, hoping to hell Holly was too distracted by whatever the Gatekeeper was doing to notice me sneak onto her territory. It was a wonder anyone could see in the driving snow, but the moment I slipped through the gate, my spirit sight snapped on. Greyness flooded my vision once more. I wished I'd had time to practise using River's useful trick to sense if there was anyone nearby, but the entire house was blurred, probably due to the Winter Gatekeeper's out-of-control magic.

Focus. Get the candles down. The sky was thick with snowflakes, and the breath felt frozen in my lungs. Urgency screamed in my ears, but I couldn't walk any faster. My hands and ears were numb. I continued my path around the garden's perimeter, heading for the fence on the house's right-hand side.

I laid down the first two candles, where they were immediately blanketed in snow. Tossing a handful of iron filings down, I hoped they were enough to counter the Winter magic assailing the place. *Maybe the necromancers use spelled candles for a reason.* I brushed snowflakes from my eyes, the bitter cold cutting through my coat. Once I reached the back, there was no chance I wouldn't catch Holly's attention. I just needed to move fast enough that it wouldn't matter.

My numb feet pounded against the gravel path. The circle was more of a crooked octagon by now, but it didn't matter as long as the points were in alignment. I slammed down the next candle, heart pounding against my ribs, breath stuck in my chest, lungs burning.

And stopped. Undead barred the way around the corner of the house—too many to count.

"Get out the way," I said.

None of the undead moved. There was no way to get around them. And the salt was running low. My hands were too numb, too clumsy, to fight.

The first undead lunged. I kicked out, hurling salt at it. Its face dissolved but it kept going anyway. Bloody creatures felt no pain. How was I supposed to take the whole pack down at once?

The book.

No. That'd definitely draw attention. I was so close.

I held the salt shaker one-handed, and punched the zombie. This time it fell, but two more took its place. Choking on the stench of dead flesh, I used my knife to carve a path through, but the press of bodies was like moving through sludge.

And then a white light appeared, penetrating my greying vision. Horror momentarily blanked out the cold and exhaustion. The undead weren't simply reanimates. Those white lights were their souls, trapped here, and furious. They collectively swarmed me, clawed hands grasping not at my body, but at my very essence. Wanting me to join them in misery.

No. Never.

"Get away!" I croaked, my vision flickering back to the real world. I threw the empty salt shaker, my free hand scrabbling at my pocket for the book and finding something else. A candle, one of the few left. Wait—they were infused with necromantic power.

The candle ignited in my hand. Though they didn't cease their attack, a few cringed away from the light.

I held it above my head, a clear warning. "I can banish you," I shouted, wielding the knife in one hand, the candle in the other.

They moved aside, slowly, and I pushed my way through the pack, finding a free spot for the next candle. *So close...*

Another flash of light came from the lawn ahead. Then another. A summoning circle. Greyness seeped across my vision, but not before I'd seen the body lying in the circle. I knew who it was without looking close—the necromancers' leader. And swirling currents of blue light spiralled from the circle to the house. Beside the circle stood... Holly. She must be drawing on the necromancer's power in some way.

"Contain them!" Holly shouted, her voice whip-sharp on the breeze.

Greaves said, "This is more than a necromancer can handle, you foolish girl. The spirits will have you."

The voice didn't come from his body but from the spirit hovering above it. She'd torn him out of his body. *Winter feeds on death energy.* What the hell was she doing—boosting the Winter Gatekeeper's power? I needed to finish the circle, but there was no way I could walk right out in front of her and not be noticed, even with all her attention on her own circle.

She killed Graves. Gingerly, I crouched down, laying the second to last candle on the snow. If I sprinted—

The icy presence of the Winter Gatekeeper's spirit burst outwards like a deadly flower in bloom. Blue tendrils snaked across the lawn from the dark space of the house.

"That's better," purred the spirit. "I see what you're doing with those candles, dear. You're hopeless."

I froze, my body locking in position. I *felt* her before I saw her, her evil presence brushing against me, colder even than the snow. She'd been watching me from within the house the whole time. *I need to move. I have to*—but my legs wouldn't obey. Her magic had frozen my body. *Move!*

The Gatekeeper's laughter rang in my ears.

Snow blanketed my fall, and everything faded to grey, and whispering. Cold air on my face... cold snow soaking through my clothes...

"Wake up!" Holly snapped.

I opened my eyes, my mind fuzzy, everything indistinct.

"I said get *up*, idiot."

"What?" I lifted my head. "I thought you wanted this."

"You thought wrong," said Holly. "I've been trying to stop her, and now—it's all your fault."

"I don't know what you're talking about."

"Get *up*. She'll drain you dry."

I was dreaming. Why in hell was Holly helping me? I twitched my hand, found I could move again. The Winter Gatekeeper's hold had lifted. With the greyness gone from my vision, blue light continued to flow from the summoning circle to the house. I'd thought she was amplifying the spirit's power... but maybe I was wrong.

"You're trying to contain her?" I asked. "Not help her?"

"Of course not," Holly said. "This is your fault, Ilsa. I should have had that book. I need it to keep her contained, but it's too late now."

"No, it isn't." I pushed to my knees. "Not if you help me get these candles into place."

"Candles won't do a thing," she said. "Nor will regular necromancy. Your *friend* killed the only people keeping her contained."

Those necromancers… "They tried to kill me, and my sister. What did you expect us to do, let it slide?"

"I didn't order them to do that," she said. "It's too late now."

"Like hell." I stumbled forwards, pushing aside my exhaustion. What'd the spirit done, fed on my life energy? Or my spirit? It sure felt like it.

Greyness slid over my vision and once again I was in the spirit world. The Winter Gatekeeper's spirit was here, too. It was leaching life not just from Winter, but from all the spirits. The undead included.

Holly knew that. Maybe her tenuous attempt at an alliance with Winter was due to her knowledge that eventually, the Gatekeeper would break free. The only place she'd be able to escape her would be in the Unseelie Court.

"Come here, child," whispered the Winter Gatekeeper's voice in my ear. "It'll all be over soon."

I shook my head, my body threatening to freeze up again. Whatever Holly had done had slowed the spirit, but not enough. She was too strong. There was a ton of rage and fury contained in that glowing spirit, a presence worse than any wraith. Her magic had survived beyond death, and if unleashed, it'd break the Ley Line. There'd be another faerie invasion, from the darkest depths of Faerie.

"Come here, Ilsa," she whispered again.

23

I turned on the spot to face the house, and the torrent of power, barely contained by the necromantic spells on the territory. I could see them now, through the grey—like ropes, holding her spirit down, confining it to the house. The lock on the grounds had been temporary. That dizzying power, the horrifying presence of it, probably wore down any necromantic defences over time. Holly had hired those necromancers to keep her in, but it wasn't enough. And now she'd killed someone as a last-ditch effort to keep her contained.

How could I have misjudged the situation so badly?

The book. Get the book. The spirit wanted the book. How it was possible for an incorporeal spirit to take it from me, I didn't know, but I knew from the sheer force of that power that when unleashed, there was nothing she couldn't do. She could crack the world in two. With the Ley Line open, she might do just that.

"Why?" I asked through numb lips. "Why do this?"

"Why else?" purred the Winter Gatekeeper. "The Courts

sought to control and enslave us, but they foolishly entrusted us with their power. I'm claiming it as mine."

"You're dead. And insane." I fumbled my coat, my fingers slipping on the book. The last candle had fallen from my pocket somewhere in the snow, along with my last hope. All that was left was numbing cold, and the knowledge that as long as her attention was on me, it wasn't on the others.

I hope you run while you can, River. But that vow of his would compel him to stay here until the end.

"You're a pathetic, powerless mortal," said the Winter Gatekeeper. "Give me the book."

"Like it'd open for you." Cold air stirred, lifted my hair from my head. "I might be mortal, but at least I'm still alive. And I claimed its power already."

"Have you any idea how many years I've been looking for that talisman?"

"I can guess." She might even have known Great-Aunt Enid had it. And she knew it was a talisman. There was no hiding anything from her.

I held only one advantage left… as a Lynn, she was bound not to fatally harm me. I could only assume that held after death, because otherwise, she'd already have tried to take me out of the equation directly. But she needed me alive. It was her orders the necromancers followed, in the end. She must have offered them a better deal than Holly. She'd become a force beyond human, even the Sidhe, and the magic that kept her alive was fed by death itself.

"They'll all die," she whispered. "The fools will come here, and perish. There'll be an end to them, and the Lynn curse, forever."

The Sidhe. She knew they could die now. And she planned to have them come here, while the veil was unstable, and take them to pieces.

There'd be nothing left of any realm to rule over.

"You could have made things easier for me," said the Winter Gatekeeper. "All the clues were supposed to tell you that you're the missing heir. Your delusions of grandeur were supposed to land you in the Courts, where you were supposed to leave the doors wide open for our people to stride in and take power. The traitorous raven must have tipped you off."

My mouth fell open. *She'd* started the heir rumour—for *me*. "Delusions of grandeur? Are you sure you weren't thinking of yourself?"

Anger pulsed from her spirit. "You dare mock me—"

"Damn, I didn't give Holly enough credit." I could hardly believe Aunt Candice even thought I'd have the audacity to make a claim on the throne of the Summer Court. But I'd hardly spoken to her. She'd made a wild guess depending on how *she* would have reacted to being the one born without magic, and it'd backfired. "The wraiths, the Vale... it was all you. She was trying to stop you."

"And she almost succeeded. I'd like to thank you for setting me free. All you need to do now, Ilsa... is die."

"Not if I can help it." Holly spoke from within the blizzard —and she held the last candle.

I drew the book, lifted it, and power rolled through me, flickering lights appearing around my vision. The Gatekeeper's terrible laughter cut through, even as the candles lit up— containing her, binding her to this space.

At the same time, the house burst apart. Bricks flew wide, roofs splintered, and the whole building cracked open as the writhing spirit within broke free. I held myself upright in the face of it—and didn't move. None of it touched me. The house was made entirely of magic, and my anti-magical shield still functioned.

The glowing orb of her spirit floated above the house's ruins, her figure now visible within it. Eyes raging with flames, mouth stretched in a grimace, hands splayed, glowing with vivid magic. *Now I'm in trouble.* Necromantic magic was exempt from my magical shield—though it would surely have killed a normal person.

The candle lights wavered. Then the Gatekeeper released a blast of magic, directly at Holly. If she dropped that candle, we were dead.

I threw myself in front of her, and magic slammed into me, knocking me into the snow. Winded, gasping, I rolled over, my vision flickering with grey lights.

The Winter Gatekeeper laughed. "Your pitiful spell won't do a thing, you mortal fools."

"Everyone's mortal," I shouted at her. "Even you."

The book's power rolled through me again, shivering, demanding. Words rose to my tongue, banishing words, like a language half-remembered. Her power pushed back. She was too strong. As long as her rage remained in this world, fuelling her power, she would, too. No wonder Holly had only been able to stall her. She'd kept her powers beyond death.

River's voice joined mine, speaking the bindings. The Gatekeeper spun on the spot, hissing in anger—and collided with River's fist. He floated in ghost form—but as a spirit, he could fight her.

And so could I.

Perhaps because I'd done it before, perhaps because the veil was so close—my spirit came free of my body in barely a blink, and collided with her at speed. It wasn't like hitting a physical body, because with nothing to land on, we both kept falling until I managed to stop myself in mid-air.

She lunged, screaming, at River. He got there first, shoving her backwards, with practised moves indicating this was far from the first time he'd fought someone as a ghost. Magic burst from the Winter Gatekeeper's palms, aimed at

River, but he dodged expertly. The candles' lights continued to burn, but the words I'd spoken hadn't been enough. I needed to do more than that. The roaring power inside her simply refused to be diminished.

Wait. What had River said? *My defence mechanism...*

"Are you too much of a coward to fight me?" I said loudly. "I thought you wanted the book."

"I don't have any use for the book while in this state," she said, spinning to face me. "But I would *dearly* like your magic."

I screamed as her magic pierced through me again. River was shouting, binding words that rang with familiarity, but while those words would bind a lesser spirit, she was too clever, too *present.* She was entirely conscious, her spirit preserved as surely as though she still lived.

But her power wasn't infinite.

"You want the magic—come and get it."

She screeched and flew at me, and I willed myself to wake into my body again.

The Gatekeeper flew through empty air, allowing River to strike her from behind. *His* magic still worked, too—but of course, he was still alive. I barely rested in my body for a second, long enough to check on the book, then I launched myself at her again, sending her sprawling in the air.

"How *dare* you humiliate me." Power brimmed in her eyes, leaking off her body, but none of it touched me. It ought to have burned out by now. Her ability as a Gatekeeper shouldn't allow her to draw on others' power. No... the circle did that. The circle held her contained. The energy was drawn into the necromantic trap. Her own magic was limited, and she'd been using it all this time. Even on top of the Ley Line, there was a limit.

River's eyes widened as I shouted at Holly— "Keep hold of that candle. Whatever you do—don't drop it."

Then I floated up to the circle's edge. In this form, it appeared in a shimmering line around the territory. Just beyond was the smaller circle where the dead necromancer's leader lay. His power pulsed in the air, a living thing, feeding into the circle. His life force had fuelled the circle around the house that I'd accidentally broken when I'd killed the necromancers, too. Life force contained death. The ghosts floating around, faerie spirits stuck on a loop... all of them were trapped within the circle as well. There was no way out. The candles wouldn't hold forever.

River floated to my side. "She's too strong," he said. "We need to get out of the circle. If we bind her from in here, we'll be sucked beyond the gates, too."

The gates.

Gatekeeper.

"Wait for me," I said. "I think I know what to do."

He gave a brief nod. Had he guessed? Or did he really trust me to know what I was doing? No time to ask. Once again, I willed myself to return to my living body, and in barely a blink, I was face-down in the snow. Fighting the numbing cold, I stumbled to my feet.

"This won't hold," Holly said. "What are you doing?"

"Keep standing there. Nobody else is in the circle, are they?"

"Only the dead. What *are* you—?"

She broke off as I stepped outside of the circle of light, holding the book, conjuring the image of those endless gates. I was going by guesswork now, but this necromantic power was linked with the faeries somehow, and the faeries tended to be very literal-minded.

Gatekeeper. The gate was everywhere, existing in every place at any one time. Even here in the between world. A paradox. The gates of death, eternally open, a siren song calling to every spirit to pass Beyond.

I fixed the image in my mind, and slipped out of my body.

The gates appeared immediately, open wide. Spirits passed in and out, not noticing the world beyond the greyness. A different plane... yet I could see the house's ruins beneath, the Winter Gatekeeper's spirit hovering beneath. And I still felt the thrum of the Gatekeeper's power in my veins even as my body remained cold and frozen below.

"*Stop that.*" The Gatekeeper's booming voice reached me. I focused on the gate. *You're there. You're everywhere, in every part of this world, and she's* dead.

The gates opened wider, and a glow enveloped my body. I heard voices shouting, maybe from the mass of spirits ahead, but I stood my ground, laser focused on the gate.

Gatekeeper.

And then my feet touched down on earth, the gate floating in front of me. Closer to the circle's edge.

"Holly!" I said, and she spun around, eyes widening. *She can see it. They all can.* As the Gatekeeper's power grew stronger, the spirit sight would creep up on everyone in the vicinity. Ghosts would appear amongst the living. The gates would try to claim them all.

Not as long as I was in control.

"Holly," I said. "Drop the candle. And hang on to something."

"What—? What in hell *are* you?"

"I'm Gatekeeper."

The candle fell from her hands. The circle rushed open, a whirlpool of magic exploding outward. Right at the gate.

Aunt Candice screamed in fury, writhing on the spot, but the gate relentlessly sucked at everyone within the circle—and outside it. The raging spirits possessing the undead went first. The Winter Gatekeeper's spirit continued screaming and writhing. Whatever force was behind that gate, though, was far too strong to resist.

Other spirits followed. Half-Sidhe and other part-faerie beings, and humans, and everyone who'd been dragged to the wrong side of the grave by the magic. Only one remained—old Greaves. No, two. The younger Greaves stood beside his father, neither of them moving, while every other spirit was sucked into the void. I stood my ground, hoping River and Hazel had got out of reach—but all the gates' focus was on the screaming, struggling form of the dead Winter Gatekeeper. My Aunt Candice shrieked, clawing at me, but her hands passed harmlessly through my body.

In a blast of white light, she was sucked into the void.

The gate kept on, open, and now my own body was pulled backwards. *No.* As a ghost, I had nothing solid to grab onto. The gate would suck me in—

A solid hand gripped mine. River. "Think about being alive, Ilsa."

I shook my head, my fingernails digging into his hand. The gate was pulling him in, too, and it wouldn't close. The book—

I let go of the book with my free hand, and it floated. The pages glowed silver, and it remained hovering in mid-air. It wouldn't float through the gates. It *was* the gates.

"Stop!" I screamed at it, pulling that power *back*, into me. The book resisted, but the grey smoke thickened, blocking the gates from view. "I *own* you."

I grabbed the book, gripped it hard, like pulling a heavy pair of doors closed.

The gates began to close, and the smoke faded, to be replaced with the Winter estate.

Silence descended, thick as the fallen snow, calm as a breeze, stark as the aftermath of a terrible battle. If I'd been in my body, I'd have fallen to the ground in relief and shock. As it was, I remained floating where the circle's edge had been, where Holly had thrown the candle aside, and my own body lay face-down on the snowy lawn.

I looked down at River's hand, still in mine. "Thank you," I said. "Is she—?"

"She's gone," he confirmed.

I blinked, and the next second, I lay in my mortal body again, freezing and aching. The thick snowflakes had disappeared, leaving grey sky and dampness. My clothes were soaked through. I'd catch my death of cold if I didn't get somewhere warm, but somehow, I couldn't bring myself to move.

The veil closed, the grey film from my vision receding. Before me, the house lay in ruins, the walls collapsed, the candle's lights out, and the dead gone.

Holly collapsed to her knees, sobbing.

She was her mother, after all.

Guilt rose, but not enough to counter the rush of profound relief. Bodies of undead lay on the lawn, on snow that was already melting. And the body of the old necromancer lay a few feet away. The candles were out, spent.

It's over.

Dizziness washed over me, and my forehead rested on the ground. The world spun, and I only looked up when someone walked in front of me. Hazel.

I sat up. She hugged me, hard. "Ilsa."

I squeezed her back. "It's okay. She's gone."

From Holly's heartbroken sobbing, the victory felt tinged with bitterness, and anger at what the Winter Gatekeeper had done. Sure, the binding to the Courts was unfair, but she'd willingly put thousands of lives at risk by drawing in so much power on the Ley Line. And she'd forced her daughter to become a killer.

Holly crawled to the circle where the necromancer lay dead. She glanced up, sensing me behind her.

"I didn't mean to kill him." She swallowed. "He came here on his own account… they all did. I—she locked me into a faerie vow. I couldn't tell anyone what had happened to her. I was trying to get them to understand what she was doing, but they didn't get it until it was almost too late."

"It's okay," I said, though it wasn't. She'd still been involved in plotting against my family, whatever her reasons. But she was Winter Gatekeeper now. And the Sidhe would punish her no matter what.

Rustling came from behind me. River approached, retrieving the candles one at a time. Aside from the snow dusting his clothes, he looked unhurt. Snowflakes settled in his fair hair, but his warm smile could have melted ice. I took a step towards him—and Hazel gasped. River stood at alertness as cold air whirled towards us. I tensed, turning to the forest, and the Winter gate swung open with barely a whisper.

Three Sidhe approached on steeds as white as the fallen snow, the same ones as before. I forced myself to keep still, though I barely had the energy to stand. The Sidhe warriors' faces were expressionless, and in my exhausted state, they blurred into one. All wore the same silver mail that glistened in the sunlight. As did their weapons. Their glowing blue eyes were the only constant. Judging, terrifying, condemning.

Hazel stepped forward. "I'm the Gatekeeper's heir to Summer," she said. "*Your* heir betrayed you, and all of Faerie. We stopped her."

A silver-haired female Sidhe spoke first. Her eyes were on Holly. "You are responsible for putting all the realms, and the truce, at risk."

Holly finally turned around. "Your people saw what had become of my mother. You chose to do nothing."

"Your trials are not ours."

"We *serve* you," she said, her voice growing louder. "My whole family has. And when she tried to steal power that wasn't hers, I tried to stop her. I was nearly too late. She'd have attacked you."

"How dare you steal our magic?" she said. "You have forfeited the right to a place in our realm."

"Good!" Holly shouted. "I never wanted to be your servant. You let my mother *die*. You left me to handle the fallout. And if you want to keep your word, you have to take me into your realm now. I'm Gatekeeper."

"You will be banished henceforth from Faerie," said the Winter Sidhe, pointing her staff at Holly. "On pain of death, you will never set foot near Summer nor Winter territory again. You are no longer heir, but you will forever bear those marks as penance."

The silvery lines on Holly's face gleamed. She stepped forward, choking on a wordless protest. But she couldn't ignore a direct order from the Sidhe. Her feet moved, and though the strain and desperation showed on her face, she turned her back on the gate and walked away.

There was no longer a Lynn heir to Winter.

The Winter Sidhe turned back to Hazel and me. I remained still, frozen.

"It seems the Winter Court owes you their gratitude for stopping that creature," she said.

Wait… she was talking to me?

She snapped her fingers, and Arden appeared beside her, in raven form.

"This one tells me you broke your own contract in acting against the Winter Gatekeeper," the Sidhe added.

"Excuse me?" said Hazel. "We haven't even seen this contract. They attacked us first, tried to frame us for murder, and killed two people. Maybe more."

"Wait," I said to the Winter Sidhe. "Arden told you? But he

betrayed us. He tried to stop me from binding the Winter Gatekeeper's spirit."

"The bird holds no allegiance to any party. Your contract, however… if there is no Winter Gatekeeper, there will no longer be a Summer one, either."

"The Summer Court will be the judge of that." Another female voice rang out as though from a loudspeaker overhead.

Three Sidhe appeared in a flash of white light. They too rode horses, and were dressed in gleaming armour in gold and green shades.

Summer ambassadors to Faerie.

Winter and Summer faced one another, not exactly with hate, more a kind of icy politeness. On the Winter Sidhe's part, at least. The group of us mortals might as well have faded from existence. For a moment, they exchanged words in the faerie tongue. From their mannerisms, they weren't declaring war, at least.

"I didn't think they'd actually show," Hazel whispered. "It'd have been nice to have their help, right?"

"Yeah, but an hour late is better than a year. Arden must have been insistent."

But where was Mum? For a brief, ridiculous moment, I'd hoped to see her there amongst the Summer faeries, but she was nowhere to be seen. The Sidhe finally turned their attention onto us. The central Summer faerie, a tall female with olive skin and gold and green finery, looked down at us as though surveying her kingdom from on high. "Which of you is the Gatekeeper's heir?"

"I am," Hazel said, "but it's Ilsa who saved all your necks."

"Is that so?" All eyes focused on me. I looked down, partly due to nerves, partly because the combined strength of their stares was too much. Too intense. Their magic could break me into a thousand tiny pieces.

But someone in Faerie made the book. A talisman.

One of the Summer Sidhe addressed River. "You," he said. "You were assigned to guard the Lynn girl, correct?"

"Actually, I was assigned to the Gatekeeper's heir," he said. "And it's true. Ilsa saved both realms."

"Explain."

It wasn't a request, but a command. Somehow, between the three of us, we got the story out. Either Grandma's restriction had lifted or the Sidhe's magic somehow neutralised it, because I told them about the book—the best I could, anyway. Finally, I stopped, feeling as drained as though I'd run a mile.

There was a pause.

"She is not to blame," said the Summer female faerie. "Neither of the Summer children are responsible for the actions of Winter."

"And us?" said the Winter female who'd spoken first. "We are without an heir and representative. You should give yours up, too. It's only right."

"Whatever your heir did, the curse is binding."

My heart sank. Maybe there'd be a war after all. "Can't you forget the contract and set us all free?" I asked. Apparently I was channelling Holly after all. Hazel shot me an alarmed look, but the Sidhe didn't move to strike me.

"Absolutely not," said the Summer Sidhe. "You swore a vow, and that holds."

"Our ancestor did," I said. "It's not our fault the Winter Gatekeeper is dead. If it bothers you that much, let Holly come back. She's better than the alternative. There are no other living Lynns."

Technically, there was our brother, but we hadn't heard from him since Mum disowned him. And he wasn't magical, so not a candidate. Only Holly had ever inherited the Gate-keeper's power.

"Find her," commanded the Winter Sidhe. "If she doesn't present herself to us by the next solstice, then you will face the consequences yourself."

The Winter faeries turned on the spot, the gates opening once more. As one, they rode into blinding light.

"Looks like we have to find an heir after all," I said, with a wry smile. "But it'll be okay. Holly stands in, nobody goes to war, and we deal with the rest later."

"Poor Holly," said Hazel quietly. "We shouldn't have any trouble finding her. It's not like she can leave the Ley Line."

I looked up at another flash of light. The Summer Sidhe had turned away as though intent on returning to their own Court.

"Wait," I called after them. "Can one of you tell me where our mother is? She's in Faerie, but she hasn't been in touch. We really need to tell her about all this."

"Word will be passed onto her," said the leading Sidhe, without turning around. "That useful bird of yours will hand her the details."

"You're still employing Arden?" My voice rose. "He's working for Winter as well."

The female Sidhe turned around, her green eyes cold. "The shapeshifter has always been neutral."

"Mum didn't tell me that," Hazel said. "She needs to know there was a threat, at the very least."

"As I said," the female Sidhe enunciated clearly, "I will see to it that the information reaches her. You need to fix the boundaries on your territory."

Oh no. Winter's magic had wiped out our defences. "But —" I ran after as she turned her horse around again. "But the book. The talisman. Can you tell me who made it?"

"No," she said. "I know no talisman but my own. That

particular talisman does not belong to Faerie, so it has nothing to do with us."

"Wait—"

Light flashed, and they were gone.

"Dammit," I said.

"Mum will come back," Hazel said confidently. "She always does. The important thing is that we're alive, nobody's going to war—oh yeah, and you're a certifiable badass."

I snorted. "Yeah, right. I'm going by instinct on this necromancer power, mostly. And I'm still not joining the guild." My smile faded when I spotted their leader's body. River stood beside him, muttering under his breath. A moment later, candles flared, devouring the fallen necromancer. I walked over to join him.

"His last request," River said. "Necromancers burn their dead."

"I know. I just—I guess it didn't really hit me that he's gone. Who will be his replacement?"

"He'll decide himself."

I blinked. Then I concentrated on letting the greyness slide over my vision, my spirit sight taking control. And sure enough… Mr Greaves floated beside his older counterpart.

"What are you staring at, girl?" he said. His eyes were on my forehead.

"Guess you know what I am, now."

"What you are is a menace."

I folded my arms. "I'm sorry I didn't get there in time to save you, but you're being a dick."

"Unfortunately for you, you don't get to choose who you meet in life or death."

"Unfortunately for *you*, I have no shortage of other necromancers to ask about my powers, and I'm not about to give up my role."

The book didn't belong to Faerie. But since when had talismans ever been forged here in the mortal realm? Usually they were made from the hearts of Faerie's most ancient trees. Unless it'd been made in the Courts and ended up here later. Mysteries only concealed more mysteries, and Holly's house lay in ruins, the only source of information buried along with it.

No. That can't be it. There'll be records. I'd ask Grandma, for a start, and now I could enter the spirit realm, I could question the necromancers, too.

I let my spirit sight recede, a thrill going through me at how easy it was. Maybe it wasn't the power I'd have chosen, but River was proof that necromancy was far more versatile than I'd originally thought.

I looked around at the ruined house. Nothing to do for the Winter estate. Presumably Holly's magic would fix it, if she came back. That could wait. We had a tremendous mess to clean up, and all I really wanted was a long, warm shower, and a decent, wraith-free night's sleep. River looked like he needed the same, though he still managed to look absurdly attractive under all the dirt and grime.

"You're a natural," he said in an approving tone. "I'd like to see what else you can do."

I grinned. "You should know, I'm an academic, not a warrior."

"Could have fooled me," he said. "My mission might be over, but you need someone to talk you through that book."

"I thought you hadn't seen it before." I lifted the book, flipping it open. The pages shimmered, but still had text on them. "You seem confident you're going to see me again."

"I'd like to see you again, Ilsa Lynn."

How did he make my name sound so seductive? How? "I won't be here," I told him. "Some of the time, I mean. I do still have a job to go back to." The thought of my normal co-workers ever finding out about this was laughable, and hell, I couldn't imagine fitting into that life the way I was now. But though I might be Gatekeeper, nothing in that title meant Faerie owned me. I was free to go wherever I liked.

"I'll come and find you," River said. "But I have to return to the Sidhe now that my task is complete." Green light shone from his palms, and his eyes gleamed with magic. His expression was a mixture of resignation and steely determination. I almost expected him to fight the pull of the faerie vow, and drag me with him. And some wild part of me would have let him do just that.

No. You've had enough close calls with faerie magic lately.

Instead, I said, "They won't punish you for what happened—right?" They'd better not. Not after everything we'd done.

"I helped keep you alive, which fulfils the requirements of the vow, and with any luck, they'll believe me when I tell them that the Winter Gatekeeper was the conspirator against the Court. I'll see you soon, Ilsa."

"What?" I said as white light outlined his body. "Oh, come on. Won't they at least let us say a proper goodbye—?"

His hand brushed mine. "I think you know by now that in Faerie, as in death, magic runs on its own rules." Behind him, light rushed in, and he was gone.

"Dammit," I muttered. I hadn't even got a real-world kiss out of our whole misadventure.

Hazel gave me a self-satisfied look. "Told you he likes you."

I blinked the light's glare from my eyes. "He's off to Faerie. I wouldn't get my hopes up on them letting him come back within the same week, or even year."

"But he will," Hazel said. "Hopefully with news of where Mum is."

"Shit," I said. "That means we have to fix the house. Otherwise, no book or magic will hide us from her wrath."

Hazel cracked a grin. "Nope. Even though you're a Gatekeeper in your own right. That makes you her equal, power-wise."

"Not in terms of training," I said. "Or wisdom, or whatever else it is she used to tell you in Gatekeeper lessons."

"You eavesdropped on our lessons?"

I shrugged. "Yeah, I did." I wasn't ashamed of it anymore —how desperate I'd been back then, to have magic. I'd let it go long before Holly had misused her own powers. But I couldn't deny that now I had magic of my own, the idea of being amongst supernaturals again... I could see it. I'd spoken to the *Sidhe* and walked away in one piece.

"Then it's only fair I get to spy on yours." Hazel ducked, grabbed a handful of snow and threw it at me.

"Hey!" I said indignantly.

"How many times are we going to get near the Winters' lawn?" She grabbed another snowball.

I did likewise. "Okay, you asked for it."

For a moment, as I doused my sister in snow, I forgot the gate at the back and the responsibilities hanging over my head. The role of the Gatekeeper. The answers lay buried somewhere in our history, and the future was unknown, but for now, none of that mattered.

ABOUT THE AUTHOR

Emma is the New York Times and USA Today Bestselling author of the Changeling Chronicles urban fantasy series.

Emma spent her childhood creating imaginary worlds to compensate for a disappointingly average reality, so it was probably inevitable that she ended up writing fantasy novels. When she's not immersed in her own fictional universes, Emma can be found with her head in a book or wandering around the world in search of adventure.

Find out more about Emma's books at
www.emmaladams.com.